Silver M[oon]

HAVE A[...]
OF 72 [...]
OF
EROTIC DOMINATION

If you like one you will probably like the rest

A NEW TITLE EVERY MONTH

Silver Moon Readers Service
c/o DS Sales Ltd.
PO Box 1100 London N21 2WQ

*Distributed to the trade throughout North America by
LPC Group, 1436 West Randolph Street, Chicago, IL 60607
(800) 826-4330*

Silver Moon Books of Leeds and New York are in no way connected with Silver Moon Books of London

If you like one of our books you will probably like them all!

Write for our free 20 page booklet of extracts from early books - surely the most erotic feebie yet - and, if you wish to be on our confidential mailing list, from forthcoming monthly titles as they are published:-

Silver Moon Reader Services
c/o DS Sales Ltd.
PO Box 1100 London N21 2WQ

http://www.silvermoon.co.uk

or leave details on our 24hr UK answerphone
0181 245 0985
International acces code then +44 181 245 0985

<u>New authors welcome</u>
**Please send submissions to
Silver Moon Books Ltd.
PO Box 5663
Nottingham
NG3 6PJ**

FUTHER PRIVATE TUITION first published 2000, copyright Jay Merson

The right of Jay Merson to be identified as the author of this book has been asserted in accordance with Section 77 and 78 of the Copyrights and Patents Act 1988

FURTHER PRIVATE TUITION
by
JAY MERSON

This is fiction - In real life always practise safe sex!

CHAPTER ONE

The professor sat at the large desk in the study of his new house. It seemed slightly strange to him to be working on the ground floor after all those years in the apartment in Regents Park. He sat back in the leather swivel chair, sipping at his coffee and looking out over the formally laid and tended gardens of the house.

Fond memories of the luxury apartment came to him, the place where he had recruited and introduced Paula and Louise to the various sexual delights and practices he so enjoyed, how he had drawn them into and had gained their acceptance into the society, his cock stirred as he recalled the satisfaction he had experienced in providing their education. Memories washed over him of how they had shrieked and struggled at first under the cane and the whip, and then how those struggles had become more sensuous as they learned to accept his domination and welcome the pain and pleasure it brought them. The central London address of the apartment had certainly proved worthwhile in his recruiting. This new address - he hoped - would help improve upon that success. It would be necessary for his next step up the ladder.

A senator now within the society, he would need to recruit five more girls to gain the position of principal. The society rules dictated this and he meant to achieve it. He pondered a moment, visualising himself holding the top position at the society meetings, it strengthened his determination to succeed.

The society needed a fresh direction, he felt, a new style of leadership - his leadership. Soon the post of principal would become vacant; the time was right to make his bid. Just the recruitment to complete and he would have all the necessary requirements to stand. Five girls, all to be recruited, trained and then accepted by the membership, it would be no mean task and time was short.

The professor placed his coffee cup carefully on the desk and again read the advertisement that he had placed in seven magazines and five national newspapers. He would use the same approach as before he had decided; the one that had worked so very well for him in the past. His cock stiffened as he thought of the replies that would soon be arriving from the naive and hopeful young girls. Then of course, there would be the interviewing. He put down the advertisement and sat back smiling, his hard cock pressing against the inside of his trousers. Silly little bitches, he thought.

***

Jenny Spires parked her old and battered Ford Fiesta at the side of the tree-lined avenue, just a little past the house and out of sight of it then switched off the engine. Anxiously she double-checked the address on the letter to her confirming the interview.

It was her first trip to London, driving through the heavy traffic had been a nightmare, she was thankful that at least it wasn't in the centre of the city. Hampstead, famous and so very nice but way out of her league though, she thought.

The address confirmed she checked her long auburn hair in the driving mirror and checked her watch. Too early, she thought, much too early. She so wanted this job - needed it actually.

Her mind was in a whirl, nervousness nipped deep in her stomach and her hands trembled slightly. Weeks it had been since she had replied to the advert, watching for the postman to arrive each morning. Wishing, hoping and almost giving up all hope at times, then the arrival of the invitation. She smiled as she recalled her delight, reading the letter time and time again just to be sure that it wasn't after all, a refusal.

Jenny took several deep breaths and composed herself; she again read the letter inviting her to attend an interview and again wondered why they had asked for a full-length picture of her. Thoughts of her lipstick being smudged distracted her; she again checked her face in the mirror. Pale pink lipstick, sober and not too bright for interviews, she couldn't remember where she had heard or read that particular pearl of wisdom, but she certainly agreed with it.

A slow walk to help kill the time, she thought and got out of the car. Millionaire's row, she had heard of it and now she was actually here. Easy to see how it got its name, she thought. The houses - more like mansions really - were huge, each set back in its own grounds mostly hidden from the road unless like her, you made it your business to look.

Silence, almost nothing seemed to move in the road, just the sounds of the birds and the distance murmur of traffic on the busier roads far-off. So very different to where she lived.

Jenny crossed the road and walked close to the high hedge of the big house to stand in the entrance to the driveway. It was enormous, Georgian in style, set far back from the road and at the end of a long, curving gravel driveway, well maintained with freshly painted walls of beige and window frames and corbelling picked out in pure white. Two rows of high leaded windows showed the upper and ground floors of the house to be both long and high, two double garage doors to one end of the house painted also in white, gleamed in the weak spring sunshine. Jenny sighed in envy, what it must be like to live in such surroundings.

Nervousness gripped her, she wanted to turn and run, she felt humble and out-of-place in the face of such obvious wealth. She smoothed her short black skirt, picking a shred of lint from the hem, it seemed inadequate in such circumstances; her one good skirt - her best one, and it seemed so pathetic in the bright light of the daytime.

Determined as always, she told herself boldly that she had come this far, she had nothing to lose - she didn't feel convinced. Jenny checked her black hold-up stockings for ladders or snags, silly really she thought, for there was nothing she could do about it even if they were holed. A glance down at her buttoned blouse reassured her that no stains or creases existed to mar her presentation and she walked forward down the driveway.

Shoulders back and head high, she walked self-consciously through the gravel, her high heels making the walk difficult and certainly inelegant. Jenny had a feeling of being watched as she approached, it did little to help her progress and she sighed with relief when at last she reached the base of the stone steps that lead-up to the front door.

The huge porch, supported by four thick, white-painted columns was as big as the lounge in a normal house. Terracotta tiles covered the floor leading to the wide and highly polished front door, a huge brass knocker adorned the centre of the heavy door, Jenny knocked lightly.

As she waited, she rubbed a tissue over her black shoes; the dust from the gravel had ruined her careful polishing. No reply came, again Jenny knocked, louder this time and cringed as she heard the hollow booming echo around the inside of the house, she waited.

Bowling-green lawns neatly trimmed and edged, flowers of all types planted in neatly planned rows gave a show-house presentation to the huge front garden.

"Jenny Spires?" The velvety voice asked as the door opened.

Jenny spun around to face the door.

"Professor Lane?"

"Yes. Do come in," his kindly voice coaxed.

Jenny flushed - he was lovely. Not at all what she had expected, professors were old with glasses and beards, they dressed scruffily and were both impatient and short in their manner; that's what she had thought until now anyway.

Clean- and well presented, he was cool and confident. About fifty, Jenny guessed, with thick silver hair brushed back to show his fine facial features. He smelled good and fresh as she stepped past him into the hallway.

As large as her village hall, the enormous size of the entrance hall made Jenny gasp. A wide central staircase like those seen in Hollywood movies curved up to the first floor giving access to the many doors visible leading off from the wide balcony that ran around the upstairs landing. Deep-piled carpet in dusky blue covered every inch of the floor and stairs.

"Please follow me," the professor prompted and lead the

way through to the lounge.

Expensive looking paintings adorned the walls, antique furniture rested around the walls and they weren't even out of the hall yet! Jenny looked around in amazement as she followed his lead.

The professor stood back politely to allow her to enter the lounge and then excused himself.

"Make yourself comfortable, Jenny, I won't be moment. '

Enormous was the only word Jenny could think of to describe the lounge. High patio doors ran the length of the outside wall giving the room a bright appearance and showing the whole of the rear gardens as a panoramic feature. Cream painted walls and a tasteful mix of antique and modern furniture made the room a joy to be in.

Jenny walked to the two large settees that faced each other in the centre of the room and seated herself nervously. She placed her small handbag on the long coffee table that stood between the two settees and sat back to look around the room in more detail.

A big chandelier hung from an ornate ceiling and heavy velvet curtains tied back at the ends of the room. Heavy glass vases filled with freshly cut flowers seemed to lift the room and the decoration to create a gentle and relaxing atmosphere.

"Please forgive me," the professor announced as he entered and sat down on the settee opposite Jenny. His eyes went immediately to her legs as the short skirt pulled back along her thighs, he made no secret of the fact that he was looking directly at her slim thighs.

The bitch is perfect, he thought. Her slim legs and slender thighs, her tight firm bust not over-large but pert and in perfect proportion to the rest of her delicate frame.

Jenny shifted uncomfortably, aware of his gaze on her legs; she pressed her knees tightly together and clasped her hands on her lap to press the hem of her short skirt down. From his position he could possibly see straight up her skirt.

"Now, Jenny," his warm velvety voice broke the silence.

He laid the folder on his lap and opened it, the cover facing her. "I see from your application that you are eighteen years-old."

He looked up at her for confirmation; his eyes dropping down to linger on her breasts as they pushed against the tight material covering of her blouse.

"Yes," Jenny agreed. She cleared her throat nervously and repeated the confirmation slightly louder. "Yes, my birthday was two weeks ago."

He nodded and continued.

"You are studying - sorry, about to begin the study of psychology," he paused and again looked at her.

His cock stirred, he loved this part. The young girl before him, in awe and under his control. Fresh and unknown to him, a challenge for him, one that he rose to in more ways than one.

"Yes I am. I started some time ago and now want to apply myself seriously to the..."

"Why psychology?"

Jenny floundered nervously, again aware that his eyes were roaming her slowly, inspecting every part of her. She felt embarrassed but at the same time flattered that such a rich and influential man such as he would be the slightest bit interested in her. She had always found it easier to relate to older men, this one in particular; he was so good looking. She flushed and tried to concentrate her mind on his questions.

"I find it most interesting, people and the way they behave. The reasons they do whatever it is that they do. I also find..."

"Sex?"

Momentarily thrown in her flow of well-practised answering, Jenny sought confirmation that she hadn't misheard him.

"Sex?"

He smiled and looked directly into her eyes. He loved these mind-games, toying with them and confusing them, all as a lead-up to the subject he sought to approach.

"People and their sexual behaviour," he said calmly.

"Oh! I see. Well I hadn't really thought of the sexual side."

He looked at her, a serious and set expression that contained a hint of question.

"Didn't you Jenny?" he said knowingly. "Didn't the thought of sex even cross your mind for an instant?"

"No, of course not," she responded defensively.

He closed the folder and placed it casually next to him on the settee.

"Very well. Let's change subject shall we. Where do you live Jenny, describe your neighbourhood to me."

Slightly bemused, Jenny relaxed a little more. She crossed her legs and instantly wished that she hadn't. His eyes moved to look beneath her skirt, to view the expanse of lower thigh that was offered from her new position.

"A good area, suburban," Jenny began confidently. "I live in a neat semi-detached..."

"A one-roomed flat above a launderette in a high street situation," he corrected firmly. "You live alone and work part-time in the pizza take-away a short distance away. Why do you feel the need to lie to me Jenny?"

Jenny sat dumbstruck, her face reddened and she cast her eyes downward. She felt dreadful for having tried to lie.

The professor came to her aid and helped ease her embarrassing situation.

"From your application, Jenny. I immediately short-listed you because of the potential you offer. I haven't changed in that opinion. We must however, be totally honest with one another, in my work and in my private life I insist on - I demand - total honesty and loyalty, I will accept nothing less."

Jenny looked up at him.

"I'm so sorry," she said with sincerity.

He smiled that warm and tender confidence-giving smile that relaxed her more every time he used it on her. His eyes fixed between her legs, looking straight up the gap in her skirt created as she had moved her hands in her discomfort.

"Shall we start again but honestly this time?"

"Thank you," Jenny said in relief that she had managed to

salvage the situation.

The way he was looking at her made her feel good. A hungry and lustful look but so unlike the ogling of the boys of her own age. He was discerning and calculating, a greedy sort of look but filled with appreciation at the same time. She liked him more for it and relaxed further still.

"I, Jenny, need five successful applicants for the position offered."

"Five!" Jenny blurted in surprise and immediately wished she hadn't.

He grinned at her reaction.

"I offer extra private tuition in psychology, an excellent salary, your own room and run of the house, days off and time for studies in addition to any college work and all food and clothing expenses paid," he paused to allow her to absorb the rapidly delivered benefits.

"In return, I would expect you - and the other four successful applicants between you - to do a few mundane chores such as dusting and cleaning. A little cooking and to effectively - serve my needs."

Jenny's mind was in a whirl, she ran quickly through the list of benefits and imagined what they could mean to her.

"I needn't remind you Jenny, that I am the top in my field of psychology and your studies would benefit greatly from my guidance."

"Yes of course," Jenny enthused sitting forward in her seat.

His eyes found the top of her thighs as her skirt rode further up the slender thighs. This time she made no attempt to cover her legs from his gaze.

He sat back, snuggling himself deeper into the thick cushioned upholstery of the settee and crossed his legs slowly as he watched her.

"Would you mind getting a drink for us Jenny?"

She stood quickly looking around her.

"Certainly, where from?"

A casual wave of his hand indicated the drinks cabinet across the room from them. He watched as she walked self-consciously to the cabinet and all the time she stood pouring the drinks from the only red bottle of wine in the cabinet.

With her back to him, she poured the drinks, hoping that her erect and hard nipples weren't obvious through the thin material of her blouse. She cursed herself silently for not having worn her thicker bra. The effect he was having on her was near hypnotic. A pounding headiness filled her; her hands trembled as she poured. A series of light flutters deep inside her vulva made her shiver in delight, the fact that she could virtually feel his eyes roaming her legs and body made the feelings all the more intense.

"Sex, Jenny," he said as he accepted the heavy cut-glass wine goblet from her.

She sat down opposite him and crossed her legs with new air of confidence about her. A challenging look and posture, her slim thighs open to his gaze, she didn't care, it was as though her strict upbringing had all gone for nought. She felt a tinge of naughtiness come over her and she actually welcomed his lustful looks.

"Yes," she replied easily, prepared to discuss the subject that she had inwardly tried to avoid.

"Your views on it."

"I don't really know. I haven't much experience," she found herself opening up and letting her true self to be revealed. The truthful and ever honest Jenny Spires, she flushed as she realised what she had said.

"How experienced are you Jenny?" he coaxed soothingly.

Jenny flushed slightly and sipped at her wine several times before answering.

"I haven't actually. I'm still, a..."

"Say it Jenny," he coaxed her, his voice low. "Say the word."

She shifted to the edge of her seat; his eyes found the tight white triangle of her panties as they pulled across her pussy beneath her skirt.

"Virgin."

"Again. Say it for me again."

"I'm still a virgin," Jenny's face flushed scarlet at the admission.

"Marvellous! Simply marvellous!" He enthused. "Innocence is such a wonderful thing and the learning - heaven itself."

She is perfect, he thought, innocent, naive, willing and ripe, exactly right to fit his strict criteria. He would push her some more, play with her a little longer. His growing erection felt too good to lose so soon. Interviewing these hopefuls was sometimes better than sex itself. The pounding headiness of dictating words and actions and coaxing the little sluts to comply.

"Does the subject of sex embarrass you Jenny? It really shouldn't," he pre-empted. "In psychology we must be able to speak freely on any topic without reservation or malice."

"It does embarrass me," she said and looked at his changed expression. "It's only that I'm not used to speaking about it - I will learn though, I really will."

He smiled, you certainly will you wonderful little bitch, he thought.

"Does it feel nice to show yourself off to me, as you've been doing since you arrived here?"

Jenny felt hurt. She responded angrily.

"I have not! How dare you say such at thing!"

He grinned and ran his eyes quickly over her body as he interrupted her.

"Allowing your skirt to ride higher and higher up your gorgeous thighs."

"No! That's not true!" she protested untruthfully.

His voice raised and his tone became serious.

"Showing more and more of your lovely legs, offering yourself until I could see your panties."

Jenny jumped to her feet; her face flushed with a mix of anger and guilt as he said all that was true about her.

"Stop this! It just isn't so!"

"You set out to excite me, to make he hard and to want you!" he almost shouted.

Close to tears, Jenny stumbled in her speech.

"No! Not right, this isn't right."

His tone softened and his voice returned to the velvety coaxing strains of earlier.

"Psychology, Jenny, psychology in action." He smiled to reassure her.

She stood confused and relieved, she was aware that he had been provoking her. She was also aware that a wetness had started in her pussy to accompany the throbbing deep inside her vulva. She had experienced feelings that until now had been unknown to her, sexual feelings, wonderful feelings. Her clitoris had jolted several times during her display of anger and defence; she flushed and sat quickly down on the settee.

The time was right now, he felt. He sat back resting his elbow along the back of the settee.

"I like you Jenny," he said as meaningfully as he could. "I am tempted - against all my usual principles - to make an instant decision and to offer you one of the positions."

Jenny's eyes widened in surprise, she couldn't contain a huge smile of delight.

"I must be honest with you however."

Jenny's heart dropped.

"There are several points about you, that concern me."

He watched her expression change, then deliberately looked beneath her skirt so that she noticed his gaze.

"Perhaps we could discuss them," she said quickly, seizing the bait. Anxious to seize the tempting offer that was dangling so very close.

He sighed unconvinced, displaying an intended uncertainty.

"I understand that you are young and inexperienced. I would be willing and patient in taking the time to train you, but..."

"Oh please!" Jenny gushed anxiously. " I'd learn quickly - I promise I would. I'd listen and do all that you said."

He shifted in his position and crossed his legs in the opposite fashion, smoothing his trousers to bring attention to the straining bulge in his trousers that his stiff cock had produced. She noticed it and averted her eyes instantly.

"I can be demanding, Jenny, he offered a hint of reversal in his stance.

"I wouldn't mind that."

"Severe punishment is my reward for failure."

"And so it should be," she readily agreed unsuspectingly.

He smiled and looked again at the slim thighs, exposed now to show the dark tops of her hold-up stockings as she had edged forward in her seat.

"I am tempted Jenny, sorely tempted," he said, his tone still portraying uncertainty.

"I wouldn't let you down, really I wouldn't."

His heart was pounding, he loved this part. When they were almost begging, pleading with him to accept them. His stiff cock throbbed, aching with delightful pulsing as the sexually charged conversation continued. She was hooked, he had her totally hooked, and anything that followed would be purely for his entertainment. He would push her further still.

He hesitated and smiled as she parted her knees slightly, aware of his gaze fixed between her legs. The bitch was responding.

The pounding excitement coursed through Jenny, she was almost there, the job almost hers. Excited feelings of such intensity flooded through her. She found herself wanting him to look at her legs, delighting in his pleasure and obvious excitement. His cock was hard for her, that had never happened to her before. Her throat was dry; she licked her lips and saw that he noticed even that small movement of her body. He liked her legs that much was certain, perhaps he liked her also. She would go for broke and try to close the deal.

Jenny parted her legs more, seemingly as a casual shift of position, but designed so that he had an unobstructed view straight up her skirt.

The professor took full advantage of her offering and feasted his eyes on the firm white triangle of her panties as it nestled between the top of her soft thighs.

"I'd demand total obedience from you," he used a cautionary tone.

"And I would comply," she said boldly, her confidence growing.

He paused, looking thoughtful and Jenny allowed him time to think.

The terrific throbbing in her pussy was sending wave after wave of exquisite pleasure surging through her. Feelings so sweet that she never wanted them to end. She felt loose and liberated from her strict upbringing, offering herself, her intimate parts only scantily covered as they were for his inspection. Her nipples aching and her clitoris hard, she found her breathing had become short and rapid as her chest pounded.

"You are fiery and reactive, Jenny. You have a temper that could bring us into conflict."

"I'd control it."

Again he lapsed into silence, his look pensive, giving her more time to fully commit herself.

"Sex and sexuality play a great part in psychology. You realise that don't you Jenny?"

"I do now," she responded unruffled.

"You have removed almost all of the doubts I had about you, Jenny. But I still need to be certain."

"Fine by me."

He uncrossed his legs, shifted to the edge of his seat and rested his elbows on his thighs; his arms crossed casually giving a pose of total interest in her. He used that warm smile on her and spoke in soft coaxing tones.

"Describe your feelings as you parted your knees just now and allowed me to look under your skirt."

Determined not to be thrown by his line of questioning, Jenny responded confidently and honestly.

"Heady sexual feelings that I have never felt before."

"Did it feel good?" he urged gently.

"Mmmm, yes it did."

"And was it good to flaunt yourself so teasingly?"

"Yes. It was good."

Jenny found herself lost in a hypnotic mist of warm sensual feelings as he spoke to her. Never had she talked so openly and freely about a previously closed subject. She wanted to say more but the reservations deeply ingrained within her prevented her doing so.

"Does it please you that you made me hard, Jenny?"

She hesitated.

"Stand up for me Jenny," his low voice coaxed.

Jenny slowly got to her feet; the pounding in her head had grown to a demanding urge for more. Her body trembled slightly with nervous pleasure, the feelings rushing through her at such a rate that her legs felt weak. Jenny swallowed, her mouth dry, the veins in her throat pumping as the blood rushed through her body to excite her further.

"Should I offer you the position, Jenny?" His voice was thick with excitement and low. He used a tone that required not only an answer but contained an unspecified condition.

"Yes," she said, her voice soft, almost a whisper.

"Why Jenny? What can you offer me?"

He sounded distant, his voice was clear but it seemed to come from a different direction and from far away. The aching in her pussy had grown now to a nagging that pulled at her very insides.

"Why?" he repeated slowly.

It was now or never, the thrill and the excitement, coupled with her need both to please and to secure the job, Jenny acted. She placed her hands on her thighs as she stood before him, she moved her hands slowly upwards, trapping the skirt and dragging it up and over her slim thighs.

"Wonderful!" he gasped to urge her on. "You're so beautiful."

Up the skirt moved, slowly revealing the dark tops of her hold-up stockings, then the creamy soft skin of her upper thighs.

"Good, Jenny, good!" He praised her as the short skirt raised higher still.

He watched intently as the tight white panties came into view. Thin and pure-white they pulled hard around her mons and down between her legs giving a tantalising indication of the shape of her delightful pussy that lay beneath. Cut high on the hip, the panties made her legs look longer than they really were, displaying her slender hips to good effect.

She stood before him proudly, her skirt bunched-up around her waist, her panties now on full display for him.

"Turn for me."

Jenny turned her back toward him. A series of electric jolts shot through her to end deep inside her pussy. She felt good and desirable, a teaser, but most of all she felt sexual pleasure and it was so very good.

He sat close, leaning his head nearer to the young girl as she stood before him. The way her firm fresh backside jutted out so invitingly. The way the tight white panties stretched across her soft skin to mould themselves so closely to the contours of her buttocks; pulling into every cleft and crease of her young body. She was delightful, he had made his decision long ago and now he was convinced. She didn't know it yet but she was a slut. A dirty little sex-hungry slut that would serve him well and provide many hours of extremely delightful sexual amusement for him.

"Turn," he commanded.

Jenny turned to face him again, still holding her skirt high around her waist. The pounding in her temples made her feel unsteady. Flashing images of couples engaged in sex came to her in mind. The throbbing ache in her lower belly had built now to a warm glow that spread down to her thighs. She tried to imagine his cock, hard and wanting. The image of him, the professor, in bed with her, his body pressed against her. Touching her, wanting her, caressing her body and delighting in the feel of her.

Great waves of sensation began to wash over her like a blanket, covering her for an instant. Faster they came, building and increasing in intensity. Jenny stumbled slightly, her legs felt weak.

Two great and powerful surges jolted through her. She gasped as she received them. Then more and then again. She cried-out and her eyes closed. She thought again of his stiff cock as the pleasure pulsed through her. Once again she cried-out, her knees buckled and she slumped to the floor in a dark warm covering of extreme pleasure.

CHAPTER TWO

Paula strode purposefully into the study at the Buckinghamshire mansion; she paused to place the riding crop on the desk before answering the phone.

"Professor!" she squealed in delight. "How lovely to hear from you."

Her voice then lowered to a husky sexual growl as she teased him.

"When are you coming see me here at the mansion? I've missed our little playtimes."

"Lovely to talk to you again Paula, is Louise okay?"

"Your sexy, blonde plaything is as horny as ever professor, never fear. She's with guest at the moment."

"Listen Paula," his voice became more serious.

Paula lifted her leg and sat half on the desk, her other long leg dangling down to scrape the heel of her boot on the wooden floor. She brushed her slim fingers over the black nylon of her stockings and the creamy flesh of her exposed upper thigh.

"You no longer need me, I'm forsaken for another," she chided brightly into the phone. A sense of humour was something the professor should acquire, she thought.

"Could we meet sometime soon?"

"I knew you couldn't resist me for long."

"Paula please! This is business."

Her long red painted nails picked idly at the treads of the leather straps that criss-crossed her chest, pushing her naked breasts up and forward.

"Okay mister serious," she sighed sarcastically. "When?"

"This week if we can."

"Here? Then I can remind you of all the things you taught me professor. I can tie you to..."

"No! Somewhere public. Somewhere that we won't be distracted."

Paula gazed out of the window as she spoke, the grounds of the mansion were beginning to brighten as the buds on the trees and plants opened up to the spring sunshine.

"Okay, you name it and I'll be there professor. Then afterwards..."

"I need your help Paula," he snapped impatiently in response.

"My, my but it must be serious for you to forego the pleasures of my body. Shall I bring Louise with me?"

His voice faded slightly and then came back loudly through the ear-piece of the phone. Paula smiled as she imagined him rubbing his cock through his trousers as he spoke to her. She had seen him doing that before in his study at the apartment, just one of the amusing little ways he had about him.

"No, you can up-date her later. Meet me at the tables outside the tea-shop in Golder's Hill park, Tuesday, shall we say at about eleven?"

"What? Where the hell is this place? You're beginning to worry me with all this secretive stuff professor."

Paula scribbled the directions he gave her on the note-pad and replaced the phone. She pondered, sitting as she had finished the conversation, half on the desk. Serious he always was, she thought, but this concerned her. He certainly wasn't his usual dry and humourless self, it was a deeper degree of seriousness - she hoped he would be all right.

***

The huge bedroom looked out over the rear gardens of the professor's house. Bright and airy it had a large double bed a small desk, two bedside cabinets and a long dressing table with an equally long mirror attached to it. Thick cream carpet covered the floor from wall to wall and bright curtains that matched the bed linen, hung at the side of the wide French-windows.

Jenny sat in one of the two small armchairs placed in the centre of the room, she was pleased, ecstatic would be a better description. It was heaven and it was all hers. The large en-suite bathroom with its over-sized bath, shower and towels that felt like cotton wool on your skin they were so soft and thick. Like a schoolgirl she giggled to herself and ran out onto the balcony for the second time since she had arrived. It was great! Simply great! There, she breathed deeply surveying the surrounding countryside visible over the thick hedge at the end of the big gardens.

The initial euphoria over, she stepped back into the room and set about the task of unpacking her clothes and filling the long fitted wardrobe that covered one full wall of the room. Playfully, she peeked at herself from time to time in the long mirror fixed in the centre of the wardrobe doors, her confidence beginning to grow by the moment, particularly when she thought back to the way the professor had looked at her during the interview. Slight ripples of those same sexual feelings began to tug at her interior. She would like it here, she just knew she would.

***

Paula approached the table along the narrow asphalt path that cut through the grassy expanses of the park. She wore a dark-blue pleated skirt that finished mid-way up her slender thighs and swished sexily as she walked; it clung to her slim thighs and hips revealing her neat shape beneath. A tight-fitting blouse in pale blue and her dark jacket slung casually over her right shoulder, the knee-length boots increased her height and stride to give her the appearance of a fashion model. A huge smile broke on her face as she neared the professor; she really was pleased to see him.

"My lovely Paula," he said emphatically as he stood to greet her.

"Professor," she breathed sexily and kissed his cheek, before both of them seated themselves.

"Are you in trouble?" Paula asked seriously.

He shook his head as he turned and waved to gain the attention of the waitress.

"No, no trouble."

Two coffees ordered they waited for the waitress to leave the table before he spoke again to Paula.

"I'm recruiting."

She sat back in her seat.

"Are you now," she said knowingly and raised an eyebrow. "Anything to do with the coming vacancy for post of principle by chance?"

He smiled guardedly.

"I taught you too well, Paula."

"Wonderful news professor. I think you deserve it. Anyway I can help?"

He looked at her; a fondness for Paula would always remain within him. She had undone the top two buttons of her blouse just as he liked. She had remembered, as she gave thought to other small details for him, it was part of her appeal.

"Finished inspecting my cleavage," she chided. "I thought this was to be a sexless meeting - at your insistence and not mine I hasten to add."

"Your breasts are as appealing as ever Paula."

He lowered his voice as the waitress returned and placed two coffees on the table between them. Then his tone became more serious.

"I have recruited one girl and am advertising for four more..."

"So principal it is then."

"Yes it is, Paula. But I wouldn't want this to become common knowledge."

She laughed.

"Ever the poker player eh!"

He shifted uncomfortably, he wished that sometimes; just

sometimes Paula could take things a little more seriously. He never did enjoy being laughed at.

"I need your help to - shall we say -help to train my recruits in the womanly ways of the organisation. I can cover most of it but there are areas - as you well know - that require your expert touch."

Paula smiled her agreement.

"My pleasure I can assure you professor."

"Excellent! Excellent!"

"The very words professor. The words you said to me during my interview with you when I replied to your advertisement at the apartment. I told you that I was virgin and you said 'excellent! excellent!'" Paula giggled as she saw him blush, one of the rare occasions that she had seen him embarrassed. "You also rubbed your hands gleefully and if I remember correctly,"

She paused and leaned forwards across the table, "you had one hell of a hard-on for me."

He moved back in his seat, the mocking was unwelcome and it showed.

"Just kidding professor. Of course I'll help you. But I also need your help."

Paula paused to sip at her cappuccino, then spoke casually.

"I'm recruiting too."

"What?" he blurted, concern etched in his expression.

"For the position of senator. Don't fret, I'm not making a bid for principal - not yet anyway."

He sighed; the relief clear on his face.

"And you want me to train the little sluts for you?"

Paula waved at the waitress, beckoning her to them.

"Another cappuccino?"

He shook his head.

"Initially I have one that needs a more experienced hand professor. She wouldn't suit my set-up but she could be perfect for yours. If I pass you the details you can have her."

Paula lowered her voice and smiled.

"And I feel sure you will do exactly that. She is wealthy,

arrogant and it will take a very firm hand to tame her."

"Interviewed her yet?" he asked, gulping his coffee.

Paula shook her head and delved in her bag. She passed him the brown folder.

"All yours prof."

He looked at her in distaste.

"Sorry, professor," she corrected herself. "You will see by her photo and the tone of her covering letter that she is a spoiled brat, just up your street I think."

He nodded as his interest moved to the contents of the folder. Paula placed a restraining hand on his.

"Later professor - deal with that later. I know," she said reassuringly, "just how important the post of principal is to you and I'll help you get it. You in turn will help me and Louise, to gain posts in the senate."

"Done!" he said flatly closing the folder and looking up at her smiling again.

"When do I get to see your new house then?"

He launched into a long and detailed description of the new house; his obvious delight with the property lasted another coffee before the details of the new arrangement were finalised. They parted as they had met, firm friends. Master and ex-pupil retaining the bond that had developed during Paula's training and had continued during his visits to the mansion and at the club's monthly meetings.

***

Responding to the call on the telephone in her room, Jenny walked down to the lounge to find the professor seated on the settee and hunched over a pile of papers on the coffee table. Jenny sat opposite.

"I didn't tell you to sit," he said coldly without looking up.

Jenny got to her feet and stood obediently, waiting for him to speak. She didn't like his attitude but would say nothing. A few minutes passed before he sat back and looked at her, a deliberate period of waiting to keep her at a disadvantage.

"Is your room acceptable?"

"Oh yes! It's marvellous. Couldn't be better, I'm delighted with it."

He nodded as if disinterested and continued.

"I have rules Jenny. Strict rules that I expect you to adhere to at all times."

"Okay," she said lightly.

"Sir," he said slowly and deliberately. "You will address me from now on as, Sir."

Jenny hesitated and then responded.

"Very well, sir."

He tore open a large brown envelope and passed it to her.

"In there you will find a charge card in your name. You will not exceed the limit at any time, do you understand?"

Jenny nodded, her mind more on a spending spree than his actual words.

"Should you exceed it, your allowance ends."

"Yes sir."

He gave a casual wave of the hand that indicated that she should now sit, and she did.

"I insist upon a strict dress code, Jenny, jeans do not form part of that code. Take them off now."

A little confused by his abrupt manner Jenny complied. She stood, undid the fastener and wriggled her tight jeans down over her hips and thighs to stand before him in red panties and her short tee shirt. He looked her up and down, taking his time to savour the firm young flesh.

"Now the tee-shirt," he coaxed.

Those thrilling sensations began in Jenny's vulva. She could hardly believe that she was again undressing before an almost total stranger. It was so unlike her but it felt so very good. The pounding throb deep inside her pulled at her delicate soft interior to send waves of tingling sensation flooding through her entire body. Jenny shuddered as she recalled the intense feelings that she had experienced at the interview. And what she knew now to have been her very first orgasm.

Crossing her arms, she gripped the bottom of her tee shirt and pulled it up over her head. The small white bra that she wore did little to flatter her neat little breasts. She stood proudly before him awaiting his approval.

"White panties, pure white and tight. Black lacy bras, Jenny. Under-wired, three-quarter cupped and tight. What you are wearing is totally unacceptable to me."

Jenny's heart sank. She so wanted to please him and she had achieved the opposite. She would do whatever he asked, but it was confusing, as he didn't actually spell it out, she made a mental note of his requirements.

A wave of his hand again and Jenny knew she had to strip. The pounding excitement was tinged with nervousness as she moved her hands up behind her back to release the bra strap.

"I will arrange for you to go shopping with one of my previous students. She will guide you as my tastes. Thereafter I will expect you to comply with my wishes and present yourself accordingly. As in any training - as you will find as you progress through life - one first has to be subjected to and to experience humiliation. It forms an important part of any psychology course."

"Yes prof...Sir."

He looked with interest as the bra fell away to reveal her naked breasts. Neat and firm, they jutted out beautifully. The perfectly formed nipples hardened and appealing pointed out toward him. Her slim waist nipped her body to an overall perfect proportion, she looked wonderful. Her young firm flesh bright in the sunlight that poured in through the high patio doors.

His eyes dropped to her panties, indicating that these should be removed next.

Jenny's heart was thumping loudly in her chest. She knew her nipples were erect, she didn't care, and it was too exciting to worry about. She loved the way his eyes roamed her. She felt good, so important and so very desirable. Her clitoris hardened in anticipation as she gripped the side-strings of her panties.

Slowly, she slid them down over her hips and thighs, the gusset pulling out from between her labia as they moved down past her knees. A terrific jolt shot through Jenny as his eyes fell between her legs. She was naked, for the first time before a man. It was so thrilling and sexual, the pumping feelings racing through her body and her mind. She again found herself imagining what his cock was like.

"Sit here Jenny," he said with some difficulty, his voice portraying his growing excitement. "On the coffee table facing me."

The neat dark triangle of her pubic hair stood out in stark contrast to the whiteness of her skin as she walked around the table and sat close to him, their knees almost touching as she faced him.

"You are perfect Jenny, simply perfect."

Jenny glowed in the praise. She didn't feel the least bit embarrassed, she trusted him, she liked him and she wanted him to do more.

"Today Jenny, we will deal with the routine details, you then have until the weekend to make arrangements and enrol for your course. I expect nothing of you during this first week; I will of course begin your education and assist you in setting up your study plan if you so wish. Call it the settling-in period if you like, a while to become accustomed to your new surroundings."

His eyes roamed back and forth over the naked girl, her breasts and hips, thighs and pubic hair all were covered in turn and then re-covered as his gaze moved slowly and deliberately over her.

"Your studies must come first, over and above all else. Your course work will be monitored closely and maintained. I shall reprimand you should you fail in this."

"Yes sir," Jenny said dutifully and stole a glimpse down at his groin. The bulge was there; she had made him hard again. It delighted her to know that he wanted her. She was beginning to feel her own sexuality awakening. A hungry need that nagged constantly as it had during the many nights following her display at the interview.

"How much does your pizza take-away job pay you?"

"Three pounds twenty-five an hour, sir."

"Part your legs for me Jenny."

A rush of sensation tore through Jenny. She was astounded, that just his words, that coaxing velvety voice of his could have such an effect on her. She slowly moved her knees apart, her thighs opening to reveal her neat little pussy.

"How many hours Jenny, your total weekly pay? Open your legs wider."

Trembling at the intensity of the feelings, Jenny complied. She parted her legs wide to display her labia and sweet little pussy for him. A jolt grabbed at her clitoris and she gasped at the powerful sensation.

"Forty-five pounds in all."

He looked at the puffy little lips of her labia. So sweet and untouched, his cock throbbed at the though of her delight when she experienced a cock inside her for the very first time. He thought also of the very great pleasure he would gain from such a young and innocent little bitch.

"Wider still Jenny, and lie back on your elbows. I pay one hundred and fifty pounds a week with no deductions."

Automatically, Jenny lay back on the long coffee table, raising herself on her elbows. Her mind filled with a visual image of the figure one-hundred-and-fifty pounds. She spread her legs wide, one foot either side of the coffee table and resting on the floor, her mons pushed up above the level of her stomach. The soft skin of her parted upper thigh and the wispy bush of soft downy pubic hair looked delightful.

"You wonderful bitch," he gasped. "You lovely, lovely little bitch."

The soft and tender inner lips of her pussy were displayed for him. Slightly moist and so pink her sweet little clitoris sticking up just below the mound of her mons. He inspected it closely for many minutes.

Those thumping heady sensations that she had experienced at the interview began pounding in her head and body, but better and stronger this time. She was offering herself, naked and open on a coffee table in his lounge. She silently willed him to touch, to increase her pleasure and to bring again that wonderful crescendo of thrilling delight.

What was happening to her? She had never been like this, she would never have dreamed of doing such things. These questions and more flashed through her mind to be discarded in favour of the delightful feelings and the sense of powerful sexuality that she was experiencing.

"Tomorrow, you go shopping with Paula. For now, you must be punished. Stand up facing the coffee table."

Disappointed, Jenny did as she was told and stood next to the coffee table. He joined her, standing and moving close to her side, he remained silent for a moment and Jenny felt sure that he was smelling her.

"Bend over and place your hands on the table."

Jenny complied nervously, her head down and her buttocks presented high in the air. It was to be her first time, she hadn't imagined it would be like this. She had always thought that it would be in bed with the light out, romantic and tender, with him on top of her.

Through her outstretched arms she could see his trousers fall around his ankles, his cock however, she couldn't see. She tensed and closed her eyes, ready to lose her virginity willingly, if nervously to this older man.

She screamed and stood upright as his big hand landed the hard slap on her soft buttocks.

"Get back down," his gruff voice commanded.

His left hand on the back of her neck pushed her back into the previous position. "That was for wearing jeans."

"But I didn't know," Jenny protested.

Again the hand landed on her, jarring the firm flesh of her soft buttocks. Again she screamed. Then again as the searing pain bit into the cheek of her buttocks.

"Stand still," he shouted and slapped her again. "That's for wearing a white bra and red panties."

"That's not fair," Jenny sobbed, tears rolling down her cheeks as she fought to cope with the stinging pain in her backside and the disappointment she felt. It was his cock that she had expected and not this.

"I told you that I punish severely," his voice was excited and his breathing rapid. "Today, as you are learning, I will limit the punishment."

He struck her again, the slap of his hand on her soft buttock resounding around the silent room. Then again but harder.

"Obedience," he panted and struck again. "Total obedience."

The blows were landing faster and faster. The excruciating pain made Jenny's body shake as she sobbed her misery. A strange wash of sensation mixed with the pain gave her an excited jolt in her pussy. How could pain be exciting, she asked herself?

"Bitch," he panted. "Teasing bitch."

Several more times he struck her. Then his hand tenderly caressed the reddened skin of her firm buttocks. His hand stroking, his fingers feelings, dipping down between her thighs to come so tantalisingly close to her pussy. She gasped and tensed.

His index finger traced slowly down the crease of her buttocks, sliding across the pink and puckered entrance to her anus. Jenny's body tensed at the feather-light touch, little trembles of pleasure gripped her body.

He groaned loudly his appreciation of the feel of her. His left hand moved around to her front, cupping her mons and pressing against her labia, the heel of his hand resting against her hard clitoris.

Jenny gasped at his touch it was so exciting. The feel of him touching her and the sensations it produced were unlike anything she had ever experienced. She drew breath as - still cupping her pussy - he moved behind her and pressed his hard cock flat against her buttocks; laying his length along the crease between them. His right hand held her hip and pulled her back hard against him.

"What do you want, Jenny?" his thick voice coaxed.

Her head hung down between her outstretched arms as she

coped with the new and thrilling feelings that the feel of his body produced.

"You," she breathed sensually and meaningfully.

"Say it Jenny."

He rubbed the finger of his left hand against her pussy lips and she gasped, the very tip of his middle finger dipping between to touch her soft inner lips.

"Your...your, thing."

"Cock, Jenny. It's a cock. Words are so important in sex, important and so thrilling. Say it!"

She was panting lightly, the finger hovering in her tight entrance to tantalise her expectation of more and wonderful feelings to come.

"Cock," she said softly.

He moved his hips back slightly so that the head of his cock pressed against the puckered entrance to her anus.

Jenny gasped at the intensity of the feelings and shuddered as the thrill shot through her. His thick finger pressed a little further into her pussy and she found herself widening her stance, her feet shifting apart to accommodate him.

"Wrong place!" she cried out as his cock pushed against her pink little entrance. "Down a bit."

"Tell me you need cock Jenny," he urged, ignoring her words.

"I need cock, now move it down please!"

He pressed harder against her, the tight muscles surrounding her anus beginning to force open.

"Whose cock, Jenny?"

He now gripped her hips tightly one hand on each of her hips to hold her steady.

"Yours, your cock. Now please...don't."

He pushed in, pulling her slim warm body back onto him.

She screamed loudly, and then again. Her head threw back and her body arched as the head of his cock parted her tight muscles and entered her.

"God! It hurts, take it out please take it out!"

He rested with his cock inside her, the tight muscles gripping the shaft of his cock just below the head. Fresh and unexplored, her innocence excited him more, her protests simply added to the pleasure.

Jenny held still, fearful of further pain should she move.

"Punishment comes in many forms, Jenny."

"Okay, okay but please take it out. It burns, it's hurting me."

Both his hands now released her hips and caressed her back. Moving slowly over her slim thighs, hips and waist, slipping occasionally around her front to cup her neat breasts all the time his cock just inside her anus.

She remained bent over, accepting his cock inside her, hoping and praying that he wouldn't push further up inside her soft interior.

Jenny felt him tense, she heard him groan several times and his hands grip her hips. A strange feeling inside her and then she realised what it was. She pulled away in reaction. Jets of his warm sperm splashed onto her skin, between her buttocks and on to the backs of her thighs. Jenny gagged at the thought and pulled further away, she looked at him in disgust as he stood there. Trousers around his ankles, his stiff cock sticking out from beneath the tails of his shirt, it jerked as the last spurt of his seed fell onto the carpet.

Jenny held her hand over mouth, stooped to pick up her clothes and ran sobbing to her bedroom.

***

Jenny packed her clothes into the suitcase on her bed. Fire and anger still welling inside her. She ignored the knock on the bedroom door and it was repeated before the door opened slowly.

"Jenny?" The bright voice enquired.

Jenny looked up at the woman as she entered her room and closed the door. Not much older than herself, but much prettier, Jenny thought. She was dressed in obviously expensive clothes, her hair neat and well groomed, she looked lovely, and it made Jenny feel inadequate.

"I'm Paula, I've come to take you shopping."

"Not going," Jenny said solemnly. "I'm leaving."

Paula sighed.

"Oh dear," she said and sat down on the bed next to the suitcase Jenny was busy packing.

Jenny noted the silk blouse and chiffon scarf, the thick gold necklace and the incredibly expensive looking earrings. The smell of her perfume drifted across to Jenny's nostrils to add to her confirmation that this woman had money. The thick skirt and those sheer stockings. This woman really knew how to dress. She carried herself so confidently, graceful and elegant, she was attraction itself.

"Problems?" Paula enquired.

"I don't want to talk about it," Jenny said haughtily and turned to clear the draw of her bedside cabinet.

"I felt the same when I first came here."

Jenny whirled to face her.

"You? You mean...?"

A reassuring smile broke on Paula's face.

"Just like you I was. Penniless, naive and in awe of the professor."

Jenny threw a handful of underwear forcefully into the case at the mention of him.

"Now, in just over a year, I live in a mansion, drive a big car. I spend freely and have no worries. I have my degree, I am a partner in my own enterprise and I am happy. How many girls of under twenty can say that?"

Jenny watched her with interest, listening as the details of Paula's life were given. In just a year! And she was then just like her, it seemed incredible, but then many things seemed so different in the short time she had been here herself. Feelings and experiences so very new and different, it had opened her eyes to another and perhaps better life.

"You're trying to talk me round - aren't you?"

Paula lay back on the bed supporting herself on her elbows.

"No,' she said firmly. "I wouldn't do that. You have to make your own decisions in life. I came here to go shopping with you, I can give you an experienced view of the life here. You know, the 'I've done it, been there and got the tee-shirt to prove it' bit.

"Look at it this way, Jenny, you might as well spend his money and set yourself up with a whole new wardrobe before you go and it can't do any harm to listen can it?"

Jenny responded to the sweet smile and sat down on the bed. Paula noticed Jenny's brief glance at her slim nylon-clad thigh. Paula envied her in a way, she remember the learning that she had done herself. The way she had reacted angrily against the professor and the thrilling excitement as he introduced her to new and wonderful sexual experiences. All of these things Jenny was about to learn for herself now, Paula wished that she could have just a little of the girl's naivety again.

"He did something to me that I..."

"And me."

A look of surprise silenced Jenny.

"He likes you. He would never have done that if he didn't. You would have been out of the door in an instant."

"A strange way of showing affection."

Paula held Jenny's hand.

"Look, let's go shopping shall we? We'll talk on the way and you can ask me anything you like - deal?"

Jenny smiled and nodded.

"Good that's settled," Paula said brightly getting to her feet. "We'll take your car."

Jenny hesitated.

"But..."

"Oh I don't mean that old thing of yours. I mean your new one that is standing on the driveway for you."

Jenny moved to the window full of uncertainty.

"But that's yours isn't it?"

"I drove it over here for you certainly, and you'll have to drop me off home - we, within the organisation don't use public transport."

CHAPTER THREE

In the corridor outside the professor's study, Jenny prepared herself to enter. She had thought long and hard about her situation following the shopping trip with Paula and had decided what her course of action would be.

Dressed as was required in a short black skirt, pleated and tight on the hips, a white blouse that clung to the shape of her body and under her breasts. Black hold-up stockings and knee-length black leather boots, Jenny felt so very good. The bright red lipstick and nail-varnish that Paula had suggested she use was louder than she would have chosen for herself, but she had to admit that it gave her an extremely sensual look.

She would, she had decided, make the most of the opportunity that had presented itself in her life and she would comply with his wishes and his actions. Engaging willingly in his activities as much if not more for her benefit as for his. She would however, not allow him to dictate fully, she had after all, to retain some degree of autonomy and fully intended to do so. Jenny knocked lightly on the study door, waited and then entered.

"Jenny!" the professor enthused as he spun his swivel chair around to face her. His expression was one of pleasant surprise. The smile on his face growing, as he looked her up and down.

Jenny's body positively throbbed at the thrill it gave her, she knew she looked good, it had taken her a long time to dress and to prepare for this moment. The effect it had on him made it all worthwhile. She walked confidently into the room and stood in the centre, her shoulders back and head high, she waited as he ogled her hungrily.

"I see your trip with Paula has paid dividends. You look wonderful Jenny, absolutely wonderful!"

"Thank you sir," she said obediently, unable to contain the delight that she felt at his pleasure.

"Hands behind you girl," he prompted and Jenny complied. "Underwear?"

"White panties and black lacy bra."

He nodded his approval and stood up, his eyes searching the top of her blouse for the two top buttons, they were open as he wished them to be.

"Paula has guided you well my little bitch. Tomorrow evening I have several important guests coming here. I want to introduce you to them and I expect you to be on your best behaviour."

He moved slowly around her, inspecting every part of her. The telltale bulge in his trousers gave Jenny a jolt as she glanced down at his groin.

"I'd like to speak to you professor, sir."

"Not now," he breathed as he circled her.

He unbuckled the belt of his trousers and dropped them to the floor, his under-shorts followed then he sat down in the chair and kicked his crumpled trousers away.

"Kneel," he pointed to the floor between his legs.

Jenny knelt, her eyes taking in the hard erection of his cock as it stuck up from his bush of pubic hair. Long and thick, its bulbous head had a purplish colour about it and veins were clearly visible along the shaft. Not at all what she had expected, it looked angry and slightly gnarled. The foreskin was pulled back tight against the shaft, which looked quite painful to Jenny.

She knelt between his open thighs, her face close his throbbing member, her vulva producing light ripples of pleasure as she imagined what it would feel like inside her. Her nipples were firm, she could feel them pressing against the material of the inside of her bra, rubbing and exciting them to hardness.

His voice was low and thick but still velvety and coaxing, excitement altering the usual tones to a hypnotic pleading.

"Look at it Jenny. Come to know and to love it, worship it and treat it as though it were your most prized possession. Lavish love and tenderness upon it and it will reward you with such wonderfully delightful feelings and orgasms. It will drive you to heights to which you have never climbed, heights that you could never have thought it possible to achieve."

The underneath of his thick shaft showed a dark vein that ran down the length of it, it twitched in slight involuntary jerks as it stood upright for her inspection.

"The nail of your little finger Jenny, run it down underneath."

Cautiously, she complied, her hand trembling slightly; she traced the very tip of her nail down the thick vein.

He tensed instantly and gasped loudly before groaning his pleasure. His knees jerked at her light touch and his cock jolted several times, his face creased and contorted in pained pleasure.

The charge that Jenny received from her action and his reaction shot through her like a thunderbolt. So powerful and heady, that a simple touch of her nail on the underside of his cock could produce such terrific reaction gave her great pleasure. Her pussy contracted its internal muscles to send rippling sensations running through her. She repeated the action, using slow and deliberately sexy movements of her hand.

"My balls," he said urgently. "Now my balls!"

With the tip of her nail, she repeated the action, stroking lightly on the underside of his ball-sac. Her slim fingers looking so white against the wrinkled darker skin of his scrotum.

He grasped the arms of his chair and his hips lifted clear of the chair, he moaned loudly, his eyes closed and opened, as did his mouth.

Spurred on by his obvious pleasure, Jenny gently cupped his balls in her delicate little hand and weighted them tenderly, her long nails teasing at the rear of the sac close to his anus. His body heaved and shifted in his seat, his loud gasp of relief coming only when she withdrew her hand.

"Marvellous. Bloody marvellous!" he muttered as he lowered himself back into his seat. "Hold it for me Jenny."

Her pussy moist and her clitoris hard, Jenny felt good and so very powerful. It was as though she was now in command; with just a finger she could bring him pleasure and control him. Wherever she touched he would respond, it was such a high. Her mouth was dry, her heart pounding, the sex simply got better and better.

Her slim and delicate fingers hovered tantalisingly close to his cock; she circled her fingers around his shaft and gripped it lightly. He groaned and slumped in his chair.

Warm and hard, Jenny thrilled as she felt it throbbing in her hand. The sight of the thick shaft, her small hand and red fingernails standing-out brightly against his skin. It was wonderful; she could almost sense his pounding excitement. He was silent and panting as she gripped it. Jenny squeezed a little harder.

"Rub your thumb across the top," he panted his excitement clear in the urgency of his voice.

Holding his cock firmly in her hand, Jenny lightly rubbed her thumb across the top of his velvety glans.

"Ahh!" he gurgled and tensed, his eyes rolled and his head fell back.

The heady pulsing in her brain, the nagging ache in her vulva spurred Jenny on; she felt her own excitement building to new and previously unknown thresholds. She watched spellbound as a drop of lubricant oozed from the eyehole of his cock and she smeared it around his glans with her thumb.

As if by instinct, she began a steady squeezing rhythm, alternately gripping and releasing his shaft whilst her thumb flicked across the tip.

He was beside himself, his hands gripped the chair, and his knuckles white and drained of blood as he tightened his grip on it in his excitement. His breathing was loud and rapid, his face flushed and his brow coated in a fine film of perspiration.

Jenny felt alive with a mix of heady excitement and pounding sexual urge. It was great to watch him in such ecstasy but to be the reason for it was wilder still. She began to move her hand up and down the shaft, marvelling at the way the foreskin rolled first up around the glans and then back tight against the shaft to show the head of his cock in all its glory.

Powerful surges ran through her to further excite her aching clitoris and nipples. The pounding rhythm urging her to do more and add to the growing sexual excitement that they shared. She used her left hand to cup his balls as her right hand worked on his cock.

"Look at me," he pleaded. "Wide moon-like eyes that hold a

touch of innocence and pleading."

Jenny lowered her head and tilted it to one side; she widened her eyes and gazed directly into his. She parted her blood-red lips and sighed softly.

He thrust his hips high, so high from the chair that she had to shift position to retain her hold on his cock. Then he came. Thick globules of his sperm jetted onto her face and chin in powerful spurts.

She released him instantly and recoiled in disgust, scrabbling away to stand clear of him. Wiping the side of her face with the back of her hand to remove the thick warm seed he had sprayed on to her.

"You bastard!" she screamed. "You filthy disgusting bastard!"

He stood, his thick cock rapidly softening as he walked to the door and locked it.

"That!" she screamed at him. "Is one of the things I will not take! You hurt me by doing my backside. And now this!"

The speed of his reaction took her by surprise, in an instant he was by her side, his hand gripping her hair and twisting it painfully. Around her he moved, screwing the bunch of hair more tightly in his fingers.

She screamed, her hair threatening to be torn out by the roots; both her hands came up to clamp over his in a vain effort to stem the rising pain. Gradually her knees buckled and she lowered submissively to her knees, then to fall sobbing heavily onto her side as he shoved her roughly away from him.

The professor stood over her, panting loudly.

"You will not defy me bitch."

He reached for a thin cane, raised it menacingly high above his shoulder and then delivered a stinging lash across the back of her exposed thigh. In rapid succession he rained seven savage lashes of the cane onto her lower buttocks and thighs as she lay screaming her agony and bucking in reaction to the blows. Finally he halted, panting hard from his exertions.

Several minutes he waited before gripping her arm and hauling her to her feet.

"Bend over the desk, slut," he snarled angrily and shoved Jenny forward.

She landed face down on the desk, her breasts crushed on to the pens and desk calendar on its surface which bit cruelly into her soft orbs.

His big hand pressed down on the small of her back and he kicked her legs sideways to widen her stance.

Jenny sobbed heavily, the intense pain the cane had produced on her tender flesh still stinging harshly and biting deep.

Her skirt was hauled up at the back to rest around her waist and she waited, her body fully tensed for his next assault on her. Jenny shuddered involuntarily when the palm of his hand smoothed gently over the soft material of her tight white panties.

He moaned softly to himself as his hand moved over the taut silky material, his fingers feeling and caressing her soft skin at the sides of her small panties. For many minutes he touched her before his fingers worked beneath the tight elastic of her panties and repeated the caressing on her soft skin.

Up his hand moved, to the top of the panties. Jenny gasped in reaction when in one swift and powerful move he ripped the flimsy material from her body. She groaned loudly in despair, as she feared a repeat of his previous invasion of her anus. Again his hand moved over her smooth buttocks, feeling and stroking with a tenderness that was in sharp contrast to the severe pain that the cane had brought. Nice, welcome feelings that stirred her insides to sexual excitement. Those rippling sensations, so sweet and so very strong. The ones that pulled her clitoris to hardness and gripped deep inside her pussy to bring again the dull and nagging ache for release.

"How many Jenny? How many stokes will your punishment take?"

"What?" Jenny sobbed in surprise. "Haven't I taken enough!"

She tensed and flinched as his hand gripped her buttocks,

his fingers digging hard into her soft flesh.

"Three," she said quickly in an effort to get him to ease his grip on her.

He pinched harder.

"Six!"

He released her and stood back. Jenny sighed as the blood returned to her numbed buttock cheek and rested the side of her face down on the cool wooden surface of the desk.

He stood beside her, his cock again hard, his arm holding the cane high ready to strike.

The breath was forced from Jenny's lungs, her face slid forward along the desk as her body jerked and tensed in reaction. She tried to scream but nothing came. Her head and shoulders threw back; she raised herself onto her hands, arching her back to cope with the searing pain as the thin cane bit savagely into her soft buttocks.

"Count them Jenny," his mocking voice breathed.

Jenny regained her breath. She wanted to react but remained as she was.

"One."

Again he struck her, the cane lashing her soft flesh. Her body jerked violently.

"Two," she sobbed.

The professor adjusted his position and then struck her again.

"Three," she wailed and fell forward on the desk.

"Four," she cried out at the next stroke and began slipping into a warm and wonderful sensation that was washing over her.

"Five, " she called out in a softer tone. Amazed that her pussy actually contracted in anticipation of the next set of shuddering feelings.

"Six," she moaned softly as the terrific surge passed through her. She was slipping fast into that warm and blissful state of pre-orgasm. It was approaching faster with each lash of the cane on her. This is madness she told herself. Orgasm through pain, how could it be?

"Seven... eight," she groaned her pleasure as the warm glow

spread throughout her pussy and lower stomach.

"Nine," she panted hoarsely and pushed her hips back to receive the next one.

A pause followed before she felt the head of his cock brush against her labia. She trembled lightly, then stronger. Her body bucked and shook as her orgasm ripped through her. His cock pushed in, parting her lips and entering her tight little pussy. The whole of the head of his cock was inside her.

"Oh god," she moaned.

The moment had arrived, she tensed lightly as her orgasm subsided and she received his cock inside her. Up it pushed then a pause, another slight push and then another pause. No pain, no irritation, but no ecstatic pleasure either. Up and up it went until she was filled, his whole length inside her soft interior.

He remained still, savouring the feel of her tightness around his cock. The soft warmth of the young girl's moist interior. His hands gripping her hips from the back.

"Today, sweet one, this will be sufficient."

She felt him tense his body and jerk inside her, powerful thrusts of his hips against her as he shuddered in pleasure. His cock pumping in short spasms as he shot his seed deep up inside her. Several moments passed before he finished and withdrew. That was when Jenny slipped into the warm and comforting post-orgasmic state of sheer bliss.

***

Paula held the door open, allowed the woman to stride past her in a theatrical gush and then closed the door without entering. It had been her idea for the professor to use the mansion for the interview, a wise decision indeed, she thought and smiled as she stood outside the room listening.

"Please take a seat," the professor said in a level tone.

The woman holding herself erect, walked to the upright chair set back a little from the desk and seated herself, looking around the room and making no secret of her dislike for the surroundings.

In her early twenties he guessed her to be, he confirmed the fact from the folder, twenty-one to be precise. The professor regarded her silently. Tall and obviously well-to-do, she was expensively dressed, simple in her choice of clothes but careful in her selection of designer names. She wore shiny knee-length boots and tight black leggings that clung to her slim hips and thighs portraying the firm muscular set of her slender body. Beneath the heavy reefer-style jacket she wore a deep blue jumper, thick enough to be classed as decent but thin enough to cling to her ample breasts and slim waist. A bright scarf wound around her long neck and her bright red hair had been styled very recently. She sat, fidgeting impatiently with her long manicured fingers resting on her lap.

"Are we about to begin the interview?" she asked in an irritated tone.

The professor retained his set expression, he would really enjoy this one, he thought. Taking his time, he studied the folder before him, closed it slowly and placed it on the desk in front of him.

"Miss Geraldine Lancaster-Symes," he said in an impressed tone that brought a flicker of a smile to her face. "Why would a woman like you apply for a position such as this?"

"Why not?" she countered smugly.

The professor sat back in his chair. He had her measure already.

"Because you are unsuitable," he said calmly.

"I beg your pardon," she replied haughtily. "How could you possible know that! I've only just walked in to the room for god's sake!"

"You are Miss...Geraldine. A self-opinionated and overbearing personality that would be out of place in our organisation. I thank you for attending today, but..."

"But you don't know anything about me. You haven't asked me a single thing. I'm entitled to a fair interview," she protested getting to her feet.

His eyes fell to the tight mound of her mons, prominent and so neat as the stretch material of her leggings pulled tightly over it, moulding to her shape. The professor was unruffled by her outburst. He smiled at her.

"Here, Miss Lancaster-Symes, you are a guest. And rapidly becoming an unwelcome one at that."

The professor watched her, hoping that she would engage him in more verbal fencing. He loved a chase and this one could certainly give him that. She was thrown by his forthright approach; he waited for her response, as a chess player would await his opponent's move.

"Few people have ever dared to speak to me in such a manner," she cautioned, shifting her weight to one leg. The mound of her mons seemed even larger and firmer than it previously had.

"I know," he said flatly.

"How? How could you possibly know that?" she demanded and sat down again, aware of his gaze between her legs.

The professor folded his arms, sighing heavily to demonstrate his disinterest. In reality she would be perfect, he would love the chance to tame this stuck-up little bitch. He could visualise her chained to a rack while he worked on her. I'll bet she screams beautifully, he thought to himself.

"It's my field Geraldine, psychology," he raised an eyebrow and noted her flush as she realised her error. He used his velvety coaxing tone now, soothing and inviting, a contrast to his former abrupt and harsher tones.

"May I suggest, Geraldine. That we begin again, with you dropping the false front that you hold up in front of you and tell me exactly why you applied for this position."

She shifted uncomfortably in her seat, her dislike for the professor all too obvious in her expression. The way he had humiliated her and gained the initiative, she wasn't used to this style of treatment.

"Very well, she said positively." Her crisp and polished accent had slipped to be replaced by a finishing school accent that had not been maintained. "My father, a wealthy and influential man,"

"Yes, I know of him."

Stunned, she paused to collect her thoughts and then continued.

"He made - insisted - that I earn my inheritance. At the age of thirty, I will inherit millions. The conditions I must fulfil are: to gain a good degree in a science and to apply that degree in paid employment for at least three years; that I work to support myself during my studies and thereby gain a worldly knowledge of life and common sense."

The professor smiled.

"A very wise man, your father. And are those your sole reasons for taking your degree?"

"I have no interest otherwise if that is what you mean."

"Exactly what I mean, Geraldine." He flashed her his reassuring smile. "You would be expected to fulfil the role equally as would others. You will be mistreated and praised alike. You would gain an education not found in any books or study course, in short Geraldine - you would become a slave."

"I expected as much," she countered lightly.

"Sex," he used his favourite gambit.

"Sorry?"

"What are your views on sex?"

She sniffed her confusion and reluctance to speak on the subject.

"My upbringing," she began in a highly polished accent.

"Is as manufactured as the false image you portray. You are Geraldine, as common as the rest of us, you simply believe yourself to be better. I ask you again, sex?"

She had no reply to his interruption and complied with his questioning.

"Which part in particular?"

"Shall we start with terms and words applied? Are you familiar with the more colloquial terms applied to sex and the body's sexual parts."

"Penis and testicles - that sort of thing."

"No, I'm thinking more of cock, balls, pussy and other such terms."

She sat silently for a moment, shocked by his frankness.

"I know of them."

"But you don't use them," he said, a note of disbelief in his voice. "Tell me Geraldine, have you had sex before?"

"That is rather a personal question which I find offensive."

"It certainly is, it was designed to be - have you?"

She sighed and shifted in embarrassment.

"No, no I haven't as it happens. Not full sex in the true sense, I find men don't really go after red-heads."

"Exactly," he persisted.

"I don't see that as relevant. I've already told you..."

"Once, twice, more?"

Geraldine sighed heavily, showing her great reluctance to answer his question, doing so only under protest.

"Twice."

The professor stood and walked around to the front of the desk, he half-sat on the edge stretching his legs out in front of him, noting her furtive glance down at his groin.

"Do you realise what would be required of you Geraldine?" his soft enticing tones coaxed.

"I think so," she uttered meekly.

"Sex, both in words and actions play a vital role in psychology. Would you be prepared for that? Could you accept being given orders. If not, you would be preventing another more interested student from achieving her ambitions."

"Yes," she responded a little uncertainly. He noted the interest in her eyes as she considered his words. She was ripe, disguising her true emotions heavily but he could recognise it in her. That hungry desire for thrill after thrill, covered and hidden beneath a harsh and brash exterior.

"Stand and slip your jacket off," he said in a level tone. She complied silently.

The professor began looking at her more closely; the way her narrow waist and the small of her back tapered down to her firm buttocks that jutted out so delightfully. The way her leggings pulled so tightly to her slim body, her long slender thighs and narrow hips. He imagined her bush of bright red hair nestling between her soft and expensively powdered thighs.

"Where will you go if I refuse you?"

"I have to be honest..."

"We must be, I insist upon it," he said flatly.

"I don't have an alternative," she said in defeat.

He remained silent, pondering the situation and Geraldine didn't interrupt him.

"Very well. Against my better judgement, I am prepared to consider a probationary period in which to assess your suitability."

Her mood lightened instantly, her face lighting up again as the smile returned. Her chest pushed out, pulling the thin material of her top harshly across her breasts. She noted his glance at them.

"I warn you though, that I am a strict disciplinarian, with severe punishment as your reward for failure."

"I would accept that."

He pondered a moment.

"Subject to a physical test that I will conduct myself, I think we may have the basis of an agreement Geraldine. Do you agree to such a test?"

"What form would such a test take?"

"Do you agree?" he said forcefully.

"Yes. Yes I do," she said quietly.

He passed her a business card.

"Come to my home address on Friday morning at about ten. Then we will test your suitability."

"If I pass?" she asked, getting to her feet.

"I will welcome you as a new member of the organisation. If you fail, then you will leave and perhaps never see your inheritance."

As the young woman left the room, the professor returned to sit in his chair behind the desk. He opened the folder and again read the letter he had received from her father asking him to give his daughter extra consideration for the vacant position.

CHAPTER FOUR

The four men sat in the big lounge, two on one settee, one on the other and the professor in a large armchair to the side. The large coffee table between them was littered with buff folders and small piles of paperwork. Business concluded, the talk had changed to the professor's new house and he bathed in the many compliments that he received from his guests.

"And now gentlemen," the professor announced getting to his feet. "I have someone I should like you all to meet."

His call to Jenny was ignored; he waited, looking towards the hallway. When no one appeared, he strode angrily to the doorway and grabbed Jenny by the arm; she struggled against him as he pulled her into the room.

Dressed in her black skirt and white blouse, her face made-up and hair neatly brushed, she drew gasps of appreciation as she was shoved along to stand before the admiring men. Both her hands were behind her back, pulled up to waist level and bound tightly together with a soft cord; her feet were tethered by a similar cord tied tightly around the ankles of her boots and giving just enough freedom to be able to walk.

"My! Professor," one of the guests gasped in pleasant surprise. "What a little beauty!"

They all sat eyeing her. Each of them running his gaze up and down the young girl, searching at her blouse buttons and the hem of her short, pleated skirt.

"She's proving to be a little difficult at present," the professor sighed as he slumped heavily down in the armchair and took a swig of his whiskey.

No direct reply came from any of the men. One, the closest to Jenny, gripped the hem of her skirt and raised it at the back;

all of them shifted to see her creamy buttocks restrained within the tight white panties.

The anger that lay within Jenny gave way to that sexy throbbing as the men's hungry looks took effect on her. She had fought hard earlier as he had roped and tied her, spitting and lashing out with arms and legs but his greater strength had eventually won. Now, the way the men - all of them middle-aged and well-dressed - looked at her felt so wonderful. Their eyes moving over her slim thighs and jutting breasts, her face and waist, her backside and her groin. A great charge of sexual arousal had shot through her as the man had raised her skirt; the heady pounding she felt as they all inspected her little backside gave her thrill after thrill. Four men! All wanting and lusting, hoping and needing her and her body. Her vulva ached; little gripping spasms excited her pussy deep inside. Her clitoris jerked into life and her breathing became laboured. It had felt good with the professor, but with so many men wanting her, it was heaven itself.

The man's hand stroked over the soft curve of her buttocks, Jenny couldn't contain a loud gasp as the electric sensations passed through her. She was flushed, she knew it, she was aroused and they could see it. She felt so good and desirable; holding them spellbound as they lusted for her.

Another hand began stroking her nylon-clad thigh, moving up the front toward her pussy. Yet another hand now undoing her skirt as the man feeling her buttocks slipped his fingers between her legs. The professor slipped forward in his seat and knelt on the floor, he untied her feet and sat back to watch.

Jenny shifted her feet apart, allowing the probing hands free access to her private parts. Her skirt dropped and two different men's hands were inside her panties. Feeling and probing, touching and stroking, the fingers moved onto her labia and between her buttocks. The heady feelings pounding through her made her sway a little unsteadily.

Fingers parting her labia now, feeling her moist inner lips and pushing up inside her. Light stroking on the puckered entrance to her anus sent shivers of delight running through her.

"Just look at the little bitch!" one of the men panted excitedly. "She's loving it!"

The words added to Jenny's thumping excitement. The fingers inside her exploring and probing. Her whole lower body now seemed to be covered by caressing men's hands.

Her blouse was hurriedly undone and pulled apart. Hands squeezed at her firm breasts through her little bra. She felt her wrists being untied. As if in a haze, detached and distant, she was manoeuvred un-resisting to lie back on the coffee table.

Hands pulled at her clothes; gradually all were removed to leave her lying naked on the coffee table, legs apart; just her black hold-up stockings and boots remained on her body.

The fingers returned, easing up inside her open pussy. Her erect nipples were squeezed and pulled, a hand cupping the other breast and squeezing painfully. Light kisses, whose? She didn't know or care fluttered lightly up the inside of her thigh. She gasped as they neared her open pussy.

Her wrists were re-tied to the legs of the coffee table, the professor that was certain. She cried out as she felt a tongue touch her wet pussy lips for the very first time. The thumping pleasure droning in her head as her body responded to the deft touch of the tongue and hands.

"Let me have her professor," the pleading voice of the man feeling her breasts called to him. Two other voices joined in agreement to plead their case.

"Sorry gentlemen," the professor said loudly. "You all know the rules - look and touch but no intercourse until she is presented and initiated."

Jenny was moaning softly as the tongue returned to excite her throbbing clitoris, building into a steady rhythm that sent shivers of extreme pleasure pounding through her. She raised her hips to meet the hungry tongue.

"But look," the voice protested. "She needs it - wants it!"

"The rules gentlemen," the professor restated firmly.

Jenny opened her eyes, the man feeling her breasts now had

one hand on her and the other gripping his erect cock. He knelt next to her, his cock close to her body, his hand pumping furiously up and down the length of his shaft.

The tongue moved inside her tight pussy, pushing far up inside until she felt the man's chin pressing against her anus. It moved around inside her, tasting and searching her soft interior. Jenny pulled against the ropes holding her, she tried to watch the man wanking himself next to her but the heady excitement made her lie back and absorb the wonderful sensations washing over her.

A thick velvety feel brushing against her lips made her open her eyes once again. She clamped her lips tightly together as she saw the long cock being offered.

The man gripped her hair roughly, twisting cruelly until she gasped. Once her mouth was open, the head of his cock slipped inside. Jenny struggled and tried to pull away but he held her head firmly. The cock moved further in her soft, warm mouth.

A thumb began rubbing at her clitoris as the tongue slid in and out of her open pussy. Her nipples were being pulled and pinched, sending jarring sensations running through her. The heady and slightly salty taste of the cock inside her wasn't so bad after all; she relaxed and loosened her lips around the thick shaft. Accepting the throbbing member in her warm, moist cavern.

In and out the thick cock moved, forcing further down her throat with each of its thrusts. She felt warm splashes of sperm coat her breasts in little erratic spurts.

She was totally lost in a wonderful warm world of pure and raw sex. Four men now, touching and doing things to her. Lovely things and terrific sensations, this really was so very good. She was being used by them and didn't care. They wanted her desperately, all of their cocks hard and aching for her. The best part was that the professor said that they couldn't. Much as she wanted them to, it held a strangely erotic power for her, the wanting and not being able to. As though she were an unobtainable prize that men would do almost anything to possess.

The cock in her mouth began a series of twitches and involuntary jerks. She tried to pull away but his hand gripping her hair pulled her on to it. Then it happened, warm jets of his seed spurted into her soft mouth, filling it quickly, the excess squeezing out between the shaft of his cock and her soft lips as they gripped it.

Jenny gagged but accepted the creamy thick sperm in her mouth. She found herself tasting the salty sperm and actually finding it not too unpleasant after all.

The tongue had stopped its wonderful teasing in her clitoris and the thumb removed. The head of a cock now took its place and was rubbing up and down over the hard little bud. Faster and harder the thick warm cock pressed against her clitoris, building a steady and excited rhythm. It jerked and the man gasped loudly. He groaned as his sperm jetted out to fall in thick globules on her stomach. Hands now rubbed her breasts and body, smearing the creamy sperm all over her body. It excited her so much. The thought of different men's sperm being massaged into her skin, feeding her with the results of their excited sexual acts.

Jenny gasped as the bolt of sensations ripped through her. Her hips bucked upward and her thighs tensed. She gasped, sperm spilling out from her mouth. She trembled in involuntary spasms and came.

Gasping and thrashing her legs in pure and ecstatic pleasure, she pulled at the ropes holding her. Her head raised up and her shoulders lifted. She cried out once, a gurgling sound came from her throat and she slumped back onto the table to twitch softly as the ripples of after-pleasure moved through her.

***

Geraldine followed the professor through the house; the long corridor that ran along the side of the house was bathed in bright sunlight that shone in through the many windows. As they entered the gymnasium, the professor closed the door and walked to the centre of the large room.

Treadmills, vaulting horses, exercise benches and weight-benches were placed in different positions around the room. One wall was covered by wall-bars in a polished pine effect and an adjustable beam jutted out from the end part of the wall-bars, supported by a thick moveable support at the free end.

"Put your bag down and take your coat off," the professor said casually.

She dropped the bag on the floor and slipped off the light cream jacket that she wore. Geraldine strode confidently to where he was standing waiting.

Her tight black leggings clung to her body, revealing her slim shape beneath and exposing every curve of her lithe body. She wore a light green blouse, short-sleeved and made of expensive silk. Her red hair glowed bronze in the bright daylight that came down on them from the skylights above.

"Lie back," he said curtly, indicating with his hand to the angled press-up bench. Geraldine sat on the end, shrugged her shoulders in a display of confusion and slowly lay back.

Her hips raised above the level of her stomach, her mons pushed upward forcing the tight material of her leggings to pull hard against and over it. The professor knelt next to the bench and remained silent for a moment looking up and down her body.

A wonderful tingling excitement filled Geraldine; she lay passively allowing him to look so closely at her prostrate body.

"You have a wonderful figure, Geraldine."

"Thank you," she said warmly, her voice thick and excited.

She drew breath and shuddered as his hand rested on her thigh just above the knee. His fingers felt her leg through the stretch material.

"Strong and firm - just as I like."

She didn't answer. Her face felt red and flushed with growing excitement. She did nothing as his hand began sliding slowly up the inside of her thigh.

"You seem more passive and amiable today," the professor

observed.

"I need the job," she replied and tensed slightly as the side of his hand almost reached her labia.

"You know of course that I am looking at your pussy, don't you?"

Geraldine swallowed and had difficulty answering.

"Yes," she said softly.

"The way those leggings pull so tightly across your delightful mound leaves little to the imagination, Geraldine," that velvety coaxing voice murmured.

"I know," she answered softly.

The thrilling excitement had made her wet. She knew that when that happened she literally gushed with juices. It was a thing that just happened to her, she hoped he couldn't see any wet patches on her clothes.

"Shall I move my hand up further?"

A slight hesitation and then she replied in a deeply aroused voice.

"If you like."

"Do you like?" he countered. "Do you want me to touch your pussy?"

The response came almost immediately.

"Yes," she said softly.

His hand moved closer, the index finger moving to the side of her covered labia then circling around and over her mons, avoiding her clitoris that was visible as it pressed against the inside of her leggings.

"Stand up," he said, his tone now cold and demanding. He removed his hand and got to his feet.

"What?" Geraldine asked in surprised disappointment.

"Stand up!" he repeated coldly.

She roused herself and sat, then got to her feet.

"Are you trying to make a fool of me?" She snapped angrily.

"No, Geraldine. I'm showing you the power of anticipation and expectation. Their relationship to and the effects of rapid changes in tempo. Remove your blouse."

She raised her eyebrow and nodded, then complied with his request.

Slowly, she fumbled at the buttons of her blouse. Undoing one at a time, conscious of his gaze searching her swell of cleavage as it became exposed. The blouse discarded, she stood before him, a small, tight-fitting bra in deep blue pushing her breasts together and lifting them to create a soft milky swell of her flesh.

"Did that feel awkward?"

"A little."

"You have a perfect body Geraldine," he soothed in that thick hypnotic voice. "Take it off."

She hesitated. Her eyes searching his face for a sign of jest, she found none and obediently moved her hands behind and up her back to comply with his wishes.

"Does it arouse you to be ordered around by me, Geraldine?"

She didn't answer. Shrugging her shoulders forwards, she allowed the straps of her bra to fall from her shoulders and the bra to fall to the floor.

He looked intently at her soft rounded orbs. Perfectly symmetrical, they were not large, but then not small either. A perfect complement to her slim waist and narrow shoulders, long rosy pink nipples stuck out from the tips.

"Does it?" he demanded an answer in a stronger tone.

"A bit."

"Just a bit?"

She pulled her shoulders back and pushed her wonderful breasts out toward him.

"Yes. Yes it does."

"Good!" he breathed, his tone full of praise. "Total honesty. I like that. Now, Geraldine. What comes next?"

The wetness in her pussy began again, her juices flowing freely as the way he was talking to her took effect. Her clitoris was hard, it had been since he had first touched her thigh. Her nipples stood out hard and proud, she was aware that he liked them. The best part for her however - and he was absolutely right - was the way he ordered her around.

"My leggings," she said casually, but inside the pounding excitement willed her to undress for him, to bring to her bigger and better thrills and sensations. She hooked her thumbs in the sides of her leggings and slipped them down.

He watched as she sat to remove her boots and then slipped her leggings off. The milky-white of her pale skin against the deep blue of her matching panties gave her a look of innocence.

"Put your boots back on again after your panties come off."

She looked up, her eyes hesitating at his groin and then up to his face. She stood defiantly, facing him, naked and vulnerable with only her boots and black hold-up stockings remaining.

She throbbed with the pulsing pleasure that came to her as his eyes moved over her naked body. It pleased her to please him. To hear his command and to obey, the charge that it gave made her internal pussy muscles grip in sensational spasms to send delightful shudders racing through her entire body.

Geraldine groaned as she looked down at what had taken his interest. The black padded material of the bench was wet where her juices had left a stain as she had sat to remove her boots. She saw him smile and then turn away.

"Press-ups, Geraldine. Do some press-ups."

Without hesitation, she got down onto all fours and then raised herself to be supported on the palms of her hands and the toes of her boots. She began lowering her body and pushing up again.

He watched as her heavy breasts swung beneath her moving body; the way her firm and tight buttocks clenched and moved as she raised and lowered.

"Are you excited now, Geraldine?" he coaxed the information from her in a low voice.

"Yes," she said quickly.

"And how does it feel? Spread your legs."

She complied. Moving her feet apart, the bright pink of her inner lips and the rose pink entrance to her anus become exposed to his hungry gaze.

"Good. It feels good."

Her excitement was obvious. Her pumping arms moved faster as she was aware of him behind her.

"Stop and kneel."

Geraldine stopped; she remained on her palms and drew her knees in to rest on the floor. She rested there as he inspected her private and most intimate parts.

"Where am I looking, Geraldine?" His soft voice coaxed.

"At my Vagina...pussy."

"Excellent! You are proving to be a worthy applicant. You are aware that you have made me hard, Geraldine."

"Good," came the confident reply.

"Okay. Up and onto the treadmill."

With heart pounding her growing excitement, she got onto the treadmill mat and pressed the switch. Immediately the motor cut in and she started running at a slow jog as the continuous mat moved beneath her feet.

He sat and watched her; the way her soft buttocks jarred with each footfall, the rhythmic movement of her hips and the bouncing of her naked breasts. Flashes of ginger-red pubic hair alternated as her slim thighs pounded her pace. Faster she ran and moved the switch accordingly.

"Enough!" he shouted above the noise of the motor.

With some reluctance Geraldine slowed and stopped, waiting for his next command. He had removed his trousers and his shirt, naked all but his shoes and socks, his stiff cock sticking out from his body. She eyed the thick member unabashed.

"The exercise bike," he breathed excitedly.

This girl was wonderful! Obedient, compliant and so very willing, better than that - she actually expected and welcomed the control he exercised over her. Beautiful and such a body, he liked her - very much.

Sitting on the broad padded saddle, Geraldine gripped the handlebars and began pedalling. Her narrow hips rolled so sexily as she moved, her slim thighs first raising and then lowering as she pedalled slowly. Her breasts swinging rhythmically with her shoulders, she looked delightful.

He moved around her taking in every detail of her slim and athletic body. The little bitch was enjoying herself, showing her body off to him. Her movements became more relaxed and sensual as she settled into her naked cycling.

"Describe your feelings," he said moving to stand in front of the bicycle.

Her red-painted lips broke into a huge smile that flashed her white teeth at him. The long eyelashes flickered and her eyes widened as her gaze dropped to his stiff twitching cock.

"Exciting, thrilling - so - sexy."

"More," he urged excitedly.

"I can feel the saddle rubbing against my clitoris," she panted and increased the pace of her pedalling. "My...pussy, is wet and it feels so nice."

"Good. More!"

"My nipples are hard, my pussy aches."

"More!"

Pedalling faster still her voice was thick with arousal. Her head nodded forward at times as her pleasure built and the thrilling sensations rushed to her.

"Oh god!" she moaned. "It feels so good. I want it. Your - cock."

"Yes! Yes!" he encouraged, his cock twitching in involuntary spasms.

"To feel it inside me," she breathed her shoulders slumping forwards slightly and her eyes half-closing. The rate of her pedalling furious now. The hair of her fringe had stuck to her perspiration-coated forehead, her body coated with a fine film of sweat that reflected the downward light.

"Oh god I need it. Please! I need it."

"More! Beg me."

Moaning and struggling now to cope with the heady excitement and rhythmic rubbing against her hardened clitoris, Geraldine pedalled on.

"Please give it to me - please!" Her voice was sincere and filled with an urgent need. "Professor - I beg you!"

"What? What do you want me to do?"

She hesitated, lost in the building orgasm that was fast approaching. The first light flutters nipping at her to raise her level of excitement still higher.

"Fuck me! Fuck me!" she screamed loudly.

He came instantly. His cock jerked and spurted his seed forcefully out of the small hole in the end of his cock. It gripped in jerky spasms as the sperm splashed down onto the polished wooden floor.

It was too much for Geraldine. She tensed and her pedalling slowed, her head threw back and she screamed aloud. Her body shook, racked with convulsions as her orgasm swept through her. On and on the pleasure went, gripping her slight body and shaking her slim frame until she was done. Geraldine slumped forward on the handlebars and then slid down onto the floor to lie murmuring softly in her sated pleasure.

***

The senator sat in the big leather chair of the mansion; naked and hard he answered the phone as Louise approached him.

"The professor," he mouthed as he momentarily covered the mouthpiece with his hand.

She straddled him, sinking down to receive his stiff cock inside her.

"Not a good time professor," he said, gasping as her warm wetness covered his length.

"Professor!" Louise squealed in delight as she snatched the phone from the senator.

She felt his hand slide under her and his finger probing at the tight puckered entrance to her anus for the second time that morning. She moved on him, riding him as his finger entered and stretched her gripping muscles, his mouth clamped onto her long rubbery nipple as she spoke on the phone.

"Great news," she breathed and then listened again, delighting in the way she was having the man as she spoke to her old friend and mentor.

The senator groaned deeply and she felt warmth spreading deep inside her moist interior.

"I think the senator has just completed his visit," Louise breathed sexily into the phone. "Okay. I'll tell Paula - see you soon."

She hung up and slapped the senator hard around the face.

"For that, you bastard! Twenty-lashes."

She got off him and pulled hard on the dog-leash attached to his collar. She then dragged him, stumbling behind her through the corridors of the old mansion, never easing in her pace as she walked quickly back to the cellar.

****

Jenny lay on her bed thinking. The session with the four men had really brought it home to her. She was hooked, hooked on sex and revelling in it, each time it got better and more - disgusting? Not really disgusting any more, before it certainly would have been but now? The thought of a cock in her mouth would have made her vomit a few weeks ago, now, since coming here; she had progressed to letting a man come in her mouth! Didn't really have much choice at that time but it hadn't been that bad, quite horny now that she could look back.

The really good bit had been the men. The fact that it had been more than one, something that she would never even have considered before. She recalled the way they had leered at her; touched her and all of them had come without actually entering her. The powerful surge of that sense of control that she had felt would remain with her, she thought. That was what she liked, the sex was great, but teasing them, offering herself and getting them to want her. That was the drug she needed.

A bath was needed, she thought, to ease that nagging ache in between her thighs that had built as her thoughts had progressed. She ran the bath, the hot water giving off great whirls of steam as the tub filled.

The professor had been angry with her. 'Throwing herself at them' he had said once they had gone. She didn't really believe it, more like a good excuse to punish her. She didn't mind that, it was becoming easier with each lash of the cane and she, at times, actually welcomed it. It was his nasty attitude that she couldn't take. Hurtful and cold, she had tried to please him and he had shouted at her for it. They hadn't spoken since.

All night she had brooded about his attitude, she had thought long and hard and had decided that she was right. She accepted his discipline and his punishments, she was anxious to please, but now he had hurt her feelings and that she couldn't forgive.

Lowering her body into the hot foaming suds, she had decided. She would do what she had learned that she did best, she would tease the hell out of him and bring him round to appreciating her more. Perhaps after that he might treat her a little better. A smile broke on her face as she lay back in the soothing water, tonight. At the study session with the professor, she would do it and watch him squirm.

The study sessions always took the same pattern. She would sit at the table, dressed, as he liked in her black skirt and white blouse, he would sit on the settee reading the paper, 'there if you need me' he had explained. She knew he watched her, she had seen him. Her thighs were the part he liked best, kinky in a way, she thought and giggled.

The thick sponge oozed suds as she raised her leg and ran the sponge lazily down over her soft skin. He would ignore her, as he did whenever he was in a mood, not speaking to her and never answering her. Is that what it is like when you are married, she wondered and soaped the other leg.

He could ignore her all he wanted tonight, it would make no difference. She had made up her mind that he would suffer, suffer in the way that she knew she could make him hurt. Teasing, that was his weakness and she would play on that - to its fullest.

CHAPTER FIVE

The tour of the house completed, Louise, Paula and the professor settled themselves in the deeply cushioned chairs around the small table on the patio. A slight chill in the air despite the bright spring sunshine made the girls shiver as they sipped at their drinks. The professor shifted restlessly in his seat, a sure sign that he was worried about something; both girls recognised this in him. They had come to know his moods so well in the time that they had known him.

"So then prof - give. Let's have what's on your mind," Louise, forthright as ever, broke the silence.

He sighed loudly, his expression serious.

"The recruiting has got off to a good start, but there have been few suitable candidates in the last few mornings' post. I fear girls, that I will not meet my target in time and therefore, I will miss the opportunity to stand for the post of principal."

"You have two already!" Paula said, unsure as to why after such a short period he was at all concerned.

He shifted again and crossed his legs.

"True, but I have been fortunate, the other three could prove much more difficult to obtain. I also have to allow for a small percentage dropout rate."

"Ever cautious," Paula stated knowingly.

"Caution has kept me safe and well all these years," he replied firmly.

"Perhaps we could help professor," Louise chipped-in. "We get applications all the time - you know, word of mouth and all that. We after all don't need girls as much as you."

"Speak for yourself," Paula quipped, trying to lighten the serious atmosphere.

The professor seemed to brighten, his face actually showing some of his old sparkle.

"I would certainly be grateful if you could help."

"How grateful? " Louise asked in a sexy tone, then pre-empted his rebuke. "I know - be serious."

Paula nodded her agreement.

"We could put some your way," she said thoughtfully, and added a note of caution. "Then the rest would be up to you."

"Thank you girls," he said beaming his delight at their offer. "I knew I could rely on you both."

He changed track as he visibly relaxed.

"Your shopping trip with Jenny certainly paid dividends Paula."

"Glad to have served," she smiled and winked.

"I'd like to send her to you for a day - to see your set-up and to perhaps watch you with a guest or two. Educate her a little deeper in the ways of the organisation."

"Do we get to handle the goods?" Louise asked, her wet tongue running lasciviously around her red-painted lips to add emphasis to her question.

"Feel free."

"Oh but we never pay!" Louise said seriously and then smiled, both girls giggled loudly.

The professor, not known for his humour, couldn't contain a smile either. He liked his two students so very much. Apart from being beautiful and sexy, they were a tonic to him, at times a little trying, but they did make him feel better when he was down. The sex that they provided for him on his rare visits to the mansion - well, that was simply a bonus.

"Do I detect that she is not responding to the training?" Paula observed.

"A slight reluctance, shall we say."

"I remember someone else like that," Paula offered.

He smiled back at her.

"The deal is struck, so when?" Louise asked.

"Next week if that's okay. We need to get her introduced to the woman's touch as soon as possible."

"Mmmm! " Louise muttered loudly and laughed. Paula scolded her before breaking into a fit of giggling with her friend.

***

Posing in front of the long mirror of her wardrobe, Jenny double-checked her make-up and her overall look. Her hair had been lovingly brushed and styled, her lipstick the brightest red that she could buy and her mascara carefully applied to add to her sensual look. She had taken much care in preparing for the coming study session.

A small black lacy bra and white panties that fitted her to perfection, pulling tightly into all the right places. She smoothed the palms of her hands over her firm buttocks, delighting in the soft feel of the material. Black hold-up stockings and small patent-leather ankle boots in black. She turned and posed, admiring her slim body in the mirror, delighting in the thought of the professor's reaction when he saw her.

A last quick glance at her blood red nails, varnished with much care less than an hour before, she blew herself a kiss and walked down to the lounge.

The professor glanced up from his reading as she entered. He watched her as she walked confidently into the room, taking in the fine shape and the sensual movements of her hips, the way her neat breasts bounced within the three-quarter cupped bra. Best of all, he liked the way the small panties moved on her like a second skin. She looked wonderful.

Jenny moved to the table and placed her study folders carefully down on the polished surface, ensuring that she bent over more than was necessary to give him full view from the back. She stood erect, her back arched and chest pushed out for his benefit, and she would make him squirm tonight, she thought.

Aware of him looking at her, she pulled out a chair, sat and settled herself to study. The pounding feelings were wonderful as they pumped through her. He was annoyed with her before, now he would be livid. Out of the corner of her eye, she could see him watching her, his head moving slightly as he covered her naked thighs and waist. She smiled as she imagined him searching the tight panties and little bra, wishing that he could be inside them - and inside her. Jenny swallowed hard as the heady sensations rippled through her. She crossed her legs and sighed loudly as she read the material on the pages before her, squeezing her thighs tightly together to excite her clitoris and savour the incredible feelings the action produced.

Each time she moved or looked aside, he would pretend to be reading the paper, uninterested in her presence. She knew him better though, he would be hard by now and in need, the thought delighted her. It increased her determination to tease him unmercifully.

After about ten minutes, Jenny selected a textbook and stood up, he noted her move and watched her. She stretched herself lazily and moved to the big armchair opposite him. Jenny sat down, conscious of his stare and engrossed herself in her book.

It was silly she knew that. Two grown-up people acting like children, him not speaking to her because she had upset him and her doing all she could to annoy him further. It was however, so very good and she delighted in his obvious discomfort. Good psychology in action, she thought and smiled.

Casually, and without looking up she hooked one leg over the arm of the chair, aware that her thighs were spread and that her panties were pulling hard across her pussy; a sight he surely couldn't resist.

He didn't. His head remained still but his eyes centred on the firm bulge of her pussy as it pressed against the flimsy white material. The shape of her labia clearly defined beneath the thin white material. The little bitch would pay for this, he thought and held his temper. The paper placed across his lap to disguise the bulge of his erection.

Lazily and seemingly idly, her hand moved slowly up and down the inside of her thigh. The red nails of her fingers bright against the white of her soft skin above the dark stocking-tops as her delicate fingers stroked.

"You push me too far, bitch," he said at last.

Jenny rested her book to one side and stared at him, her hand moved to rest between her legs, the red nail of her index finger resting down the centre of her labia.

"What's that professor?" she asked sweetly.

His eyes moved with her index finger as she slowly traced over the crack of her pussy through the material. Long sensual strokes with just the very tip of her slim finger.

"I said," he repeated in irritation. "You push me too far."

"Oh my!" she mocked. "Testy because the professor won't get his rocks-off tonight? Because his little sex-slave has withdrawn her favours?"

A dark and thunderous look on his face told Jenny that she had succeeded in annoying him beyond her expectations. He then relaxed more, a confident and calmer look about him.

"You over estimate yourself, Jenny. But you will learn."

She ignored him and eased the gusset of her panties to one-side to show her sweet little pussy. The swollen lips of her labia and the soft downy pubic hair with the vivid pink of her moist inner lips open to his gaze.

"This, professor," she breathed. "This what you will be missing tonight."

Silence filled the large room for a moment as Jenny waited for him to explode, instead, he burst-out laughing. She had never seen him laugh before, it threw her.

"Geraldine!" he shouted.

Through the doorway, Geraldine entered. Tall and erect, confident and elegant, she strode into the room and came to his side.

Jenny was stunned; she withdrew her hand and sat back in the chair, both her legs now together. She looked at the tall girl and felt inadequate as she matched herself against the gorgeous newcomer.

Red hair and well made-up face with thick sensual lips, the girl was so pretty. She wore a thick collar around her neck, made of black leather; it had a large silver D-ring fixed to the front. Shiny black straps ringed her arms and upper thighs, both joined around her hips and waist by thicker straps of the same material; silver rings were attached in various places on the straps. A tight leather bra and panties stood-out dark against her pale skin, long black boots completed her outfit.

"As you see, you naive little bitch," he addressed Jenny. "I anticipated your pathetic little attempt to mock me."

Jenny didn't answer. All her plans were shattered, she hadn't even considered that he had anyone else - she didn't know. A pang of jealousy ran through her, tinged with a reluctant hint of admiration for his timing.

"This is Geraldine, my latest recruit. Tie her!" he barked angrily.

Geraldine picked up the coil of soft cord from the floor behind the settee and moved to the armchair. Jenny sat passively and stunned as her hands were tied behind her back, pushed then to kneel on the floor, her ankles were bound tightly together.

"Join the two," the professor urged.

Geraldine stretched a length of the cord from Jenny's ankles to her bound wrists and pulled hard.

"Bitch!" Jenny muttered as the girl secured the ropes tightly. Her hands now pulled hard down against her heels, she was bound immovably in a kneeling position. Her shoulders erect and pulled back as her arms were forced back to her feet.

Grinning broadly, the professor got to his feet. Bending over her he wrenched the lacy cups of her bra down to expose her quivering breasts and then he pulled from his pocket a length of thin cord, just a hint thicker than sewing thread and began looping it. His fingers worked deftly as he squatted close to Jenny.

She watched in silent horror as he held the loop over her right nipple, the thread surrounding it dangled there menacingly.

"You really must learn not to defy me, slut," he said, his voice calm and even.

Jenny screamed as he pulled the loop tight around her nipple. The thread biting harshly into her tender flesh about halfway along her erect nipple. He passed the thread around her shoulders and the back of her neck and began looping the other end of the thread. The process was repeated on her other nipple.

"Pain is the reward for your defiance, slut!"

He pulled tight and again Jenny screamed. Her body racked

by the searing pain that shot through her. She gasped at the pain produced by any slight movement as he adjusted the thread and stood back. Her nipples were pulled harshly upward, lifting her breasts to bear the weight of them on her erect buds held so tightly by the thread; no easing of the pain was possible, the ropes pulling her shoulders backward allowed no movement at all.

"My turn now to show you a thing or two, slut," he sneered as he watched her face crease in agony.

Jenny held still, fearful of any slight movement; she wanted to speak but dared not. She wanted to call him all the names that were racing through her mind, but it would do no good, it would only bring more pain.

Geraldine watched fascinated as the young girl bore her pain. It gave her a terrific surge, better and more powerful than even the tying of the girl and that had been sensational in itself. Binding someone, actually tying the knots and rendering them helpless had been so exciting and sexy. She felt a trickle of her juices pass the gusset of her leather panties, her clitoris was hard, she wanted the professor's cock. The heady excitement was pulsing through her to excite her inner depths. Her vulva throbbed its delight and her nipples rose to display their interest. She didn't hear the command the professor snapped at her until he repeated it in a louder voice.

Breaking her thoughts, his command brought her back to the present and she responded. Geraldine passed him the buttplug and he held it up for Jenny's benefit; he tied the end of thread around the thick rubber finger and allowed it to dangle before Jenny's face. Thick as a man's finger and about four inches in length, it had two wide side flanges attached to the end that he had secured the thread to.

"Any guesses as to where this fits?" he asked smiling sardonically.

Her eyes wide with fear, Jenny watched the dangling rubber plug move before her face. She swallowed hard, the fear sounding in her voice

"No!" Jenny blurted, flinching with the pain that shot through her nipples.

He laughed in response and moved behind her. Jenny felt her panties being forced down and off her buttocks, then she froze as she felt the thick rubber plug press against her anus. She tried to tense her buttocks to prevent the invasion but her widely spread thighs made her defensive move ineffective.

Jenny sobbed as the thick plug pressed in, forcing her tight puckered entrance to open and accept the thick intruder. Burning and searing the pain was immense; it seemed to push right up into her insides before it was fully inside her. He then tied the end of the thread to that which was around her shoulders and it was pulled tight.

Jenny was bound immovably, the threads holding tension to her nipples and anus so that even her sobbing brought new and fresh sets of pain shooting through her. The burning ache in her backside was even worse; she knelt erect and still.

"Now my little slut. We will demonstrate how things should be, bearing in mind that Geraldine has only been here one half-day!"

He waved his hand casually and Geraldine responded, she removed her bra and then the small panties, untying them at the sides where they gripped her hips.

Even through her pain, Jenny felt compelled to watch. The sight of this tall girl's ample breasts and long rubbery nipples gave her an involuntary jolt, she had never really seen another woman naked; certainly not in any circumstances remotely connected with sex. A ginger bush of pubic hair nestled between her slim thighs, the black straps that criss-crossed her body added to the overall sensual look of her. A feminine yet menacing appearance increased by the black-leather strapping on her body.

"What do you think Geraldine?" the professor asked as he undressed.

Geraldine's face was flushed with excitement, her eyes flicked back and forth from the bound girl to the undressing professor, dropping to where his erection was forcing his under-shorts to poke out in a sharp point.

"God! It's so powerful!"

"Your type of sex games, eh?"

She looked down at his stiff cock as he removed his shorts, the desperate sexual need within her all too obvious in her hungry gaze.

"Kneel bitch," he said suddenly. Geraldine complied and got down on her hands and knees.

"Part your legs, arch your back, stand up, turn around."

All of his commands were obeyed instantly and in silence as the young woman moved to his precise directions.

"Face away from me and bend over."

Geraldine turned her heart pounding hard, she moved her legs apart in a wide stance and bent from the waist, placing her hands on the floor in front of her. With her legs and buttocks stretched wide, the reddened lips of her labia and the pink inner lips of her pussy were on full show from behind. She remained silent as he and Paula inspected her private parts. Her hard clitoris jerking in light convulsions as the heady sexual feelings grasped her.

"You see, Jenny. Obedience, without argument. Total compliance with my wishes and desires. This girl already knows the delights that come from serving. You too will come to acquire the taste. Stand."

Geraldine stood up and faced the pair. He moved behind her, pressing his erect cock into the crease between her firm buttocks, trapping it between their two bodies and pressing into her. She gasped at the feel of him. Both his great hands circled her waist and moved up to cup her heavy breasts, weighing them in the palms of his hands like prized and delicate objects.

Moaning softly as his hands caressed her, Geraldine pushed her backside hard against him. She drew breath as he gripped her long nipples, pinching them and rolling them between finger and thumb, increasing the pressure each time he pinched. Her head moved back to rest on his shoulder as the pleasure raced through her. It felt wonderful; his touch on her, the feel of his hard cock against her and then - then there was the pain. Strange and wonderful feelings came to her, the fact that Jenny was watching made it all the better. She gasped and moaned softly to add to Jenny's discomfort and arousal. Together they could perform and the girl could only watch in heated envy, the thought excited Geraldine more than ever.

One hand moved down, sliding over her taut stomach to cup and cover the firm mound of her mons, the heel of his hand pressing against her hard clitoris, his middle finger slipping between her labia and into her soft wet pussy.

"So wet!" he breathed and pushed another finger in to join the first one.

His hips pushed hard against her, he moaned his pleasure as he pleased her. Fingers moving inside her, the feel of her warm body against him, she was lovely.

Guiding her gently down onto all fours, he knelt behind her and pushed straight inside. She gasped loudly as his hard cock slipped in, gliding easily over her copious flowing juices.

Geraldine's face was close to Jenny's, so close that Jenny could feel her breath on her face. It was an erotic sight, the beautiful girl kneeling before her with the professor's cock buried deep inside her pussy; she could do nothing but remain tethered and motionless.

He began thrusting, gripping her hips and lunging into her. She grunted loudly with each hard thrust of him inside her. The red lips gripped hard together, her teeth clenched as the bitch was sated. Warm and sweet, her breath washed over Jenny's face, forcing closer as he pumped his cock in her from behind. She was whimpering in sheer pleasure as he brutalised her, his powerful hips banging against her buttocks and his big hands pulling her hips back onto him for extra purchase.

Faster and faster the pace steadily built. Jenny was filled with a mix of emotions. The pain had numbed now to a dull ache, the sight before her as she witnessed a couple having sex for the first time excited her. Her own arousal now moving with the jerking movements of the heaving couple. Increasing as she watched Geraldine's face first contort in extreme pleasure and then relaxing as the first waves of her orgasm were felt.

Faster the professor grunted as he moved into her and faster she moaned as she received him. Her face at times actually touching lightly against Jenny's.

Panting hard in time with his thrusting, Geraldine was building fast. Her breathing increased to a series of excited gasping short breaths, her mouth now open and panting. She cried out in sheer pleasure and clamped her soft moist lips onto Jenny's as she came.

Unable to move, Jenny was repelled at the contact. Her initial disgust quickly gave way to a heady and exciting surge as she shared in the racking orgasm as it ripped through Geraldine's shaking body. The lips softened as her orgasm gripped her, sensual feelings being transmitted through to Jenny, who both received them and then came herself. Their lips joined, their saliva mixing as their tongues met in deep and heated passion.

A strange and different type of experience. So very powerful and wonderful yet mixed with shards of sharp stinging pain as the shaking of her body brought agony shooting through her. Once again that exciting blend of pained pleasure that drew every sinew to breaking point and then released to flood her with wonderful warming sensations. Both women gasped and panted heavily, their lips sucking hungrily at one another as the climax was reached and they relaxed.

Geraldine slumped, her face to the floor. Her backside remained high in the air as the professor twitched and grunted, he locked rigid, his whole body tensed momentarily and came. Grunting and slowing his strokes he enjoyed the orgasm, his warm seed jetting deep inside Geraldine's accommodating pussy.

Geraldine was busy, first releasing Jenny and then tying her again as she had been instructed. A collar had been fitted around Jenny's slim neck and a dog-leash attached. The leash had been threaded through the back slats of a dining chair and pulled through to be tied tightly to the lower crossbar.

Jenny was kneeling before the chair; her head pulled down,

the side of her face pressed hard against the soft seat of the upholstered chair. Her hands gripped at the legs on either side as she steadied herself and braced ready for the inevitable punishment. The stinging pain of the thread around her nipples continued and the plug sticking out from her anus pulled hard against her soft interior as the tension on the thread increased.

Geraldine stood beside her, a thin cane in her hand. She was trembling with a mix of reluctant nervousness and pounding urgency to experience caning a person.

"I've never..."

"Do it Geraldine!" he snapped.

"Oh god," she mumbled and raised the cane high above her shoulder.

Nervously, she lowered the cane to shoulder level and struck lightly.

"Harder, much harder!" the professor shouted.

Again Geraldine lashed at the soft buttocks as Jenny knelt before her. This time Jenny cried out as the pain gripped her. Her hands grasped hard on the legs of the chair, knuckles bled white by the power of her grip.

Geraldine felt a jolt in her vulva at the cry from Jenny and she lashed her again. A thrilling surge passed through her entire body and she struck once more, harder this time and then again harder still. The powerful pumping sensations made her internal pussy muscles grip in great spasms with each lash that stung the soft flesh.

The pounding excitement raced through her as she lashed the young girl harder, cruelly aiming to hit the end of the plug that jutted out of her anus. She drank in the sight of the buttocks rippling under each lash, amazed at the reddening weals that appeared on her white skin, she lashed again and again. Her breathing hard and excited, Geraldine handled the cane well. Lash after lash she dealt to the crying Jenny, spurred on by the whining sobs of the tethered girl as she suffered her punishment.

"Enough!" The professor said at last.

Geraldine dropped to her knees panting from her exertions. Shuffling toward him on her knees, she reached out urgently and gripped his now hardening cock. In one swift move she moved her mouth over it and began sucking greedily and hungrily on the thick throbbing member. Feeding more and more of the thick cock inside her wet orifice. By instinct she worked on him, a new and thrilling experience for her that felt so very natural and so very good. She murmured softly as she closed her mouth around his thick member, savouring the taste of the throbbing flesh and the remaining sperm mixed with her own juices.

She wasn't good at it, he thought. But god! Was she willing, a little tuition and practise would see her an expert at the art of milking a man of his sperm.

From her low and uncomfortable angle, Jenny watched in silent amazement. The things people could do to each other simply astounded her, but she felt no revulsion this time as she watched Geraldine bobbing her head up and down the length of his cock. It did in fact, hold a riveting fascination for her, her hand moved from the chair leg to between her open thighs. She began pressing her clitoris as she watched.

***

She walked along the pavement with the grace of a fashion model; the long leather coat doing little to hide her slim shape beneath. Happy and laughing as she and her friend talked, the two women turned to go through the park gates. Obviously enjoying each other's company and delighting in the subject of their conversation.

The professor noted the time, got out of his car and followed. This was one part of the recruiting he enjoyed, the secretive way he watched them; knowing all their personal details from their applications and them not knowing him. An intrusion into their personal life and without them even suspecting, it pleased him very much.

He could see them at a distance, settling themselves on a bench over by the tennis courts, he increased his pace and walked quickly across the grass toward them.

To watch them was wonderful, he did this ÊΣ had done this, with each applicant that he had short-listed, all part of his cautious nature. He needed to be sure before any interview would be offered. If he could sit next to them that would be great, if he could engage them in conversation, that would be wonderful. For three days, on-and-off he had followed her, he already knew the details of where she lived, worked and went; now he had seen those places and her for himself. She seemed ideal, his mind was the next part of his approach and that was one thought, he particularly relished.

"Would I be disturbing you two ladies if I sat down?" he asked as he reached the bench.

Both girls giggled and shifted along the bench to make room for him.

He thrilled as he caught a glimpse of Natalie's slim nylon-clad thigh as her coat opened when she moved. The dark coloured tights or stockings looked so smooth and sexy as they pulled tight across her firm flesh.

"Dirty old sod!" her friend whispered as she noticed his glance at her leg.

"Certainly not dirty, young lady," the professor said firmly. "A middle-aged man with an eye for beauty and a perfectly healthy sex drive, nothing more I assure you."

The young woman flushed red and fell silent.

"Sorry," Natalie offered sweetly, obviously embarrassed by her friend's remark.

"No need to apologise Natalie"

She stood abruptly, fire blazing in her eyes.

"What? How the hell do you know my name?"

The professor crossed his legs casually.

"Would psychology be a clue."

She pondered, her initial anger subsiding. Her deep blue eyes now searching his.

"Psychology? You mean...?"

"Paula and Louise."

She relaxed and sat down again blushing heavily.

"Look. I'm so sorry if I reacted angrily."

The professor smiled reassuringly.

"Really, there is no need to be sorry. You have simply confirmed my initial thoughts from the details in your application Natalie. I should like to offer you an interview."

"What interview? You didn't say anything to me about any job!" her friend interrupted.

Natalie shifted uncomfortably, her friend obviously hadn't been aware. The professor came to her aid.

"Many of my students in the field of psychology attend interviews before I agree to accept them. Standard practice in the higher echelons of science."

Natalie sighed with relief, she and the professor then talked on the details of the venue and date. She felt herself warming to this charming man, psychology she smiled and thought to herself. If some of the things Paula and Louise had told her were true, then psychology was worlds away from what she would be studying.

CHAPTER SIX

Paula came down the wide stone steps of the mansion to greet Jenny as the car drew noisily to a halt on the gravel driveway. She waited patiently as the girl got out of the car and moved to greet her.

"Hey, what's this? Got the miseries?" Paula asked in concern for the sour-faced girl. Jenny simply shrugged in response.

The two women walked silently into the hallway and through to the study. Tastefully decorated, it had two small settees next to the high windows, they settled themselves on the one nearest the door. Paula looked in amazement at the hundreds of books that filled the heavy mahogany shelving that covered most of the wall space.

"The professor is upset with me," Jenny offered, breaking the silence.

"And you?"

Jenny looked at her, question in her eyes. She had expected sympathy.

"Me!?"

Paula crossed her legs, the split in her skirt widening to show almost the entire length of her thigh; a sight that did not unnoticed by Jenny.

"You're pissed off because he has recruited another girl."

"No!" Jenny protested.

Paula stood up and walked to the window between the two settees. She spoke knowingly as she looked out over the driveway.

"I felt like you when I started with him. He has that sort effect on you; drawing you in and making you feel special. When another comes along to threaten the situation, it hurts."

"That isn't how it is," Jenny said shaking her head slowly.

Paula turned and sat again on the arm of the settee, her slim thigh displayed as it rested casually along the length of the thickly upholstered arm.

"Isn't it? So tell me how it is then."

A slight pause and hesitation followed before Jenny replied.

"He does things."

"And?"

Jenny looked up at her.

"You mean you know what he does?"

A smile came to Paula's face; she reached across and gripped Jenny's shoulder reassuringly.

"I will talk about it and listen to all that you have say Jenny, I'll help you all I can - but later. For now, have a look around and see what we do. You can spend the night and a couple of days here..."

"He wouldn't like that!" Jenny said quickly.

"He's already agreed, so relax. A few days away from him will let you see things more clearly."

"Do you mind?"

"I offered didn't I? It will be great to have you here. I'll introduce you to Louise and leave it to her to show you around."

"But..."

Paula slipped easily off the arm to sit next to Jenny on the settee.

"Don't worry, she doesn't bite you know. I've known her for years, you can rely on her."

Jenny half smiled and nodded her agreement. She liked Paula; she felt she could trust her.

Paula slipped a comforting arm around Jenny's shoulder and squeezed her in reassurance.

"We'll get time together before you go back, once you've seen around this place the talking will be much easier and I will be able to answer all of your questions. Just remember that Louise and I started exactly as you did, we felt and experienced all the things that you are."

"Thanks Paula."

She hugged the girl tightly and smiled.

"You can thank me later."

***

Louise, tall and blonde, her long hair falling down around her shoulders, stood outside the bedroom door. She looked terrific Jenny thought, in a tight fitting long-sleeve blouse that pulled tightly around her waist and bust, a flared black skirt that finished half-way up her enormously long slim thighs and black high-heeled boots. Louise had a sexual aura that seemed to radiate from her. Deep blue eyes and full red lips that positively glowed with the deep red lipstick on them.

"He's already in there - his name is Gordon - I prepared him earlier," Louise said in her low husky voice. "When we go in, sit on the chair to the right of the door and do or say nothing. He likes to think that I'm his and that we are alone, It's important that you don't interrupt, understand?"

"Okay," Jenny said, her voice cracked with the dryness in her throat. She felt a tinge of nervousness fluttering in her stomach, what she would find inside, she didn't know.

The tall girl smiled confidently.

"Just watch and learn, okay? Come on then."

Louise opened the door and walked straight into the centre of the room. Jenny followed and sat down on the straight-backed chair as she had been instructed.

A naked man sat on a straight-backed chair similar to the one she was on, except that he was tied securely to his, his arms behind his back and his ankles tied to the front legs of the chair. He faced the end of the huge bed and was set back about three feet from it, his cock, long and thick, rested lazily across the top of his thigh.

"I see you've provided some fresh meat for me," he leered as they entered.

Louise struck suddenly, the flat of her hand landed a stinging blow across the side of his face, and the force of it jerked his head aside.

"You were told that she doesn't exist. I am the only one here with you. You will ignore her, otherwise there will be no goodies for you, understand?"

He nodded, hanging his head down but still casting a furtive glance across at Jenny.

Suddenly, Louise's voice and manner changed. Low and sensually she purred sexily as she moved slowly, hips rolling, she sidled towards him. Standing about a foot away from his knees, she moaned softly as she gyrated her hips close to his face. Her hands smoothing down over her waist and hips to stroke her long slender thighs.

"I'm feeling naughty, Gordon," Louise purred huskily.

"You always are, you bitch," he snapped.

She slid her hands slowly up the length of her thigh, trapping the hem of her skirt and pulling it up slowly to gradually expose her long legs.

He watched her, the way her slim delicate finger dragged

the skirt ever higher up her thighs. The tops of her hold-up stockings now visible as she moved her hips so sexily and the creamy white flesh of her upper thighs.

"I need a cock, Gordon," she breathed throatily.

Louise pulled the hem of her skirt up to show her tight black panties, so tiny that they were little more than a string with a small piece to cover her pussy.

"I give you enough," he said, a rising excitement sounding in his voice.

Jenny watched spellbound as the act continued and the story began to unfold. She found herself being drawn in to the heady excitement that was building; a ripple of sensation floated through her and her clitoris began to stir into life.

"I wasn't thinking of yours, Gordon," Louise breathed sexily and dropped the hem of her skirt back down to cover her legs.

"You rotten little bitch," he said in mock annoyance, his cock twitched visibly.

With slow movements of her slim fingers, Louise unbuttoned the blouse; her red painted fingernails standing-out brightly against the white of her blouse. She pulled the two halves of her blouse apart and tugged it free of the waistband of her skirt. Open at the front and cuffs released, she slipped the blouse off and tossed it aside.

Louise cupped her breasts through the lacy black bra and moaned softly as she kneaded and squeezed them. Her excitement now becoming evident.

"Does it excite you to think of another man seeing me like this, Gordon?"

He shook his head slowly, his eyes never leaving the firm swell of her breasts as they moved with her caressing.

"It excites me," she breathed sexily and gasped softly.

"Dirty bitch," he spat at her.   His cock moved as it began to harden slightly.

Jenny was astounded; the room was filled with an atmosphere thick with sexual heaviness. She was totally absorbed as they play-acted the horny scene. Her nipples now fully erect and tingling with sensation, her pulsing clitoris fully hard.

Louise un-clipped her bra and threw it aside. Jenny gasped at the wonderful shape of her ample breasts and the ever-so long rubbery nipples that stood out so proudly. Firm and pink within a darker outer circle that surrounded the base of each one, the nipples were large but in perfect proportion to her ample breasts.

"Do you think other men would like these, Gordon?" Louise purred in her low voice. "Perhaps to feel them and kiss them."

His cock jerked, growing harder, it now lay between his open thighs semi-erect. Long and thick, strange how the size and shape of men's cocks differ, Jenny thought.

"No! No they can't," he protested.

"They could if I were to let them, Gordon," she said softly massaging the palms of her hands over the erect nipples.

"But you wouldn't," he said uncertainly.

Louise moaned aloud as she pulled and pinched at her nipples. His cock rose, sticking up now, but not quite fully hard.

"I might," she teased.

He groaned loudly.

"I see the thought excites you, Gordon," Louise moaned softly and moved to straddle his legs. She stood over him, one leg either side of his chair and his thighs, her pussy hovering tantalisingly above his lap and close to his face.

"No!" he said firmly. "It does not."

Jenny was filled with a pounding excitement. Her cheeks burned with the blood rushing to them, she watched in fascinated silence.

Louise draped the hem of her skirt across the end of his rapidly hardening cock; the feel of the material on him caused him to groan loudly.

"Oh god! Gordon," she gasped loudly. "Do you think other men would react like that if I were to do this to them?"

"No," he murmured quietly and then groaned loudly as she pulled the skirt back and forth across his cock. Stroking the soft material up and down his throbbing shaft.

Gathering her skirt around her waist, Louise lowered her

hips so that her pussy just touched the tip of his now rigid cock.

"Feel good? Like to be inside me?"

His head fell back and his eyes closed.

"Yes," he moaned, lost in the heady feelings.

Louise began a rocking motion of her hips; back and forth she rubbed the gusset of her panties over the tip of his hard cock, pressing the lips of her pussy down on him. Slow thrusts of her hips added a sensual baseness to her body movements, her slim thighs tensed and working in time with her hips.

"I think other men would get hard for me don't you?" she teased.

"No! No!"

"Yes, yes, I think they would," she breathed and lifted herself off. Louise stood back and slipped her skirt and panties off to stand in front of him in her boots and stockings, otherwise she was totally naked.

Jenny shifted in her seat she was wet. Her pussy nagging with that now familiar ache as she watched this beauty teasing the man mercilessly. She empathised, visualising herself in Louise's role, the incredible charge she received from the thought shot through her entire body. Jenny squeezed her thighs together to put pressure on her clitoris and gain at least some relief. To be doing those things to a man, one that couldn't respond. A hungry and wanting man, filled with desire and able to do nothing except beg, her thoughts thrilled her immensely.

Louise's long delicate fingers slid slowly down over her body towards her mons, her red fingernails leading the way. Finally, she cupped her pussy in her right hand, shifting her legs apart to allow her hand to cover it.

"I need a cock. Oh god, I need one so badly."

Gordon was trembling with excitement, his cock hard and twitching in little involuntary jerks. His excitement now at fever pitch as she teased him further.

"Come here," he pleaded urgently.

"Not yours, Gordon," Louise purred.

"Rotten little bitch," he sneered.

Louise sat on the edge of the bed and shifted to lie back, her head and shoulders supported on three pillows so that she could look down over her body to see him sitting facing her. She raised her knees and parted them, drawing her feet up and placing them on the bed. Her wonderful soft pussy pulled open and apart for his hungry gaze. She looked between her open thighs at the man, her index finger stroking lightly up and down the parted lips of her pussy. Sexily she stroked, taking her time to move around her swollen lips, panting and gasping as her excitement increased.

"Other men would like this wouldn't they, Gordon?"

"You teasing little bitch!" he said venomously, looking straight at her open pussy. "Lying there thinking of another man's cock."

"Perhaps I've already had one," she said softly and sighed sexily. Louise shifted her hips and moaned softly.

His cock jerked and he started visibly, pulling against his bonds. A drop of lubrication squeezed from the eyehole of his cock.

"What? What did you say?" he demanded angrily.

She giggled and rolled onto her side, delving beneath the pillows before resuming her previous position, he watch her naked body as she moved.

Louise held up the huge black dildo and smiled broadly.

Jenny gasped. It was enormous, far larger than any man could ever be. Thick and made of shiny black latex, it looked awesome as Louise held it by the base for his benefit. A large bulbous head at the top and an ever-so thick shaft that was sculptured to resemble a man's cock.

"One just like this it was, Gordon," and she sighed wistfully.

"No! It's not true!"

Louise began smearing the huge phallus with lubricating gel, spreading it all over and around the thick shaft with the very tips of her fingers. Moving sensually over the big cock as thought she were touching a man.

"Yes, Gordon, yes it is!" she provoked. "He had me - and it

was so wonderful."

"But you're mine, you bitch."

She turned the big cock-like dildo upside down and allowed it to hover above her open pussy.

"Are we married Gordon? Engaged perhaps? Have we been having a relationship of any kind?" she asked sweetly as she lowered the dildo slightly.

"No. We are not in any kind of relationship," he responded. "But you're still mine."

Jenny sat on the edge of her seat, her gaze fixed on the big bulbous head of the dildo as it moved so tantalisingly close to her open pussy lips. She was transfixed, willing the huge cock-like phallus to enter Louise's waiting pussy. A slightly sadistic streak filled her as she imagined Louise taking it in her and screaming at the pain it would give her. She silently urged it into Louise as her own need grew to terrific heights of excitement. Her heart thumped loudly, her body positively throbbed with the rising need within her.

"And I was his, Gordon," Louise breathed sexily. "Shall I tell you how it was?"

"No you bitch, I don't want to hear it."

He fell silent as the big black head of the cock moved to push her labia apart further still. Louise gasped loudly as it entered her open pussy; the big bulbous head just inside, she began pushing further up herself.

Shifting her chair to the side a little, Jenny craned to watch as the soft pink lips of Louise's pussy expanded to accept the huge girth inside her. As it entered, her lips stretched tightly around the big cock-like dildo to grip its great girth. Pink against black, the contrast had a sexuality of its own, showing clearly just how much it stretched her pussy.

"Oh god!" Louise gasped loudly. "I can feel him in me again."

Gordon sat silently. His face portraying the disbelief he was feeling. His cock stood upright and hard, the head a purplish colour and the thick veiny shaft pulsing with excitement.

Louise lay still on the bed, her knees raised and apart, the big dildo resting fully inside her pussy. She held it by the thick base and began to withdraw it slowly.

"This is how he fucked me Gordon! Nice and slowly, his warm throbbing cock felt so good inside me."

"No!" he snapped instantly and fell silent again as she began moving the big cock inside her.

In and out she pushed and pulled, the pace increasing slightly as she found her rhythm.

"He wanted me on my knees you know, Gordon, to come in me from behind just as you like it."

"Bastard!" he grunted, maintaining his watch on the fast moving hand as it worked the dildo in and out of her.

"Mmmm! His cock feels so good. He was so strong and energetic, Gordon."

Gordon was panting now, pulling against his bonds in an effort to get closer. His forehead coated in a film of perspiration, a set and determined look on his face.

Louise grunted with each inward thrust of the big dildo. Her back arched to raise her hips to meet the pounding cock. Faster and faster her pace steadily built.

Jenny's hand was between her own legs, pressing hard on her clitoris. She was lost in a dreamy mist of pounding sexuality as she watched the beautiful Louise pleasure herself. She found herself unconsciously grunting softly with each lunge of Louise's hand, fulfilling the role and wishing that she could dare to try that big dildo inside her own throbbing pussy.

"Ahhh!" Louise cried-out and then again.

She bucked her hips upward, lifting her body so that she was supported only on her shoulders and her feet. Her hips thrust high and her buttocks clenched, the hand moving between her open legs a blur as she pleased herself so excitedly.

"This how he fucked me, Gordon. Hard and fast!"

Gordon was so excited, it looked as though he might pass out. His eyes rolled with pleasure, returning often to see the exciting sight before him. He was breathing rapidly, his strong chest rising and falling with the effort; he licked his lips often.

Faster the hand moved, crushing against her clitoris as she pounded it into herself. The heel of her hand hammering against her hard bud in a fervent passion to reach her peak.

Jenny realised that she had slipped forward during her watching, off the chair and was on her knees. She didn't care; this was just so enthralling. Her hand remained between her legs pressing and gripping as the wonderful exciting spectacle continued.

Louise gasped loudly, her hips bucked high and she groaned. Her body shook in light quivers as she reached her orgasm. The pounding phallus still driving into her.

"Ohhh!" Louise screamed and came.

Her whole body tensing and then locking rigid suspended above the sheets on her feet and shoulders. She gasped loudly twice move and slumped back onto the bed sighing softly.

At the sound of his voice, Jenny came back to the present, her cheeks flushed red as she realised that she had moved and had been rubbing herself furiously. Slowly she moved back to her chair and sat silently hoping neither of them had noticed.

"Bloody marvellous, Louise!" he enthused. "Each time you use that scenario to tease me like that, it just gets better and better."

Louise roused herself, removed the dildo and sat up dreamily.

"You certainly did enjoy it," she stated emphatically, casting a glance at the thick globules of his sperm that coated his thighs.

Jenny hadn't even noticed that he had come. So wrapped-up in the sight of Louise in orgasm was she, that she had missed the part that she had silently promised herself to watch for. Inwardly she cursed, she hoped they wouldn't be long, the burning need inside her nagged incessantly deep in her vulva.

***

The professor sat on the wooden bench beneath the ivy-covered arbour towards the end of the rear gardens. Geraldine knelt between his parted knees, completely naked save for the thick collar around her neck and the attached lead which the professor gripped tightly to pull her close to him.

Geraldine shivered, the cold spring air had teased her nipples to erection, her fair skin covered with little goose pimples as she knelt before him.

He undid his trousers and freed his semi-erect cock, holding it for her to look closely at.

"I am pleased that you sucked it for me the other evening, Geraldine. You do however, need some guidance as to the finer points of pleasing a man with your mouth."

"Yes professor," she answered automatically.

"I always tell my students to worship it, and that is exactly what you must do. Regard it as the centre of your pleasures, the very reason for them, let it fill your dreams and serve to delight it."

Geraldine nodded her acknowledgement of his words.

"Slow and sensual, use your tongue and lips in sexual harmony. Your face too plays an important part in the act."

"My face?"

The professor fed out a little of the leash so that she could sit-back on her heels.

"Look at me."

"I am," she answered a little puzzled.

"Now, Geraldine. Look at me again, but this time tell me with your eyes and your expression that you want me - without using words. Convey to me that your sweet little pussy is aching to feel me inside you. Entice me, tease me, make me hard and draw me to want you."

She gave an impish smile, titled her head slightly and widened her eyes.

"Your mouth," he prompted.

Geraldine parted her lips slightly, pouting gently and mouthing silent words to him.

"Good! Good! Now really make me want you."

The look she gave him made him shudder involuntarily. The

sexy little bitch learns so fast, he thought.

"Now grip my cock, hold it as though it might break."

She closed her slim fingers around the thick shaft, just below the head.

The facial expressions continued and she used her eyes to good effect. Her hand moved slowly up and down his shaft, squeezing lightly and savouring its warm pulsing firmness.

"Your tongue - just the very tip - circle the head."

The naked girl did as she was bid and lowered her head. Close to the end of his cock, she used her soft wet tongue to run tight little circles around his glans.

He groaned loudly.

"Look at me, not my cock," he coaxed in his velvety voice.

The tongue moved slowly and sensually around and under the head of his cock, pressing and searching beneath the folds of his foreskin. She gained in confidence as she watched the expression on his face move through the various masks of pained delight and ecstasy.

"Drill the tip into the end," he urged, his voice thick with arousal. His hands now held her shoulders as the pleasure increased for him.

The firm wet tip first flicked across the tip of his glans drawing gasps of delight from him. She then located the small eye-hole of his cock and pressed inward.

He bucked his hips upward in pleasure, groaning loudly he gripped painfully on her slight shoulders.

Geraldine was delighted with the response and repeated the act. Again and again she dipped her tongue into him, each time drawing the intense set of reactions from him.

"In your mouth," he urged breathlessly.

Her eyes held his stare as she lowered her head; her red lips parting sexily as she covered the head and then closed her mouth over it. His wild groaning urged her on; she used her tongue to flick across the tip as she held him in her mouth.

He was panting now, his eyes half-closing as she worked on him. His hands moved to his sides, gripping the edge of the seat to steady his body as the waves of pleasure passed through him.

"Now, Geraldine," he said in a low and excited voice. "Soft and loose with your lips as you move down the shaft, then grip it and move back up tightly. Milk me, draw it from me and taste my seed."

Down her head moved, slowly, as the soft wet lips slid down his rigid shaft. She gripped it with her lips and drew back up to the head. Repeating the process, her head moved down again.

"Perfect," he groaned loudly and slumped back to rest his head against the wall of the arbour behind the seat. His hips slid down in the seat, his legs stretched full out and spread wide. The soft mouth on his cock sending him to a misty world of delightful sexual bliss.

On and on she moved on him, milking him of his seed, she said to herself. At last he tensed his body and following a loud groan he came.

Geraldine sucked hungrily, swallowing his warm thick sperm, allowing it to slide easily down her throat. The jerking of his cock continued for a moment and then he relaxed. She remained kneeling as she was, licking all around his wet sperm-coated cock, tasting and searching for every last drop of his salty fluid.

"Wonderful, you little slut! You are proving to be an excellent student. Later, you will reap your rewards for learning so rapidly. Does the thought excite you, slut?"

"Yes, professor," she said sitting back and releasing him. Geraldine ran her tongue around her lips to clean the very last of his seed from her.

"You like to be ordered around, yes?"

"Very much!" she said brightly.

He looked thoughtful for a moment and them smiled.

"Very well then. I have to go out for the remainder of the day and evening and I won't be back until late. Jenny, my other girl, is away and you will be alone. These then are my instructions: you will now go into the garage, collect the necessary tools and weed the flower beds, you will of course, remain naked at all times. Later, during the evening, complete and bring your studies up to date. I shall inspect the flower beds tomorrow."

"Yes professor," Geraldine answered smiling.

***

It was all so casual, Jenny had difficulty taking-in the ease and the casual air with which Louise made the coffee and seated herself at the large table in the kitchen of the mansion.

"Hope that's how you like it, Jenny," she said as she seated herself opposite.

"Fine," Jenny answered after she tasted the hot liquid.

The nagging ache in her vulva had lessened but just wouldn't go away.

"He's one of the senators of the society."

"Senator?" Jenny questioned. "What society?"

"Syndicate, society or club - even organisation sometimes, we all know what we mean. The professor is a senator and Paula and I hope that in the not too distant future, we will be too."

"What happens in this...club?"

Louise sat back and lifted one leg casually to rest it on the table.

"The membership meets one a month usually and we get to do all sorts of naughty things together, much same as we did today."

"Really!" Jenny gasped.

"All this, yours and my salaries, the cars - all courtesy of the organisation."

Jenny looked perplexed.

"Prostitution?"

"Absolutely not!" Louise said firmly. "We do it because we like it, Paula and I live well and choose who we want to have sex with. There is never any pressure and it's a far cry from the meagre existence at the campus."

Jenny nodded her acknowledgement.

"Am I part of this?"

"Certainly. When you and the others are ready, you will be

presented to the membership. Full membership brings with it your own place, bigger car and a much bigger salary."

"So the professor recruited me for that reason?"

"Yes."

Many thoughts ran through Jenny's mind all at once.

"Anyway, enough about that, let's change the subject shall we? What did you think then, about today," Louise asked smiling.

"What would anyone think?" Jenny gasped as she tuned her mind back to the heady events of earlier. "It was fantastic! I'd never have thought that it could be so powerful and that...that huge thing!"

"Dildo," Louise stated easily. "It was of course rather nice for me too."

"My god!" Jenny gasped. "How you took that thing inside you I don't know."

Louise smiled broadly and sipped at her coffee.

"Easily is the answer. When you are turned on, it's easy - but you need to relax."

"I'd be terrified," Jenny stated, inwardly wishing for an hour alone to experiment with the huge cock for herself; the nagging in her pussy had increased again and she wished upon wish that she could do something about it.

"In time, Louise," soothed knowingly. "And you? Were you turned-on?"

Jenny flushed and hesitated.

"Yes," she said softly, her voice little more than a whisper.

"Judging by the way you were rubbing yourself, I thought so."

"Oh god," Jenny groaned and flushed bright red.

Louise reached across the table and held her hand.

"Look, Jenny," she stated firmly. "We have no secrets here and no embarrassment. All of us do the same things - and boy do I enjoy it!"

Jenny chuckled at the wisecrack.

"Are you in need yourself?" Louise asked gently.

Jenny nodded.

"Like time alone to do it yourself?"

Jenny nodded and then flushed again.

"I don't know what...I've never done it to myself before."

"No problem," Louise soothed her voice kind and reassuring. "You seemed to be doing pretty well earlier. Like a demonstration?"

Jenny didn't answer.

"Come with me girl," Louise said softly as she stood up and Guiding Jenny by the hand. "You're in for a big treat."

CHAPTER SEVEN

The professor answered the door to Natalie and guided her through to his study; he seated himself at the desk and offered her a seat alongside him.

"Let us dispense with any formality Natalie and get straight to the point."

The tall girl crossed her legs casually and sat back in the chair, her hands placed on her lap. She was calm and un-flustered, a confident air about her.

"Fine by me."

"We both know what the job entails and having now spoken to Louise and Paula, I am certain that you are fully aware of the precise details of our operations here."

"Yes, yes I am."

He rested back casually and crossed his legs also.

"You look ideally suited for the post and from the details on your application you seem to fit the required criteria. I do however, need now to talk to you to establish beyond doubt that you are suitable," he raised the pitch of the last word to indicate that confirmation was required.

"Fine, ask away."

"Talk, Natalie. I said talk, not questions."

"Okay, we'll talk then."

He looked her up and down. The tight black boot-cut trousers hugged her slim frame portraying the slender shape of her beneath. A tight black T-shirt pulled over her breasts and her long dark hair cascaded over her shoulders to give her face an angelic appearance. The fine structure of her cheekbones made her face look slightly hard yet still radiantly beautiful.

"Talk to me - sexually."

"What about exactly."

The professor settled himself in the deeply upholstered chair.

"Let's try describing your own sexual preferences."

"Okay," she shrugged lightly. "The man needs to be..."

"Only one?"

She hesitated casting him a questioning glance.

"I've had more than one sexual partner."

"Fuck."

"Sorry?" she couldn't resist a smile.

He watched her reaction.

"Your descriptions need to be more basic and direct. If you mean fuck - then say so."

Natalie looked at him, her expression one of mixed relief and surprise. This interview was different to any other she had attended, she thought.

"Okay," she said easily and began. "I dislike straight sex. The thrill for me is the variation and experimentation with new and exciting things."

"Such as? With more than one man at the same time?"

She fell silent for a moment.

"I don't know, I've never tried that."

He looked down and fixed his stare on her firm thighs as he spoke.

"Does the thought excite you?"

She un-crossed her legs and made herself more comfortable, stretching her legs and offering the tight bulge of her mons to his fixed gaze.

"Yes. It has occurred to me in the past, I have wondered what it would be like."

"Good. I applaud your honesty."

She smiled sweetly and relaxed more, he was an easy man to talk to, and he had a way of getting you to open up and relate your thoughts and feelings.

"I've tried oral - on a man, but haven't received it. I've also tried light bondage."

"And did you like that?"

She sat up in her chair, a huge smile on her face.

"Oh yes! It was fantastic. Being completely at his mercy and receiving such wonderful feelings. It was out of this world."

"Okay," he said with a note of finality to indicate that he had heard enough. "Stand up for me."

Natalie stood, her heart pounding wildly. Tall and slim she towered over him as he sat looking up at her.

"Did our talk excite you Natalie?" His thick coaxing voice probed.

"Yes," she answered softly and then confirmed it more positively. "Yes, it did."

"Good, very good. Raise your T-shirt for me so that I can see your waist."

She quickly pulled the thin T-shirt up with both hands and held it, exposing her mid-drift for him to view. Shards of electric sensations ripped through her as she showed herself to him. She felt naughty, as though she were doing something wrong, something that others might frown upon, something that as a younger girl she would have been punished for. It felt good though, so very, very good.

"Higher," he stated simply.

Without hesitation, she rolled the T-shirt up and over her breasts. A tight black bra pulled tightly to restrain the swelling orbs of flesh. Young and fresh, firm and creamy, her skin looked so soft and so very appealing. The way her breasts pushed forward proudly above her neat waist and slender hips.

"Take it off, Natalie," his velvety voice urged.

She struggled to work the tight shirt over her head, folding it neatly; she placed it carefully over the back of her chair.

"And my bra?" she asked casually without a hint of embarrassment.

He nodded and watched as she removed it. Firm rounded breasts with small neat nipples that stuck out hard from her soft skin. Even without a bra, her breasts had a natural cleavage as they came close together in the centre of her chest. So firm and taut, the skin seemed to stretch beautifully and perfectly to form her attractive mounds.

"Does it bother you to be naked before me?"

"Not especially," she responded easily.

She stood close to him, proudly showing and displaying her body to him. The veins in her throat pulsed visibly with her growing excitement.

"I particularly like the firm mound of your pussy, Natalie."

It hit her suddenly. The terrific charge of powerful sensation that his words had created, it ripped through her entire body. She felt so tall and in charge as she towered over this older man. He leered at her, wanted her, lusted for her. It felt fantastic. The way he inspected her, firm and young flesh, it must be a real treat for him, she thought. Natalie swallowed hard as she looked down at his face, he was excited and it showed.

He looked up at her and then back down to her trousers, she obeyed without hesitation and undid the fastener on the waistband. Natalie wriggled her slim thighs and wiggled her hips until at last she stood before him in only her little pink panties.

"You are truly fantastic!" he said sincerely.

Natalie felt a tight gripping in her vulva, her clitoris jolted and she shuddered with the pleasure that she experienced at his reaction.

He stood up, sweeping with his arm to brush the items on the top of the desk to one side and clear space for her.

"Sit up on there," his voice portrayed his growing excitement. That thrilled Natalie. To hear him in arousal simply added to her own excitement. She trembled slightly as she lifted herself to sit on the edge of his desk, her thighs apart.

The professor sat down again and wheeled the chair close to the desk, his hands instantly rested on her thighs, caressing and stroking the soft firm flesh. His thick finger feeling the soft silky skin of her upper thighs.

"Lovely," he moaned and dipped his head.

Natalie gasped as his lips kissed lightly on her thigh. First one then the other, alternating to create a series of exciting ripples that ran up her thighs to excite her pussy. She rested back, supporting herself on her hands, her arms locked out straight behind and to the side of her. She shifted her hips and eased her legs further apart.

"Oh! That feels good," she breathed hoarsely as she relaxed into the swirling mist of pleasure that was enveloping her.

She gasped loudly and tensed her body slightly as he planted a light kiss on the very tip of her erect clitoris through her panties. He continued to plant soft kisses on each of her labia, tracing the shape beneath her little panties.

Co-operating and working as one, they removed her panties and she resumed her open-legged position on the edge of the desk. Both his thumbs eased her swollen labia apart and his tongue dipped in to taste the wetness of her soft pink inner lips.

Natalie moaned softly as his warm tongue searched all around her entrance, dipping lightly into ever fold of her sweet smelling skin. The sensations she felt were beyond belief, heady and pounding, quite unlike anything she had experienced before.

In long cat-like stroke of his rough tongue, he scraped across her clitoris, pressing harder with each long lick. Two of his thick fingers probed at her pussy and slipped inside to savour her wetness and to explore her soft interior. Palm-down he pushed the fingers fully inside and teased at her anus with his thumb.

Natalie responded by resting her head back and lifting her feet to rest the heels on the very edge of the desk; opening her thighs fully to allow him unhindered access to her pussy, savouring the delightful heady feelings of his ministrations.

"Please!" she moaned urgently. "Please."

He maintained the unhurried licking, the slow thrusting of his fingers and the light teasing of her puckered entrance.

"Oh god! Please! Do it faster!"

He ignored her pleading and continued his slow and deliberate pleasing of her. He was stiff, his other hand fumbled with his trousers as his excitement increased.

She was talking non-stop now; gasping between her urgent pleas and making emphatic statements of how fantastic the feelings were that she was receiving. "Faster," she urged, then "wonderful, so wonderful." Her pleading gained momentum, it changed in pitch and urgency.

"Do it! Make me come, please - make me come."

The thumb teasing at her tight entrance pressed inward. She cried out as the muscles parted and slid around to grip his thick thumb. Natalie shuddered several times, her head thrashing from side to side. She cried out and moaned softly, before her body locked suddenly. A great gush of air was released from her lungs and she jerked her hips. Her whole body was racked by wave after wave of violent jerking and then she came, wailing aloud to the otherwise silent room.

The professor gripped her legs to steady her and to prevent her thighs closing around his head. The thumb pushed far inside her tight warm anus and she screamed her pleasure loudly, the echo reverberating around the room.

As she slumped back onto the desk, he stood and moved closer. He guided his erect cock into her relaxed pussy and slid easily up inside her.

Slow and unhurried he fed it into her, withdrawing almost completely before moving back up inside her. She lay moaning softly, her body twitching gently as her orgasm subsided, she was only vaguely aware of him inside her.

The professor looked down on the twitching body as he moved in a slow but steady rhythm; she was wonderful, he thought. She will make an excellent addition to the required number of girls.

***

Jenny sat naked on the bed, she felt self-conscious, undressing before Louise. The girl had been very good, busying herself with her own clothes and then the bed so as to ease her embarrassment a little.

"Lie down," Louise said brightly, patting the thick duvet on her huge bed.

Jenny complied and lay rigid on the bed, her legs clamped tightly together.

"You look as though you're about to be shot! Relax and think sex!"

The nervous Jenny forced a half-laugh and maintained her tensed position. Louise knelt on the bed next to Jenny; she parted her naked thighs and smiled down at the trembling Jenny.

"Watch me," she said kindly and slid her hand down between her own thighs. "Rest the heel of your hand just above your mons and let your fingers rest on your pussy."

She waited for Jenny but there was no response.

"Do it with me, she coaxed and guided Jenny's hand down between the girl's thighs. "Grip your clitty between the two outer fingers and press the middle finger down on the top of it. That's it," she praised gently.

Jenny's face was flushed, part embarrassment and part excitement. She found that her fingers located the spot easily, it felt good as she touched her own clitoris.

"Good," Louise guided. "Now, just using the fingers, begin stroking it up and down."

Jenny complied and gasped at the strength of the sensations that rushed through her. It was fantastic; at last her nagging ache had gained some relief. She moved her fingers evenly and in a steady rhythm.

Louise watched the young girl experimenting, she remained silent for a moment before taking a pillow and sliding it under Jenny's buttocks to raise her hips. Jenny moved to assist her, raising her hips until the pillow was beneath her, supporting her body and forcing her pussy high and open.

Jenny's thighs parted gradually, as her excitement and pleasure increased, she allowed them to open more until they were thrown wide, her pussy forced upward and open.

"Good, Jenny, good," Louise coaxed. "Now in circles, tight little circles."

Jenny complied automatically, pulling her hard clitoris up and around and then down and around. The feelings got better, she moved faster, gasping softly as she relaxed to pleasure herself. A pumping urgency filled Jenny as she lay before the beautiful girl, offering herself and longing for her touch.

Louise panted softly for the girl's benefit, urging her onward to her first self-induced orgasm.

"Wonderful, Jenny, you look so gorgeous doing that. It makes me wish that I were doing it for you."

A loud groan came from Jenny as she rubbed speedily now on her clitoris. Her eyes closed and she was rapidly losing herself in the warm pleasures of sexual bliss.

"I'm doing it to myself now, Jenny. Seeing your wonderful body has excited me so much! I'm rubbing with you Jenny, wishing it could be your lovely pussy that I'm rubbing.

Jenny groaned and increased her pace; her slim body jerked as she rubbed herself, her hips rising to meet the waves of pleasure that shot through to her pussy.

"Mmmm. So soft, so sweet, so horny."

Louise rested her left hand on Jenny's thigh, a light and sensual touch.

Jenny moaned softly in response, her body shuddered in delight. Her pace quickening again as her excitement built. Her mouth was open now, gulping air desperately into her body to feed the frantic exertions of her pleasing.

Louise slid her hand slowly down the inside of Jenny's thigh, edging closer to the young girl's pussy. Stroking lightly and caressing softly.

"Lovely bitch," Louise groaned huskily and covered Jenny's hand with her own, taking up the same rhythm, their hands working in tandem.

Pounding excitement so powerful and draining, Jenny thrashed her hips up and down as Louise's hand guided her. She panted heavily as the sensations washed over her. She felt Louise's other hand gently ease her own away. The exciting rubbing on her clitoris continued as Louise's hand now worked on her erect clitoris alone.

A stabbing surge of heady delight speared Jenny as she realised that it was Louise rubbing her to heady heights of pleasure. That beautiful girl, her delicate and experienced hand and fingers touching her, rubbing so delightfully on her pussy. A woman touching her, bringing so much pleasure to her. Her mind flashed back to when Geraldine had kissed her in the height of passion and the incredible feelings it had brought to her.

The heady sexuality increased, Jenny was losing herself in the blissful feelings. Silently she willed Louise to touch her, to enter her soft open pussy. Louise's other hand stroked inside her thigh and moved closer toward her waiting pussy. At last the contact she sought, long slim fingers entered her wet pussy and moved inside her.

Faster and faster the waves of sensation washed over her. Light, gripping flutters nipped at her deep inside. Without thinking and without hesitation, Jenny raised herself, circled her arm around Louise's shoulder and kissed her full on the lips.

Louise responded instantly, her other hand going immediately to Jenny's breast to cup it and caress it. The girl's tongues entwined, mouths open and hungry, they remained locked in a passionate embrace as Louise continued to rub on Jenny's clitoris and finger her to climax.

Jenny gurgled and came. Her grip on Louise's body vice-like as she tensed and gasped. She shuddered and twitched, then broke away from Louise to gasp loudly, cry-out and then slump back on the bed completely sated.

***

The professor placed his briefcase on the small table in the hallway and picked up the message pad next to the phone. The journey back from the barn in Buckinghamshire had been tiring and fraught with frustration in the heavy traffic. He had avoided going to the mansion even though it was close by, for now he wanted to keep his preparations to himself.

"Professor!" Geraldine said brightly from the top of the great staircase. She ran quickly down the stairs to greet him, obviously pleased to see him.

"This message on the pad. A Mrs. Mornay. Did she say who she represented?"

Geraldine looked at him in surprise and then smiled.

"You kid me professor, she's your next door neighbour! Wants to make an appointment to see you." Her voice changed to mimic an upper class and polished accent. "At your earliest possible convenience."

He pondered a moment then looked Geraldine up and down, a look of displeasure on his face, his icy glare showing fully his deep disapproval.

"Why are you not dressed as I require you to be?"

The girl looked crestfallen. Geraldine looked down at her loose grey jersey-wool skirt and pulled at her white sweatshirt.

"But it's my free-time," she offered.

He strode into the lounge without waiting for her.

"Come!" he snapped curtly.

As she followed and moved to his side, he sat down on the settee, grasping her wrist and pulling her down with him to lie facedown across his lap. Swiftly her skirt was pulled up to her waist and a stinging slap of his great hand burned on her right buttock.

Geraldine cried out and struggled against him but to no avail, his other hand pressed firmly into the small of her back to pin her in position. Another slap landed on her soft flesh and again she cried out as the searing pain burned her backside. Slap after slap, hard and meaningful stung at her soft rounded buttocks, then he paused to pull her panties down to her knees.

The young girl lay passively as she waited, bracing herself for the next bolt of pain to cut through her; instead, she felt the light brush of his fingers, circling lightly around her creamy, firm buttocks. His middle finger traced up and down the crease of her backside, dipping almost to touch her labia when it reached between her thighs, then to move back up again to the very top of the crease.

Geraldine moaned softly as the ever-so pleasant feelings began to excite her, she relaxed and bathed in the wonderful sensations that washed over her. A warm and exciting glow spreading around the tops of her thighs and to her pussy itself.

She screamed as the spanking started again, harder and more stinging than before. Again she struggled and lashed out wildly with her legs, held firm by the pressure of his left hand in the small of her back. Eight more slaps Geraldine received before he again paused and the soft caressing of his fingers returned to excite her.

His left hand this time, the fingers moving further now, lightly down over the firm cleavage her tight buttocks created, he paused close to her pink little anus. The muscles surrounding it tensing and relaxing as the pleasure came to her. She was wet, her pussy gripping as the sensations tantalised her to full arousal. The alternating pain and pleasure was having a dramatic effect on her, to thrill and to jerk her clitoris into life. She panted softly, expecting and perhaps welcoming the next stinging pain of his spanking.

The fingers of his right hand slid between her thighs to rub against her wet pussy, the index finger of his left hand located the sweet little entrance to her anus and pressed against it.

Geraldine gasped loudly at the contact, wild pounding delight pumped through her, she arched her back and raised her head as the finger pressed inward. A burning sensation surrounded her little entrance, as the muscles were forced apart by his thick finger, the sweet agony producing a thrilling charge that shot through her vulva and jerked at her hard clitoris. She ground her mons hard down onto his knee to gain the pleasurable feelings of having her clitoris pressed.

The air was forced from her lungs as the next slap stung her backside. It jarred her buttocks around his finger sending tremors deep into her soft interior. Again he slapped her and forced the finger further up inside her. Then again and again, harder and more brutally with each hard slap.

Geraldine was gasping now, urging the terrific feelings to come to her. Welcoming the pain and the pleasure as they combined to give her the sexual release that she now sought.

Slap after slap rained down on her reddened buttocks. She wriggled her hips to move against the finger inside her and to grind her clitoris harder onto his knee. Geraldine screamed as he forced the finger fully up inside her. She bucked her body, thrashing her arms and legs violently - then she came.

Wave after wave of sheer blissful ecstasy washed through and over her. Bringing with it the wonderful warm feelings that she now had come to love. She slumped forwards and murmured softly to herself as she savoured the thrilling sensations.

"One more session of training and I think you are ready to be presented to the group," the professor said as she stood up and straightened her clothes.

Geraldine smiled broadly at his comment.

"Great! Just great!"

"There is a meeting next week, do you feel confident?"

The beaming smile and her rapid nodding assured him of her answer.

"You have learned quickly and well, Geraldine, you have pleased me with your rapid progress. Your rewards will come if you are accepted."

"Do you think they will? Like me and accept me I mean."

The professor smiled warmly.

"I feel certain that they will. It is of course conditional on the progress at the next training session and to your course work being fully up-to-date."

"Rely on it," she said brightly and walked from the room humming.

***

Paula was stretched out on the waist-high table, padded and upholstered, it resembled a doctor's inspection couch. Spread-eagled, Paula was tied tightly by the wrists and the ankles, her knees raised and her buttocks lifted by a thick padded bolster pushed under the small of her back.

From the chair in the corner of the room, Jenny had watched the naked man take much time and care in his tying of the knots, checking and re-checking until content that she was pinioned helpless to the couch.

He moved confidently, his body slim and muscular for his age, about forty-five Jenny guessed him to be. A thick head of hair that showed signs of white at the sides, his handsome, rugged face set in an expression of deep concentration.   T h i s man, Jenny thought, not only knew what he was doing but he was in total control, he seemed used to things being his way.

Between his legs his limp cock dangled, long and thick, the foreskin rolled back to reveal the huge head.

Jenny watched the pair, taking more interest in the lovely Paula and her thick bush of dark pubic hair, as she lay helpless on the padded table, the taut muscles of her slender thighs and the way her breasts rested on her heaving chest, the nipples pointing up erect.

The man worked methodically and in silence, he was busy now with his back toward Jenny, working feverishly on something that lay on the small table just behind the bed. At last he straightened, his pace slowed and he turned to face the bed. Held in his fingers was a shiny silver crocodile clip, small but savage looking with its saw-like serrated teeth. A strong spring operated the jaws; his fingers added the pressure that held them open.

Reverently he stepped forward and bent to kiss Paula's left nipple once before he gripped the erect bud and attached the clip to the rosy point of flesh, he released the tension, the jaws closed tightly around her tender bud.

Paula grunted and clamped her teeth tightly together as she accepted the incredible pain. Her body shuddered and her hips raised, the toes on both feet curled as she tensed in agony. Her leg muscles gripped and relaxed then gripped again.

Jenny was horrified, she almost jumped up and hit the man, such was her shock at his actions. Only Paula's insistence as a condition of being present, that she should remain silent and still, prevented Jenny from acting to assist her.

Around the table, the man moved to stand now at Paula's right side. He was almost fully hard now, his cock sticking out from his body as he walked. Another quick kiss on Paula's right nipple and he attached the second clamp.

Again Paula's body heaved and struggled as the searing pain shot through her, she grunted but didn't cry out.

The man stood next to her, smiling and looking down at the helpless girl. His expression sardonic and slightly evil, he seemed to revel in her discomfort. Bastard! Jenny thought as she struggled to control her temper. If it were her doing those things to the lovely Paula she would be sensual and kind, stroking and feeling, caressing and touching. Jenny came back to reality with a start, she blushed automatically at her thoughts. Since experiencing the touch and feel of Louise, a woman's body no longer seemed repugnant to her.

Slowly and deliberately the man returned to the table and working like a surgeon, he pulled on the thin latex gloves. Taking his time as he had with each of the actions Jenny had seen so far, it made Jenny shuddered.

He moved to Paula's side and attached a thin thread to each of the two crocodile clips clamped onto her nipples; he tied the two ends together and precisely arranged the knotted end to lay gently on her mons. Next, he pulled Paula's labia apart with his left hand and attached a third clip to her erect clitoris.

Paula's body bucked wildly, she grunted loudly several times and half-uttered a cry of pained despair, her head thrashed from side to side as she fought to cope with the pain she was experiencing.

Jenny cringed as she imagined herself being subjected to this torture, it was evil and cruel, and nothing would ever induce her to be subjected to such pain herself.

The man paused, watching and waiting until the thrashing of her body receded and she fell still. With deft and practised movements of his hands, he tied the ends of the threads to the third clip, securing all three by the same thread.

Jenny felt helpless, she wanted to end Paula's misery and suffering but recalled Paula's stern warning. She remained silent, anger boiling inside her.

He now placed a small, clear plastic cup on Paula's stomach and produced a second piece of thread. He tied the thin thread to the centre of the other cord and pulled it slightly to test it.

At the small amount of tension applied, all three clips pulled slightly, Paula gasped loudly as the renewed series of pain rushed through her.

Satisfied that his preparations were correct, he looped the thread around his hips and buttocks then tied it fast. He entered Paula in one move, his stiff cock sliding easily into her open pussy and pushing fully up inside her.

Paula moaned and sighed and uttered a loud groan of satisfaction as he began thrusting into her. The thread pulling on all three clips at the same time and in tandem with his thrusts.

"Beautiful," Paula cried out excitedly. "So wonderful!"

Jenny was stunned; Paula was actually enjoying this wicked and sadistic abuse. She felt nothingness, a numbing amazement that anyone could even consider this as sex.

"More! More!" Paula panted as she received his cock and the pain of the clips on her most sensitive parts.

Jenny watched as his clenched buttocks drove into her, gaining in pace and force as his excitement built. She watched the thin threads pulling at the clips, the way her pinched nipples were stretched and her hard clitoris pulled seemingly horrifically during their act.

He groaned and tensed, his shoulders drooping forwards. He withdrew from Paula's wet pussy and quickly grasped the small plastic cup from her stomach to hold it over the end of his pulsing cock. He grunted and came, his thick seed spurting into the transparent plastic.

Jenny watched in repulsed silence as he moved around to Paula's side and tipped the contents of the small cup over her breasts. With the palms of his hands he massaged the thick liquid into her soft rounded breasts, humming gently as he worked.

CHAPTER EIGHT

The professor passed her a glass of white wine and sat down on the settee, crossing his legs and taking his time getting comfortable. It was a deliberate move on his part; he could sense her nervousness and lack of full commitment to her reason for visiting. She was, he summed her up to be a waffling busybody and he had listened to her whining long enough.

"So, Mrs. Mornay. Is there a point to all this, I am after, all rather busy."

She was in her mid-thirties, neatly dressed and was rather petite in her build. She had small neat breasts and a slim figure that matched her short height. With her brown hair neatly brushed in a short modern style, she had an almost impish look about her.

"Yes!" she stated more firmly, more firmly than she actually felt, the professor thought to himself as she said it; he resisted a smile. "There are - have been - since you moved in here...should we say strange goings on."

The professor retained an expressionless stare as she searched his face with a knowing half-smile. The type of look that indicates that the recipient is supposed to blush bright red and shift uncomfortably before offering profuse apologies; the professor did none of these and her smile disappeared.

"Strange goings-on," he restated. "Such as?"

Mrs. Mornay sipped at her drink and placed the glass down on the table for emphasis before answering.

"Things that no decent person would wish to repeat."

"But you will," he said calmly.

"I beg your pardon?"

"If I am to fully understand your complaint, Mrs. Mornay, I need to know exactly what it is that I am supposed to answer to."

She shifted uncomfortably.

"Very well. Embarrassing though it is. Your activities with a young girl in the garden, nudity and...and sexual practices."

"Really?" he questioned sarcastically.

"Don't try to deny it," she said quickly. "I saw you, I saw the whole thing! I could report you for it!"

The professor drained his glass and placed it on the coffee table.

"Far from denying it, Mrs. Mornay, I positively admit it. And yes you could report me. Proving it however, would be a little more difficult for you."

The woman sat back deflated, aware of his gaze moving up and down her thighs. The neat dark-blue trousers and small sweatshirt showed her body beneath to be well proportioned and firm.

"In short, Mrs. Mornay, my sexual practices are none of your concern."

"They are when they offend public decency," she snapped in response.

The professor remained calm and controlled his voice letting it contain a hint of an offer of reconciliation. She was interested; he could sense it in her. There never was any intention on her part to report him, it was simply her reason to get to know him. Many times he had seen her watching him, with more than just a passing interest. He would enjoy this one, she needed it and he would provide it.

"Mrs. Mornay," he changed the tone of his voice to use his velvety coaxing tones. "I have no wish to be at logger-heads with you, we are after all, neighbours. We both, through different circumstances in our lives, live alone and I feel we can between us come to some arrangement that suits us both."

She sat silently, considering his words, noticing the way his eyes roamed her body without the slightest hint of embarrassment or effort to disguise the fact.

"Would it help," he continued in his hypnotic deep tone. "If I were to explain to you my activities here, then perhaps you might see things a little more clearly and understand a little better the reasons for the...er...strange goings-on?"

"Very well," she agreed readily, the tone she used was one of willingness to compromise. Some of her defensiveness had gone; she seemed ready to discuss things in a more amiable fashion.

The professor stood up smiling warmly.

"Let's begin shall we, with a tour of the house. I can explain in greater detail as we go."

Mrs. Mornay stood, there was no resistance from her as the professor slipped his arm around her waist and guided her toward his study.

***

All three girls stood in line, all were dressed identically in black pleated skirts and white blouses, and all three wore thick leather collars with silver D-rings attached to the front. With hair neatly brushed and styled, bright red lipstick and nail varnish they all looked adorable. He looked each of them up and down longingly, lingering on the slim thighs of each of the girls.

"Welcome back Jenny," the professor said meaningfully. "I hope your visit to the mansion was educational."

Jenny nodded her agreement, it certainly had been every bit an education. More than you think, she thought to herself.

"The introductions have been made, it is the first time that all three of you have met and from here on in, I insist that you co-operate and get along well together. I will not tolerate bitchiness and petty arguments so avoid these like the plague. Each of you has their own room, which is strictly out of bounds to others except by invitation - one rule that brings instant dismissal if broken. One other rule, if one of you should displease me - all three of you will receive the punishment equally. Are there any questions? '

There were none. The girls remained silent.

"I have to go out for the day and you girls may have the day free to get to know one another. Geraldine, I will wish to see you later for your final assessment'

"Yes, professor."

"Your course work is up-to-date?"

All three nodded and with a casual wave of his hand he dismissed them. The girls turned as one, the short pleated skirts swishing as they turned, soft material brushing against nylon stockings as they walked from the room. The professor watched them until they were out of sight and then picked up his briefcase to check that all the information he needed was inside. He lifted the phone and dialled, giving a curt instruction when the phone was answered; he replaced the receiver and sat back deep in thought.

***

Mrs. Mornay stood still in the centre of the barn as the professor removed the blindfold. She rubbed her eyes and looked around her, taking-in the high ceiling and thick wooden walls. Musty and smelling of straw, the barn looked dry and felt warm despite its huge size. A wooden stage with a long narrow catwalk jutted out from one wall at about waist height. She turned to face him.

"And all those things that you told me about, they all happen here?"

Throughout their tour of the house and his graphic descriptions of the ways and practices of the organisation, she had shown a growing interest, unhealthy, perhaps it could have been termed if the subject matter were different. During the drive to the Buckinghamshire barn her interest had grown steadily, questioning, probing and delighting in the details given to her. The bitch was in need - desperate need, it amused the professor to see her face flushing with excited interest, the way she tried to conceal her inner feelings. She was a bitch, a dirty little bitch but didn't want to portray the fact.

"Lots of them happen here, but many also at the house."

He stood close to her side now as she looked around the rest of the barn, the arm around her waist moved down to cup one cheek of her neat little buttocks through her tight trousers.

She looked at him with longing wide eyes that said so much more than words.

He smiled knowingly, teasing her further.

"At the initiation ceremonies, until recently that is, we used this."

He pressed a switch on the wall and an electric motor started up on the other side of the barn, it hummed as it came to life. The curtains on the stage parted automatically and pulled fully back.

A full-sized model horse, complete with a covering of coarse black hair, a full mane and tail, moved out on its base onto the stage and out along the cat-walk. Tall and powerful looking the jet-black beast moved slowly along as the motor hummed to drive it along.

Mrs. Mornay stood spellbound. Her eyes wide and staring, her mouth open in surprised interest. No resistance was offered by her as the professor's fingers slid down around her buttocks and between her legs, he gripped her tight buttocks and pressed his fingers against her labia through the thin trouser material.

Tanned leather reins, full tackle and a leather saddle completed the huge real-looking beast. One addition though had taken her interest, fixed to and sticking up from the saddle was a thick black latex dildo. Sculpted to resemble a man's cock, it was long and thick with an even thicker base where it was attached close to the horn of the saddle.

Silently, she walked slowly forwards, a distant and detached look about her, she was lost in wonder as she viewed the great beast and pondered its possibilities. Step by slow step she moved, up the small flight of steps and onto the catwalk to stand beside the tall beast, she stroked it lovingly, in awe of its strong muscular build. The professor waited a moment watching her and then joined her to stand close to her.

"How long has it been, Caroline?" his soft voice probed gently.

She felt a jolt run through her body as he used her first name. Her eyes looking up longingly at the thick dildo above her. She liked this man, very much. It had been so very long since she had had a man in her life and he now fitted the bill exactly.

"A very long time," she said almost absently.'

His hands rested lightly on her waist, as he stood close behind her, deliberately he pressed himself against her firm buttocks. She sighed at the contact, the feel of his body against hers. His erect cock resting between her firm buttocks.

"Try it," he coaxed, his voice low and thick.

"Oh but I couldn't," she murmured hesitantly, her hand moving over the saddle to stroke the thick phallus delicately. It held her mesmerised; the cock-like dildo was all that filled her thoughts at that moment. What it must feel like to have that inside and in such strange and exciting surroundings.

"You want to," he soothed gently.

She didn't answer, her soft delicate fingers continued to caress the phallus longingly.

His hands moved up to cup her breasts from behind, his big hands covering them, the thick fingers feeling her firmness through her sweat-shirt and bra. She made no move to prevent him and pressed her backside harder back into his groin.

"I'll leave you alone for an hour," he breathed softly into her ear, gave her breasts a last squeeze and released her. "The door is locked and no-one comes here, I'll go into the village and be back in exactly one hour."

Caroline didn't seem to hear him. She moved slowly around the great beast, stroking and caressing as the professor backed away and walked through the curtains of the stage. He opened a door at the back of the barn and slammed it loudly, locking it noisily with the big key; he remained inside the small back room of the barn, hidden behind the curtains, the video camera pointing through the small hole towards the end of the catwalk.

Silence filled the barn; Caroline looked around her suspiciously, assuring herself that she actually alone, her hand gripped her mons and she squeezed her legs together. The idea appealed to her so much, she wanted so desperately to try it, and uncertainty filled her, a conflict of emotions that tore at her insides.

The professor watched though the viewer of the video camera; his hand paused over the 'on' switch. He smiled knowingly as he positioned the camera to record the coming events.

Caroline looked all around her; she walked over to the two locked doors at the other side of the barn and tried the handles to assure herself that they were locked tight. She was alone; the heady pounding running through her body was so incredibly strong it made her heartbeat fast and her breathing laboured. Her nipples were hard and the nagging ache in her vulva that she had harboured for so long now, threatened to consume her completely in a sexual haze.

At last she decided as she walked quickly back to the catwalk, she crossed her arms around herself, gripped the sweatshirt and pulled it over her head.

The professor smiled to himself and switched the camera on.

With a growing urgency, Caroline removed her bra, throwing it aside as she mounted the catwalk steps, her neat breasts standing out firm, the nipples erect. She pulled at her shoes and dropped one of them as she hopped closer to the great tall horse. Her other shoe discarded, she fumbled hastily with her trousers, cursing loudly as the zipper stuck.

She was panting heavily as she wriggled the tight material down over her slim hips and thighs, pulling frantically with her legs to free them from the restricting legs of the trousers. Her small panties quickly followed until she stood naked and alone in the huge barn. The thrilling sexuality had changed her now into a lust hungry slut who simply needed satisfaction by any method.

The professor adjusted the lens of the video camera, bringing the zoom into play and focusing closely on the saddle of the horse.

Pressing and grinding, Caroline was rubbing herself against

the coarse hair of the great beast. Pushing her mons against the thick hind leg, her hands rubbing sensually over its great flanks as she leaned against the tall horse. She gasped loudly, groaning her need into the stillness of the barn, a hungry and desperate series of wild grunts.

Her small white frame was dwarfed by the great size of the black beast; she looked far too slight in her build to even mount the tall model.

Trembling with excitement, Caroline put her foot into the left stirrup, gripped the saddle with both hands and hauled herself up, her right leg swinging over to allow her to sit astride the saddle just behind the thick dildo. She sat there for a moment, her thighs forced wide apart to grip the wide body of the best and to savour the feel of the cool leather on her open pussy.

The professor watched in fascination. He had guessed that the bitch needed sex, but in reality she was more desperate than even he had realised. She showed an animal-like hunger to be pleased, his cock stiffened as he watched her next move.

Standing up in the stirrups, Caroline hovered above the dildo, her legs wide apart, she then lowered herself slowly onto the thick shaft of the cock-like phallus. Using her right hand to ease her labia apart and guide herself onto the big cock.

"Oh god!" she cried out as it penetrated her wet pussy. Her gasps of pleasure and delight echoing around the still barn. She paused hovering with the big bulbous head just inside as she accustomed herself to the huge intruder. Giving time for her inner lips and muscles to adjust to the huge girth.

Gradually lowering herself, she accepted the thick dildo into her moist interior, down and down she moved until the whole length was inside her and her clitoris rested against the thick base.

For several moments nothing happened, then she gripped the reins in both hands and adjusted herself by shifting her hips. One hand moved to the switch and the model horse burst into life, the motor whirred and the beast began a jerky series of movements that resembled a horse in motion. Her thigh muscles contracted tightly as she used her knees to aid her grip on the huge pounding body.

It was an erotic sight to the professor, he had seen the horse used many times during initiation ceremonies, but this was different, she was alone and pleasing herself. Gone were the baying crowds of members usually present at initiation ceremonies, she was alone and enjoying herself. Better still, she believed herself to be alone and unseen, it made his cock jerk to full hardness, causing him to adjust its position in his trousers to ease the pressure on it.

Her hips jerked forwards with the motion of the horse, soft buttocks quivering as it thrust her body in the saddle. He watched as she straightened her back and began to take up the rhythm of the movements, grinding her hard clitoris onto the base and horn of the saddle.

The thick cock inside her felt wonderful; so long it had been since she had felt anything like this deep inside her pussy. The jarring movements that crushed her hard clitoris against the base of the dildo sent stabbing shards of exquisite pleasure rushing through her. The naughtiness and the heady excitement urged her on; she rode the great beast with increasing pleasure as she relaxed into the pulsing sexy rhythm.

Alone in this strange and different place, with always the remote chance that someone would enter, the thought thrilled her so much. Caroline moved more easily now, the muscles of her pussy settling down to suit the girth of the big cock. The vibrating dildo inside her sending different sets of delightful sensation tearing through her as it brushed the insides of her moist depths. The thumping powerful jarring of the big beast sent tremors of delight passing through her entire body to excite her further.

Her slim thighs gripped the thick body of the horse; Caroline grasped the reins harder, pulling against them to steady herself then moved the switch to the second position on the dial. A low wailing moan filled the barn as the beast bucked faster and Caroline felt the new series of feelings it produced. Bucking her fast now, she had difficulty holding herself steady in the saddle. Her clitoris crushed hard against the thick base with every forward movement, she gripped the thick cock with her internal pussy muscles and experienced sweet and wonderful feelings that brought her close to her peak.

She looked so small, the professor thought as he watched the thrilling spectacle. Her slight body thrusting and jerking, naked and so frail looking yet hard and hungry with the urgent need inside her that continued to build. She was wailing loudly as she rode the great powerful beast. Her breasts wobbling in great thumping jolts as the big horse jerked her almost violently.

Faster and faster the beast moved, faster Caroline sensed her orgasm approaching. She wanted it, would welcome it but she also wanted the wonderful feelings to continue. Her head rested back and her mouth opened wide. Her shoulders gripped and her body locked. She made desperate and urgent thrusts against the rhythm of the horse with her hips as she urged her climax on.

"Yes!" she cried out. "Wonderful, wonderful!"

Faster she urged herself, pulling hard on the reins and lifting herself out of the saddle to plunge down hard on the thick stiff rod that probed inside her wet pussy. Again and again she rose and then descended, impaling herself on the stiff warm rod. Perspiration coated her silky skin; frantically she rode the machine now. Her head slumped forward, her chin on her chest. She cried out once and then locked her body rigid momentarily; her head jerked back and her mouth opened to scream aloud as she came to her climax.

Thrusting her hips furiously against the dildo she savoured every last sensation that ripped through her. Grunting and moaning in an animal-like fury she gained every sensation and held it for as long as she could. Lighter sweeter flutters came to her, sensitive feelings deep in her pussy made her begin to relax her body, she turned the dial down and rode more slowly as her post-orgasmic surges washed over her.

The professor switched off the video camera and removed

the cassette, he wrote on the label, 'insurance, C.M.' and placed it on the shelf amongst the others.

Caroline was lying; murmuring softly to herself on the wooden boards of the catwalk when he entered the barn, lying on her side with her eyes closed she looked angelic.

The professor moved her legs gently apart with his great hands and knelt between her open thighs. His tongue dipped instantly into her wet pussy to taste her sweet juices that coated her lips so liberally.

Caroline's hands went to his head, holding him gently, she urged his head further down and onto her wet pussy. Moaning gratefully she lay back and spread her legs wider.

***

"My god, Jenny!" Geraldine gasped as the three girls sat around the coffee table in the lounge.

Jenny was relating the things that she had witnessed and experienced at the mansion, bathing in the admiration and shocked interest of the other two girls.

"And with women?" Natalie questioned a hint of disgust in her voice.

Jenny nodded.

"Never would have even considered it before, but my god! Does another woman really know what you need."

"Tell us!" Geraldine urged her excitedly drawing her legs up underneath her to sit upright and attentive. "All the gory details."

Jenny delved in her bag and pulled out the big black dildo that Louise had used and held it up for the benefit of the other girls.

Silence reigned for several moments before Natalie broke it with a great gasp of amazement.

"Did you use that thing, Jenny?"

Jenny shook her head and passed the huge phallus to Geraldine whose out-stretched arm and hand was indicating her need to hold it for herself.

"Not yet, but I certainly intend to."

"Mmmm," Geraldine moaned sexily. "Mmmmmm!"

All three burst out laughing at her lightening of the situation.

"I'm game for it," Geraldine announced.

Natalie jerked her head to look at the red headed girl.

"You're not serious! That thing could split you in two!"

Geraldine stood up and slipped down her shorts and panties, she kicked them aside and sat back down on the settee.

"My God!" Natalie gasped. "You are aren't you!"

Shifting forward so that her buttocks rested just on the edge of the settee, Geraldine parted her legs wide and lay back. She held the dildo upside down and rested the tip against the open entrance to her pussy. Her face flushed and excited, her heart beating wildly, she eased the great head of the cock-like dildo inside.

Natalie moved closer, sitting next to Geraldine to get a better view and watch the incredible sight of the thick black rod moving slowly up inside her stretched pussy. She gripped the bottom of Geraldine's tee shirt and pulled it up onto her breasts to expose her bare mid-drift and naked hips.

Jenny moved forward and knelt on the floor the other side of Geraldine's out-stretched leg, her hand resting seemingly innocently on the girl's slender thigh.

All three watched as the ebony black latex contrasted against the white of her skin itself producing an erotic sight. In, the thick dildo moved, forcing her tight pussy lips to stretch around the thick shaft of the dildo. Geraldine gasped as the length moved up her, further and further until the whole of the big dildo was inside her and only the thick base of the handle was visible. Geraldine rested there panting rapidly.

"Well?" Natalie asked excitedly allowing her hands to rest against the soft swell of Geraldine's breasts as she held the tee shirt. "What's it like?"

"A bit like...can you imagine Robert Redford up inside you?"

Geraldine said lightly.

"Oh god, that good huh?" Natalie answered seriously and them all three giggled loudly as one.

Seriousness returned as Geraldine began to withdraw the dildo, slowly it moved out of her. Coated in her juices, it glistened in the bright daylight of the lounge. Geraldine gasped loudly as the sensations it produced rippled through her.

Jenny cast a glance at Natalie, she was flushed and excited, the veins in her throat pulsing her excitement, her eyes staring down in wonder at the thick cock protruding from the young girl's pussy.

"Doesn't it hurt?" Natalie asked, her interest growing.

Geraldine shook her head and closed her eyes; she rested her head back on the settee and began pushing the thick cock back up again.

Jenny made her move, edging closer on her knees; she allowed the hand resting on Geraldine's leg to slide along the soft thigh, closer to her pussy. A groan of appreciation came from Geraldine's lips as the light touch of Jenny's hand added to her building excitement. One girls hand resting on her breasts and another on her thigh so close to her pussy. Innocent touches, light and sensual, the thought of girls wanting her thrilled her more so. In her steadily building sexual haze she recalled the tremendous thrill of her kiss with Jenny. Her hand began a faster movement to work the dildo back and forth inside her pussy.

Geraldine's hips shifted slightly to receive the huge intruder; her back arched and she sighed loudly as the pleasure washed over her.

"Oh god!" Natalie stated softly in her heady excitement. "It looks so good."

Faster now the hand moved to work the dildo. Geraldine was lost in the heady excitement and the warm covering of sexual thrill, spurred on by Jenny's hand that crept slowly along her thigh, edging ever closer toward its goal.

Without words, Jenny's hand moved to take over the grip on the dildo; Geraldine allowed the changeover and lay back, her hands resting on the edge of the settee gripping the cushions.

A heady silent atmosphere now charged the room, the musky smell of sex hung heavily in the air and pounding excitement filled all three young girls.

Natalie watched Jenny working the big cock up and down to please Geraldine. Her own pussy ached for attention and she wished that she herself had taken the initiative and been enjoying the heady experiences.

Jenny's other hand moved to cover Geraldine's mons, slim fingers with red painted nails began stroking and caressing, moving down to touch and press on her clitoris.

Geraldine gasped loudly and then sighed with deep pleasure in response, she shifted her hips upward to increase the pressure on her hard bud.

Natalie was trembling with pounding pleasure and excitement; she pulled at the tee shirt, easing it over Geraldine's head. Her hands covered the ample breasts through her bra and began to tease and squeeze them. She lifted them, easing them out of the small bra to touch and rub the rubbery nipples to further excite her. Geraldine was panting now, grunting as she received each thrust of the huge cock inside her. Her hands gripped at the cushions of the settee and her hips moved to meet the thrusting shaft as she raced towards orgasm.

Jenny lifted herself to sit on the settee next to Geraldine, her hands still moving to pleasure the panting girl. She paused to get the timing just right, then leaned across and kissed Geraldine full on the lips.

Thrashing wildly, her hips bucking and thighs jerking, Geraldine came. Her noisy gasps and moans smothered by the soft sensual lips of Jenny who kissed her hard as the excitement burst through the three of them.

***

Jenny and Geraldine were asleep on the floor, Natalie was kneeling, and her body slumped forwards on the coffee table, the big dildo half-hanging from her stretched pussy as she slumped dreamily.

The professor and Caroline stood in the doorway to the lounge.

"Now we are four," he announced with a hint of pride in his voice.

***

In the study, the professor scribbled the details that Paula was relating to him over the phone.

"Well aware of our activities and raring to go she is, if you'll forgive the pun," she said with a hint of laughter in her voice.

The professor ignored it and re-checked the details, reading them back to Paula in confirmation.

"Training?" he asked.

"We've done our part, the womanly side and she is very responsive indeed."

"Not exclusively I hope."

Paula giggled.

"Never fear, professor, there is room in her life for both. By the way, she is not unaccustomed to the taste of the cane."

"Excellent," he breathed in an impressed tone. "Paula, she isn't..."

"Don't worry professor, I know your preferences. She is, shall we say, almost new."

"I owe you one Paula."

"And I professor, fully intend to collect. Talk to you soon."

After replacing the phone, he sat back staring out of the window. Things were going well, if this one proved worthwhile he could soon make his bid for principal. His mood brightened and he whistled jauntily, smiling at the sight of Caroline in her garden next door, dressed only in bra and panties, she was weeding the flowerbeds close to the fence. He began to chuckle, his laughter growing louder and deeper as his pleasure increased.

CHAPTER NINE

The naked young girl was hanging by her arms, her feet secured to ringbolts in the floor. She had been pushed forwards to lean at a forty-five degree angle, her arms pulled back and stretched painfully behind her, suspended by the ropes from the ceiling. Small silver weights hung from both her nipples, swinging on thin thread attached to the crocodile clips that bit cruelly into her soft firm buds.

The professor entered the small basement room of the mansion behind Louise and closed the door gently behind them. Slowly and deliberately, he moved around the young girl inspecting her and admiring Louise's handiwork. The way her legs had been pulled apart to stretch her buttocks, the deep curve of her back and the firm mound of her backside that looked so very fresh and tempting. Her thick bush of inky black pubic hair spread wide over mons, lower belly and upper thighs.

"I congratulate you Louise," he uttered slowly, impressed by her handling of the girl.

"Thank you professor," Louise said dutifully as she stood in the corner taking no further part in the proceedings.

The professor ran his hand down over the girl's buttocks, his fingers feeling into the crease and brushing against the tight entrance to her anus. He picked up the short cane, positioned it so that it hovered over the girl's buttocks. Upright and in line with the crease of her parted cheeks, he flicked the cane hard down on the tight little entrance so temptingly exposed.

She screamed into the ball-gag in her mouth, her body bucking and twisting against her bonds. Again he landed a stinging blow, harder this time to renew her frantic thrashings as she struggled. Twice more he hit her, then felt around her very hairy pussy, pushing his fingers inside to test her wetness.

"Excellent," he said delightedly to Louise. "Her name?"

"Sasha. As you see, she's part Asian."

The professor moved around her again, looking over the deep olive-skinned girl, the dark colour of her skin showing clearly the fine texture and suppleness of her body. Raven black hair that hung down long and shiny to hide her face, slim and muscular in her build, she was delightful. Deep dark rings surrounded her nipples, almost black in places, they stuck-out wonderfully from her ample breasts as they dangled, pear-shaped beneath her.

"She is totally willing?" the professor asked, he squeezed her breast as the girl struggled violently against both him and her bonds.

"Absolutely. It's her thing, she loves to play against it. The pseudo-rape bit is what brings her off - mistreatment of any kind sends her wild, so do most things really, as long as she can fight against it."

"Interesting," the professor muttered as he gripped her hair and pulled her head up to face him.

Stunning, her beauty took him by surprise. Deep black eyes and soft rounded lips coated in shimmering bright red lipstick. A thin nose and high cheek bones set nicely into her almond shaped face, her look was one of simmering temptation and total sexual abandon; both combining to radiate sexuality and pleasure, it gave him an instant hard-on.

"Remove the gag, Louise, I want to hear her talk - and scream."

Louise did as she was bid, handling the girl roughly as she pulled the gag from her mouth.

"Bastard!" the girl screamed at him, she fought frantically against her bonds and twisted her head in an effort to bite him.

"Fiery!" the professor commented.

Louise landed a sting slap across her face to quieten her whilst the professor made his assessment.

"Are you? Willing?"

"Try me," she hissed in response.

Grabbing hard and twisting, the professor yanked her head cruelly. He leaned his face close to hers, his voice low and menacing.

"You like to suffer do you bitch? Well let me tell you that

you have seen nothing yet. If you are as willing as Louise says you are, I must know it now."

"Yes," she hissed and then spat at him.

The professor released her hair to let it fall down to cover her face; he stood back away from, and slightly to the side of her.

The piercing scream within the confines of the small room made Louise's ears crackle. The girl's mouth hung open, she gagged and her body slumped momentarily in pain before she again resumed her fighting against the ropes that held her fast. The weighted clips on her nipples tugging them cruelly as the serrated teeth bit in to her flesh. The more she struggled the deeper they bit.

The professor had landed a savage blow with the cane on her presented buttocks, a deep red mark instantly appeared on her skin.

"When I ask you a question, bitch. You will answer me properly."

His voice was level and calm, just a hint of excitement sounding at the tail end of his sentence. He repeated his question to her. "Are you willing?"

"Yes," she responded instantly, her voice trembling and faltering. "I am willing and I offer myself for any mistreatment with my full consent."

The professor smiled broadly and lashed her again, slightly less hard this time.

Sasha grunted loudly as she accepted the stinging pain in her backside, hard and painful but nowhere near as agonising as the first one. Again he struck at the pinioned young girl.

She gasped loudly in pleasure as the cane bit deep.

Eight more lashes stung at her soft backside before he stopped. Panting heavily, the professor undid his trousers and moved behind the girl. His cock, rigid and pulsing brushed against her soft brown flesh, it thrilled him immensely, to find a girl so young and so willing to accept pain; he groaned at the feel of her on his pulsing cock.

Forcing her labia apart, he entered her, pushing straight in up to the hilt. He remained motionless savouring the warm feel of her body around his thick cock.

The girl was still also; hanging limply on the ropes that bound her so securely in position.

The professor cried out and tensed his body.

"Bitch!" he gasped. "Wonderful bitch!"

"Thought you'd like that bit, professor," Louise giggled from the corner of the room. "It's her speciality."

The girl had gripped him hard with her internal muscles, trapping his cock along its entire length deep inside her slim young body. She began a steady rhythm of gripping and then releasing, pumping his cock to previously unknown heights of exquisite pleasure simply by flexing her inner muscles.

The professor rested his hands on her back to steady himself as she sent him into spasms of ecstatic pleasure. The warm wet muscles of this bitch were literally milking him. Squeezing his thick shaft so that he could feel her insides enveloping him in soft but firm flesh, then releasing him to allow the blood to flow back into his cock with a pounding urgency that was building rapidly inside him. His mouth opened and he gasped for breath, his eyes rolled in their sockets as he savoured the extreme pleasure and sensations of this young girl's body.

He cried out, his body gripped by light, yet powerful convulsions that made him tremble and twitch in ecstasy. The professor gripped her hips but didn't thrust into her; there was no need to. He tensed and came to his climax, her internal muscles continuing to grip and relax, alternating to draw every last drop of his seed from him and receive it willingly into her soft interior. The involuntary jerks of his cock as his sperm jetted out produced indescribably delightful sensations such as he had never before experienced. The girl was perfect - absolutely perfect.

***

Caroline protested nervously as the giggling girls tied her wrists and ankles to her bed.

"Relax," Natalie soothed as she forced two pillows under Caroline's backside to raise her hips and pussy upward. "You'll really like the little surprise we have in store for you."

Jenny held the big dildo behind her back, smiling at the thought of this older woman getting something that would put the fear of god in to her.

They had planned it for a day or so, the motherly and overbearing way that Caroline tried to order the younger girls around had made her a figure of fun amongst the others. Whilst a pleasant enough person who fitted in well with the younger girls and was welcomed by them, Caroline tried to use her age to her own advantage and suffered their constant ribbing as a consequence.

"Me first!" Sasha offered excitedly and moved to stand by the side of the helpless woman.

Her slim dark fingers began massaging Caroline's rubbery nipples to bring them to erection watched silently by the other three girls. Red painted nails teasing the soft buds to firmness, becoming increasingly sensual in their movements.

"I'm a woman!" Caroline protested, horrified at the touch of another female on her. "You can't do this!"

Laughter from the others drowned her further objections and Sasha resumed her massaging of the Caroline's pert breasts.

"Here's a treat for you Caroline," Sasha moaned huskily. "One to get the juices flowing if you understand what I mean."

A chorus of light gasps came from the others and then the room fell silent. Sliding her first two fingers either side of Caroline's nipple, Sasha gripped it and brought the thumb down on the tip of it, as a doctor would use a syringe. Squeezing the hard bud between her fingers, Sasha dug the long nail of her thumb into the very tip of Caroline's nipple.

The woman's body bucked and thrashed, pulling against her bonds. Her hips jerked violently upward and her thighs gripped to push her feet hard against the bed - only then did she scream. A pained, tormented wailing that echoed around the room.

"Noisy old bird isn't she?" Natalie observed.

Again the nails bit into her flesh and the scream was repeated, a long and wailing scream that portrayed her exquisite agony. Caroline panted heavily as she coped with the pain that was racing through her.

"She's wet," Geraldine gushed excitedly as she pushed her middle finger into Caroline's open pussy. "Rather tight too!"

Caroline groaned in deep embarrassment and turned her head to one side to try to hide herself from the smirking onlookers.

"Make way for the tongue queen," Natalie giggled and pushed her way through the others to kneel on the bed between Caroline's open thighs.

Wide-eyed, Caroline pulled her head and shoulders clear of the bed to look between her open thighs in stunned amazement at Natalie's smiling face. Caroline screamed as the first of Natalie's feather-light kisses touched the inside of her open thigh. She screamed again and again as the soft lips moved upward, edging closer to her open pussy. Caroline gurgled and then gagged as the flicking tip of Natalie's soft wet tongue touched her swollen labia.

The other girls watched in silence, their own levels of excitement increasing as they enjoyed the sight of Caroline, helpless and unable to resist, fighting against her bonds as the wet tongue dipped inside to taste her juices. The repulsion she showed at another woman's touch simply added to their excitement.

"Mmmm!" Natalie murmured as she pushed the whole of her tongue up inside Caroline's stretched pussy and moved it around searching the moist inner depths of the woman's soft interior.

The struggling had lessened, a warm flush came over Caroline's face, and she slumped back onto the bed, as her need for release became greater. The wriggling tongue inside her had made her clitoris hard, it ached for the touch of the soft teasing tongue, she wriggled her hips to try to direct the licking to her desired spot.

A loud gasp exploded from Caroline's open mouth as Natalie pulled out and licked upward toward the waiting bud of the clitoris. Her body tensed and she pulled at the ropes, sighing heavily as the contact was at last made.

"The bitch likes that!" Sasha gasped as she watched the erotic sight of the two women in pleasure.

Hard teeth gripped lightly on the hardened bud to send searing shudders of extreme pleasurable sensation ripping through Caroline's body. She panted heavily as the teeth pulled and tugged at her pulsing clitoris. The older woman cried out as the tip of Natalie's tongue flicked across the very tip of her hard bud.

"What are you doing tonight, Natalie?" Geraldine quipped in a serious tone.

Delighted squeals of laughter came from the other girls in response to her remark.

"Don't take her too far, "Jenny cautioned. "It's my turn soon so don't spoil it for me."

Caroline was thrusting her hips in time with the movements of Natalie's tongue, urging her onward with soft mewing murmurs of pleasure. She was moving her head from side to side, her eyes closed, a pained expression of extreme pleasure etched on her face. Light convulsions began gripping her body, she shuddered and relaxed.

"No more, Natalie - she's coming."

Instantly, Natalie stopped licking and withdrew.

"Taste good?" Sasha asked quietly as Natalie got off the bed and stood next to her.

"Not as good as I think you would," Natalie answered smiling.

"With a licking like that, you can visit my room any time!"

Natalie winked slyly in response.

"We have a date then."

Moaning her disappointment, Caroline wriggled her hips, moving her mons in a circular motion as she offered herself for any of the girls to finish her and bring her to the orgasm she so desperately needed. She was panting, animal-like in her urgency for fulfilment; pleading eyes searched the other girls' faces in the desperate hope of a sympathetic response. She slumped back, closing her eyes and whimpering her disappointment.

Jenny stepped forward holding the huge dildo high for Caroline to see and to fear. In a soft and coaxing voice, Jenny called to rouse the dreamy woman.

"Caroline. See what mummy has for you."

All the girls giggled as they eagerly awaited Caroline's shocked reaction, the naive older woman being offered a cock the size of which she would never have seen nor expected. The thought of her horror-stricken face delighted them all.

Caroline opened her eyes slowly and looked at the huge dildo.

"Oh god yes! Please now - please!"

The girls were stunned, not the reaction from her they had expected, and an air of disappointment filled the room.

"If she wants it - then give to her - good and hard," Geraldine hissed sadistically. The others added their agreement in a series of loud cheers.

Jenny lowered the huge phallus, holding it close to the entrance of Caroline's pussy, nudging the great head against her open inner lips.

"Please, quickly," Caroline pleaded.

Geraldine untied the ropes to free Caroline's hands. Immediately her hands were free, Caroline grasped the dildo from Jenny's grip and pushed urgently into her open pussy. She groaned loudly in pleasure as the big bulbous head forced inside to stretch the pink inner lips tightly around its great girth. Greedily she fed the thick shaft up into her waiting pussy.

"My god!" Sasha breathed in disbelief at the sight of the huge black cock forcing its way inside the panting woman.

Up and in, Caroline pushed the dildo, she eased her thighs further apart to accept the full length and girth of it willingly inside her.

Silence filled the room; the girls watched with growing interest and arousal as Caroline began a steady pounding rhythm with the big cock. Fast and furious were her movements as she pleasured herself, the heel of her hand crushing hard against her hard clitoris with each inward thrust. She wailed in delight and thrust her hips upward to receive the wonderful sensations that the great phallus brought to her.

"My god she's insatiable," Jenny gasped.

Caroline's head was thrashing from side to side and her back arching in ecstasy, she grunted as she rammed the dildo into her wet pussy. The woman gave several cries of pained pleasure; her body trembled with violent shudders. Her breathing rapid and heavy, she was lost in a fantastic dreamy world of sexual bliss, pumping the cock frantically into herself as her pleasure built.

Faster and faster her panting and grunting became, more urgent her thrusting hips rose and fell, her body tensed, locking rigid in orgasm. She cried out several times as the pounding sensations filled her, then she screamed and gave one final and terrific upward thrust of her hips and gasped loudly as she came.

"Fantastic," Sasha breathed quietly.

"That was something else," Natalie offered, more to herself than to anyone else in particular.

All of the watching girls were highly aroused, their cheeks flushed with excitement, all feeling envious of the older woman's obviously tremendous orgasm. They filed from the room quietly; Leaving Caroline to bathe in the sweet sensations of her post-orgasmic state as light convulsions shook through the sated body on the bed.

***

All five women sat around the patio table in the bright and now warming spring sunshine awaiting the professor's arrival.

"What's all this about?" Sasha asked, a little fed-up with being kept waiting.

"His bid for the position of principal probably," Geraldine offered as she lay back, her eyes closed lazily to take the sunshine.

"It's been over a week now since - well, you know since we

had any contact with him," Jenny said solemnly.

"Got an itch you just can't scratch?" Geraldine teased.

Before Jenny could respond, Natalie interjected.

"If you haven't then I have, I'm not a nun. This waiting is driving me mad!"

"Your hungry little pussy more like," Caroline added.

Natalie stood and stretched.

"It's like he's starving us of sex."

"Male sex maybe," Sasha commented and winked at Natalie.

Geraldine sighed heavily and offered her view.

"All week he's been going out for the day, coming back and locking himself in his study only to go out again the following day."

"We'll find out when he's good and ready," Caroline offered wisely.

Geraldine responded with sarcasm.

"So speaks the voice of experience."

"Experience can be very rewarding," Caroline snapped back. All the girls knew instantly the meaning behind her words and remained silent.

The professor stepped out onto the patio; he paused to look at each girl in turn and then approached the group and sat down in the remaining chair set slightly back from the girls. His expression was set, but it portrayed a calm confidence and extreme pleasure, something that none of the girls had seen in him all week. It was a satisfied and complete look that seemed to show a side of him that had been long absent, returning to him now in a welcome gush of quiet controlled pleasure.

"Each of you now knows of the organisation and the club that meets in the barn in Buckinghamshire," he announced loudly to gain their full attention. "You also know of my intention to bid for the post of principal, an event in my life that is so very important to me and the very reason that you were all recruited."

He paused, his eyes moving from girl to girl to test their expressions. Jenny's face showed signs of disapproval but she said nothing. She fiddled idly with her fingernails avoiding his gaze.

"I had intended to introduce you individually for initiation as and when each of you became ready. So rapid and satisfactory has been your progress that I have decided to offer you all at the same time in a grand and previously unknown ceremony of initiation."

A muted response came from the girls.

"Where does that leave us afterwards?" Natalie asked suspiciously.

The professor was stunned at their lack of enthusiasm; he sat silently for a few moments, looking in astonishment at each of his pupils before he realised what was troubling them. So wrapped-up in his own arrangements and delight with their response to training that he had neglected to fully inform them of all the details.

"Forgive me Ladies," he said formally and sincerely. "I should have explained, your futures are all secure. Once initiated, your salaries will double..."

Delighted gasps and applause interrupted his flow.

"You all have now seen the very nice set-up that Paula and Louise have - well, you too will have the opportunity to live in similar surroundings, alone in your own properties or as a team, that is for you all to decide amongst yourselves."

"And you, professor. Do we lose all contact with you?" Jenny asked.

He shifted in his seat, crossing his legs and clearing his throat.

"Not at all. Your tuition continues as before, both in psychology and in other ways," he raised an eyebrow as he added emphasis to the last part of his sentence.

"As principal I will of course, have full and unrestricted call on your time and devotions as and when I require it."

"Often I hope," Geraldine offered lightly. A round of giggled laughter broke the serious tone of the meeting; a welcome and relaxing quip that made all of them feel brighter.

"What happens at this ceremony?" Sasha took the opportunity to question.

The professor smiled and replied easily.

"Wait and see my dark-skinned little slut."

The girls appreciated his rare joke and then squealed in delight as Paula and Louise walked out of the house and towards them; each carried a tray, one full of drinking glasses and on the other several huge bottles of champagne.

The drinks poured, the professor proposed a toast. Holding up his glass and glowing with pride, he said simply.

"To my girls."

***

The professor moved around her in silence, Jenny was laid back over his desk naked and bound. Her legs dangled down the front of the desk and the ropes that were tied to her ankles looped tightly under the desk and up the other side to secure her wrists. She lay helpless and bound; her soft skin pulled harshly down on to the cool hard surface of the desktop awaiting his next move.

"I have to say Jenny, that I still hold slight reservations as to your suitability."

"What? After all I have been through!"

The professor moved to stand between her open thighs, gazing down at the slim body and the soft downy covered pussy that was on offer to him.

"You show a reluctance to comply with my wishes."

Jenny pulled her head up to look at him.

"But I do everything you ask of me," she protested.

"Not however, as willingly as the others."

"Comparisons now is it?" Jenny snapped icily and rested her head back, a pained expression on her face.

"Very much so!" the professor responded, slightly annoyed at her remark. "You comply but there is within you a reluctance - and I might even say - an obstinate and vengeful view towards me and the things we do here."

"Never said that before the others came along did you? Only too pleased to use me weren't you?"

"And you me," he stated calmly.

"What? What do you mean?"

Unbuttoning his trousers, the professor dropped them around his ankles and laid his flaccid cock to rest on top of her mons. When he continued speaking his tone was harsh and reprimanding.

"You also used - and continue to use me and to benefit from our arrangement."

Jenny paused and reflected.

"I'm sorry. I shouldn't have said that, I didn't mean it."

He didn't answer her on that subject.

"This ceremony is highly important to me Jenny. I need to be sure that nothing will mar it - I need to be certain that you..."

"Thanks for not trusting me!"

"I do trust you Jenny. I need to know that your temper and disobedient streak will not ruin my one and only attempt at gaining the principality."

"Doesn't sound like trust to me."

"You must see yourself, in the way that you ignore my point and ride rough-shod over it in your attempt to satisfy your hurt feelings. I need to know Jenny."

"Or what? You'll replace me?"

He stroked her thighs lovingly, one hand on each of her legs close to the top.

"It would pain me to do so. But if necessary, yes, I would replace you."

A long silence followed as he caressed her thighs, his thumbs almost brushing the sides of her labia.

She was sobbing softly to herself. She adored him, he was hers - not the other girls', they just used him - Jenny was devoted to him.

"Prove it to me Jenny," his soft velvety voice coaxed. The tone of voice that he knew would soothe her and bring her around, responding to his wishes as all the young girls eventually did.

"But how?"

He held the candle up and lit the wick, holding the flame

against the side to ensure a good amount of liquid wax was ready.

"That, Jenny is for you to decide. Tomorrow evening I will arrange to be alone in the gym at eight o'clock. By then you will have had time to consider and be able to demonstrate to me your total allegiance and compliance."

Jenny looked up at him and froze in horror, her eyes wide and staring as she looked at the burning candle.

"And now, Jenny," he cooed softly. "A little pain and delight to feed your thoughts."

He leaned forward over her, the candle hovering above her right nipple. His cock stirring slightly as his excitement rose.

"Sweet delight," he murmured and tipped the candle.

She screamed a wailing and screeching that surely must have been heard all over the house. Hot searing pain burned her tender nipple, an intense and deep pain that lessened as the wax hardened and turned white to form a hard crust over her flesh.

His cock reared to full stiffness, throbbing its delight at the terrific sensations the girl's pain brought to him.

The other nipple suffered the same treatment; a hot drip of the wax falling down to hit her nipple on the side, splashing her breast. Again the screaming, it took on a new and stronger pained content, her body writhing and thrashing within the restrictions of her bonds. Two white-coated nipples stuck up from her soft breasts as testament to her torture.

He entered her, forcing his thick cock into her soft interior. He remained still inside her, savouring the feel of her around his erect cock as she struggled to cope with the searing pain. Her body movements bringing fresh and sensual feelings with each slight tension or contraction, her suffering made it all the better.

The professor pulled out of her slightly, leaving two thirds of his stiff cock inside her, he directed the next drip of wax to fall on her hard and prominent clitoris. It missed its mark, falling half on her soft inner lips and half onto her peeled open labia and she screamed aloud.

Again and again he dripped the wax close to her clitoris,

each time drawing a series of wild and frantic screaming from the young girl. His excitement built steadily, delighting in her agony and suffering, to watch this young girl fight against his ministrations was delightful; to experience the feel of her soft body around him and to share in her pain was heaven itself. Then he came.

Spurting jets of his sperm pumped into her, one final drip of wax, hitting the tip of her hard bud brought her to her peak and he shared then in her thrashings of exquisite pleasure as her slim body shook to orgasm.

Jenny's screams now took on a different tone, a panting and excited pleading scream that helped force her orgasm through her body. She hungrily sucked in great mouthfuls of air as she convulsed to the most powerful orgasm she had yet experienced. A pounding surge of relief and pleasure combined to sate her every sinew. She bucked and groaned, twisted and gasped as the continuing racking pleasure washed over and through her, then she relaxed and slumped back drained.

***

In her bedroom upstairs, Geraldine lay on her bed, her legs thrown wide and her hand rubbing furiously on her hard clitoris. Her short skirt lay crumpled up around her waist and her small panties dangling from one ankle, such had been her need. In time with each of Jenny's screams, she felt powerful surges of exquisite pleasure pump through her. At the last of Jenny's wild screams, Geraldine hooked her slim fingers down and pushed two of them into her wet pussy as she came to a crashing orgasm. She lay there fingering herself to the very last ripple of her climax, delighting in the terrific experience of listening to Jenny's pain.

CHAPTER TEN

Sasha busied herself in the kitchen; it was her turn to tidy the area today, it didn't happen too often with five of them to share the tasks. Not that she minded doing it at all, it gave her a purpose and she immersed herself enthusiastically in the task. Cleaning was something that she had done since childhood; it seemed natural to her, not at all a chore.

Dressed in the standard requirement of white blouse and black pleated skirt, she had rolled up her sleeves and donned an apron to maintain her crisp clean appearance. It was a few moments before she was aware of the professor standing in the doorway watching her; polishing of the wall cupboards had been absorbing stuff that had filled her mind until that moment.

"Professor!" she said pleasantly as she noticed him

"Kneel before me bitch," he snapped coldly and stepped several paces forward on the quarry-tiled floor.

Sasha looked at him in surprise and shook her head.

"I will not," she said calmly and continued cleaning.

In one swift move he was behind her. His big hand gripped her hair painfully at the back, his fingers pulling hard and threatening to rip the hair from her head. Sasha sank submissively to her knees; her hands going to the top of her head in an effort to ease the pressure and excruciating pain he was creating.

"When I command you bitch - you will obey."

She winced as he tightened his grip on her raven hair still further.

"Go fuck yourself," she spat venomously and tried to claw at his hand with her long fingernails.

Pulling her back to put her at further disadvantage, his left hand gripped the front of her blouse and pulled hard, ripping the flimsy material and exposing the firm swell of her neat breasts within the tight restraining bra.

"Nice tits," he gloated as he ripped the blouse from her shoulder so that only the remaining shreds hung from her slim brown body.

She twisted around, grabbing for his groin; he avoided her attempt and slapped her across the face. In the instant that she took to collect her thoughts, his hand clamped onto her breast and began feeling her roughly through the lacy bra. Squeezing and groping coarsely on her soft firm orb.

The professor was hard, his cock jerking into life the very moment she had begun to resist. He preached co-operation to his students but harboured a deep love of their unwillingness to comply; it gave him ample opportunity to punish for the refusal and she certainly was doing that.

Spitting and clawing, kicking and biting, she tried to attack him in any way that she could. Her nipples were erect and pumping sexual arousal, her clitoris was hard and aching for more. Her pussy wet and flowing her juices readily as the contest continued.

Her arms were held firmly at the wrists, forced cruelly high up her back, she was lifted bodily, her feet clear of the floor and propelled towards the marbled work-top.

It was only then that she became aware that there were more present than just the professor. Hands ripped at her clothes, pulling and tearing roughly to rip all of the covering from her slim body. Rough hands groped her breasts and felt between her thighs as she was hoisted onto the worktop and held down on the cold surface by the strong hands of four excited men. Hands and arms pinioned, she was held down by the men, naked and at their mercy.

"Bastards!" Sasha screamed in pounding excitement. She spat and kicked against the strong grip of the men as they held and felt her.

Hands pinched and pulled at her nipples, stinging pain and thumping excitement sent wonderful sensations of extreme excitement rushing through her. Fingers groped at her labia and forced their way inside her pussy to feel her wetness. Her legs were pulled apart and her wrists held so tightly that the blood seemed to stop flowing to her hands.

Lips slobbered on her mouth and the fingers in her pussy

pulled out to be replaced by a thrusting cock that rammed forcefully inside her.

The high excitement made her light-headed as she struggled to close her thighs against the pressure. Sasha pulled hard with her hands and managed to free one foot to deliver a hefty kick into soft and yielding flesh before the free leg was once again clamped fast by strong hands.

The pumping cock inside her gained momentum, the head of a cock brushed against her mouth, she turned her head and spat in disgust. A thick finger probed roughly at the entrance to her anus and then pushed inside. She gasped loudly at the intrusion, giving the cock at her mouth the chance to enter. Once inside her mouth, Sasha began sucking greedily on the large bulbous head as her excitement grew. A cock in her pussy and another in her mouth, all against her will as she played the part to its fullest.

Events were a blur, so many things happening at the same time to produce a dizzy haze of whirling sexual frenzy. Emotions peaked and changed, as did the sensations rushing through her body to excite and stimulate her brain. This was like nothing she had ever experienced; it superseded any previous sexual encounter many fold.

She felt him come, the cock inside her pussy spurted its seed deep inside her, she bucked against and with it, fighting against it but at the same time welcoming the thick warm seed and the heady excitement it gave her. Another cock pushed into her to replace the first. The thought of its thick shaft sliding over another man's come brought a terrific jolt of sudden pleasure to her. Her clitoris jerked its response to the pounding excitement.

Salty thick seed in her mouth as the sperm shot to the back of her throat, she gagged as the unexpected rush caught her midway through swallowing. Stinging pain in her anus and rectum added to the abuse. Pinching fingers on her clitoris and nipples brought her to heights unknown.

Another cock now forced into her mouth, Sasha was aware of sperm trickling from the side of her mouth to run down her long brown neck and behind her head to soak the small hairs on the back of her neck.

It was too much, she struggled and fought, straining to break free and then she came. A draining and shaking orgasm that wrenched her body into contorted spasms of delightful ecstasy. More sperm jetting inside her, it broke her dreamlike state only to send her to another deeper and softer in raw sexual bliss. The thrill and the surprise combined to send her to greater heights, and orgasm unsurpassed in its intensity.

Another cock inside her, pounding and pumping, the grip on her clitoris unrelenting as she tried to enjoy her climax. On and on it went, more sperm shot into her mouth, splashing over her face and chin. The hands roaming her body to feel and to grope her every crevice, pure heaven and hell mixed in one to produce such wonderful and powerful sensations.

"Turn her over," a familiar voice commanded.

Harsh and uncaring, the hands picked up her slight body, turned her in the air and pushed her facedown on the now wet surface of the work-top. All fight now knocked from her, she responded willingly to the handling of the men around her.

"Spread her thighs," the voice ordered, thick with excited arousal.

Almost instantly, she felt the big head of his cock pressing against her tight little anus.

"Give to her!" another voice shouted excitedly.

In it pushed, forcing her brown-ringed muscles to stretch to its thick girth and he pushed up inside her.

The air was forced from Sasha's lungs both by the weight of the hands pressing her back down hard and by the extreme pain that burned in her backside. The pumping cock gave no thought to her as it pounded in urgent search of its own pleasure. Savage and uncaring he brutalised her, it was wonderful, and she felt herself building once again.

Several minutes passed before she felt him begin to stiffen and slow, her own second orgasm was close, the pounding excitement pumped through her. A cock brushed against her face and then she gasped loudly before coming.

As she locked her body in the spasms of orgasm, she felt him come, his warm seed jerking deep inside her rectum. Blackness enveloped her and she slumped forwards, the gripping hands released, she curled into a foetal position to savour the delightful feelings that follow such intense sexual excitement. Sperm trickled from between her labia and the lips of her mouth as she slumbered in a warm mist of sexual bliss.

Moments passed before she was dreamily aware that all was silent, the men had gone but someone remained, she felt his presence. Sasha shifted her bruised and abused body slightly in warm discomfort without looking around.

"Thank you professor," she said gratefully. "That was wonderful."

A moment passed before he answered.

"My pleasure," his soft velvety voice purred and then added. "My wonderful oriental bitch."

***

Jenny lay on her bed thinking deeply as she was prone to do, recounting every detail and considering her options of the events as they had happened and analysing her feelings.

She wanted him, adored him, yet he was a bastard. She liked him so much, yet she wanted so desperately to gain her revenge. He abused her, but she enjoyed it. He played with her emotions and again, strangely, she liked that too and yet hated it at the same time. It seemed a conflict that had no solution.

Time and time again she had been over the same details in her mind before arriving at the final chosen solution. She was certain now, perhaps she always had been, she would comply with his wishes and take the future for what it was - rosy indeed. The thirst for revenge however, remained within her, more a matter of pride now, she intended to follow it through. To make him suffer a little, to let him know what it was like to be treated in such a way and she knew now just how best to go about it.

The way she could prove her allegiance to him had been a little more difficult to solve, she had pondered long on the final choice and then she had done it. Now, it was clear in her mind. Paula was a veritable mine of information, almost an authority on the professor's likes, dislikes and preferences. She would be eternally grateful to Paula for the secret she had shared with her Jenny thought and smiled. She cast a glance to the clothes on the hanger that she had made ready, Jenny couldn't resist a giggle as she imagined his reaction.

Jenny roused herself, looked at her watch and went to the bathroom, humming contentedly to herself; she ran a hot bath and looked forward to her test - very much indeed.

***

Timed to arrive outside the gym at precisely eight o'clock, Jenny peeped through the small square glass panel set into the door of the gym. The professor was already there, just as he had said he would be, Jenny smiled, dress sense was one thing he lacked - casual dress anyway. Thick green corduroy trousers and a pale shirt open at the neck, such a contrast to when he wore a smart suit.

He was sitting on a weights bench, his back half-to the door, several times he looked at his watch impatiently.

"Don't look professor or the surprise will be spoiled," Jenny called through the half-open door.

He didn't reply, sitting instead unmoving as she had wished. It was her test and she could, for the moment at least, dictate how it would be. He would and could take over control at any stage; he reserved his option for the time being.

Jenny stepped into the room and placed the small sports bag on the floor behind the professor. Silently she worked, slipping the velvet material of the blindfold over his eyes from behind; she took great care not to allow her body to touch him as she fitted it into place around his head.

"Stand and strip," she coaxed softly, imitating his velvety

tones to good effect.

He stood and quickly stripped off his clothes until he stood naked and blindfolded, he waited a moment and sat back down a little self-consciously.

"Give me your right hand," Jenny purred sexily.

"Don't tie me Jenny - I won't be tied. I must remain in command."

She had expected opposition at this point and used her stock reply that she had practised several times in her mind.

"But of course you are in command - always. It is however, essential to my test that I tie you."

He hesitated; Jenny waited a few seconds and then added quickly.

"If you are to give me a fair opportunity to prove my loyalty then you must trust in me."

His hand came up to his shoulder in resignation.

Jenny bound his thick wrist back and above his shoulder, securing it to the chromed crossbar resting ready to accept weights. The other wrist was secured in a similar fashion and he sat, back straight and upright, his arms pinned back in short crucifixion. Jenny knelt and tied each of his ankles to the legs of the weights bench and then moved back behind him to stand silently for a moment.

"Are you still there?" the professor enquired impatiently in the silence.

Jenny didn't answer; she wanted him to suffer silent anxiety, thrilling at the fact that at last she had him at her mercy. The pounding throb low in her vulva had begun, the excited surges of anticipation pumped through her. Jenny felt alive with arousal; a heady and powerful pumping that made it difficult at times for her to breathe quietly.

She leaned forwards and planted a light and sensual kiss on the back of his neck; he shivered in delight at her touch.

"Who am I professor?" Jenny asked in a low and husky voice.

He paused before replying.

"Why, Jenny of course," he answered, a little bemused at her question.

Another kiss touched his skin higher up his neck, closer to the back of his ear.

"Wrong," she breathed. "A little friend of yours tells me I am someone else. Can you guess who?"

He sat silently in confusion as Jenny moved around to stand close in front of him. The scent of her heady perfume floating across to fill and tease at his nostrils.

"I will remove the blindfold now professor, you must keep your eyes firmly shut until I say to open them, Okay?"

He nodded and helped ease the tight blindfold off by dipping his head as she pulled it free, his eyes remained closed.

Jenny stepped back a pace and prepared herself, the throbbing excitement had reached almost fever pitch. It was her time, the chance to both convince him and to seek revenge for all the anguish he had caused her. Her heart beat fast and her clitoris ached as she adopted a child-like and innocent pose.

A short pleated skirt in light grey showed her slender thighs and legs to good effect, helped by the short white socks and patent-leather lace-up shoes. Her tight white blouse and school tie made her face seem much younger, the pigtails in her hair and the freckles so lovingly added to her cheeks with her eyebrow pencil, completed her overall seductive look.

Jenny lisped sexily, "Have you guessed yet sir?"

He sat gob-smacked, his cock twitched and he shuddered visibly at her words.

"No, it can't be!"

"Yes, sir. It is," Jenny lisped brightly and excitedly.

He opened his eyes and sat spellbound at the beauty of the young girl before him.

"Cynthia!" he gasped in shocked amazement and then groaned loudly in desperate deep pleasure and shocked realisation.

Jenny idly tugged at the hem of her short skirt, pulling it up to reveal the soft thigh and the line of her pure white tight panties beneath. She tilted her head and looked at him with wide eyes, her long red thumbnail teasing at her mouth.

"Oh god!" he groaned loudly, his cock jerked and moved to half erection.

"Sir," she breathed sexily, increasing the heavy lisping. " Little Cynthia has been a naughty, naughty girl."

She pulled her skirt high on her waist the show her hips and panties completely at the top of her seemingly long legs.

"Cynthia has wetted her knickers."

She paused shifting her weight to one leg, her expression one of guilt.

"Naughty girl," he responded in a reprimanding tone. "You naughty little girl."

She hung her head and shuffled her foot idly.

Her little voice lisped full of shame, "Does that mean that I have to touch sir's big willy for him?"

"Yes!" he snapped instantly. "Yes, touch it."

His cock stuck up from his lap, hard and throbbing, he was so excited it positively radiated from him. He could hardly contain his delight and began losing himself deeper into his fantasy.

Jenny released her skirt to hang down again covering her panties and thighs; she moved closer and sat on one of his widespread thighs, her arm looping around his shoulder.

He gasped at the feel of her warm backside on his naked thigh, her strong scent adding to his excitement, she felt so good to him, so young and so very innocent. She smelt so clean and fresh, appealing and so very delightful.

With the red nail of her little finger, Jenny idly touched the twitching tip of his cock. He groaned and shifted as the pleasure raced through him.

"Sir's willy is too big for little Cynthia," she purred.

"No!" he said instantly in an effort to reassure. "It will be alright, Cynthia, don't worry, it won't hurt you."

She changed track, pulling roughly to free the blouse from the waistband of her little skirt.

"Cynthia has grown little boobies," she giggled excitedly. "Would sir like to see them?"

He couldn't answer, his pounding excitement created a thick lump in his throat, he watched instead as she stripped to the waist baring her pert little breasts. Tossing her blouse and bra aside with a casual ease to sit close to him her nipples hard and erect.

Jenny moved closer so that her erect nipple was just inches from his mouth. Teasingly close yet so innocently unaware of its provocative look.

"Big boobies aren't they?" she teased.

"Touch it you bitch!" he snapped angrily in excitement.

She looked down at him, a pained expression on her face.

"Sir's angry with little Cynthia. Perhaps little Cynthia should leave," she lisped solemnly. Pain and hurt sounding in her voice.

"No! No, please," he said quickly to restore the sexual situation that might escape him. "Sir is sorry. He didn't mean to shout at you. Please touch his willy Cynthia, please."

She slid off his thigh to kneel between his legs; she moved her chest so that his upright cock fitted snugly between her breasts. Using both hands, she pushed her breasts together trapping his stiff cock between them.

"Oh god!" he groaned at the feel of her soft warm flesh on his throbbing cock. "Wonderful."

"Cynthia has homework to do," she lisped sexily as she massaged her breasts around his stiff member.

"No, leave it. Stay as you are," he panted urgently.

She withdrew and stood back looking at him, her face showing an impish and tempting smile that mocked him deeply.

"Is sir getting worked-up?" she asked huskily, lowering her head to one side.

"You fucking know I am!" he screamed at her. "Now get back here and finish me!"

Jenny shrugged and bent over to look in her bag. The short grey skirt pulled high up at the back to show her white panties pulling tightly across her neat firm buttocks. The shape of her labia was clearly visible between her legs as it pushed against the thin material, the crease of her firm buttocks clearly defined.

She unrolled the rope and began skipping lightly. Her body moving in a hypnotic rhythm as her breasts bounced and her skirt flicked up to give tantalising glimpses of white panties and creamy thigh. Several minutes passed before she stopped and put the rope back in the small bag.

Jenny pulled out an exercise book and pencil, went to the vaulting horse and bent over to start writing. Her back to him, she stood showing her panties beneath the hem of the pleated skirt. A tantalising hint of white beneath the grey, added to by the long legs of firm creamy flesh.

"Bitch! Bitch! Bitch," he shouted angrily, he was pulling against his bonds, struggling to get free but to no avail. "You'll suffer if you don't get back here now!"

"But I suffer anyway," she replied sweetly without looking up.

Jenny shifted her weight to one leg and wriggled her backside sexily as she scribbled in the book. Her buttocks shifting so tantalisingly beneath the short skirt. She half-turned, the end of the pencil in her mouth, her neat naked breasts jutting out in profile.

"How do you spell willy?" she lisped innocently.

He groaned deeply and slumped against his bonds. He knew it was useless to fight against the ropes that bound him so securely.

"Oh dear," she gasped sweetly. "Sir's angry with little Cynthia."

She lay facedown on the floor, presenting her side to him, her legs raised behind and above her as she scribbled in the book, her body raised and resting on her elbows.

"Please, Cynthia, please," he pleaded pathetically.

Her breasts pressed against the floor and her neat backside jutted up to show just a hint of the swell of her buttocks beneath the short skirt, she looked adorable.

"Okay, Jenny. You win. I trust you completely and accept your commitment to the organisation. Now please touch me!"

She looked at him questioningly, tilting her head to one side so that her pigtails wobbled.

"Who's Jenny?"

His face flushed red, he looked about to explode as she taunted him mercilessly. His eyes held a threatening stare of wicked revenge once he was freed.

For five full minutes she posed and wriggled before him, teasing him, tantalising him and listening to his whimpering and groaning. Her pussy was so wet, she thrilled in the sensations that rushed through her, the way she had him simply begging for her. She moved her body to afford him a better look up her skirt, scratching herself on the thigh on occasions to further give flashes of the delights that lay beneath the heavy grey material of her little skirt.

Slowly she got to her feet, her naked breasts swinging free as she moved towards him. Again she knelt between his open thighs and lowered herself to bring her face level with his cock.

"Is it aching sir?" she asked in innocent wonder.

"Yes," he panted, fighting to control himself. "Yes, it aches."

"Would sir like Cynthia to touch it?" she almost sang the words.

He fought to control his rising temper and impatience.

"You know I would you silly little bitch!"

She feigned a look of shocked surprise at his tone.

"Beg me," she purred almost as a whisper.

"Please, Cynthia, touch sir's cock for him," he pleaded in his sweetest coaxing voice.

"Is that really begging?" she lisped laying her head to one side and widening her eyes as she looked into his.

"Just do it you teasing little slut!" he blurted, losing control.

She remained calm and looked sensually at him.

"Oh dear. I think I ought to go to my room."

He changed track instantly.

"No, please, no! I beg you please Cynthia, touch sir's cock."

"Okay then," she said brightly.

Using just her first finger and thumb, she gripped it lightly just beneath the glans. He groaned in appreciation of her soft touch and shifted his hips to try to gain further pressure.

"Harder!" he moaned urgently.

"Is it?" she toyed sexily.

He snapped angrily and then tempered his voice to softer pleading tones.

"Squeeze it harder for sir, little Cynthia, please."

Jenny gripped it in her hand. His pulsing warmth filling her palm and sending exciting spears of pleasure racing through her. It was pumping with excitement, a throbbing urgency that delighted her. Inwardly she rejoiced at his discomfort.

She slid her hand down to the base of his cock and placed her thumb against the big vein where she pressed hard to restrict any flow. Now she would really make him beg.

"Oh sir," she lisped in wonder. "It's such a big willy!"

Her head moved forward, her soft wet tongue reaching out to flick across the tip.

He trembled and shifted his hips, groaning loudly in what sounded like pain. His head was shaking slightly and his eyes rolling in their sockets as the pleasure ripped through him. His thighs jerked and his buttocks clenched tightly together.

With wide moon-like eyes she stared into his eyes, holding his gaze as she opened her mouth and moved close.

"Yes," he urged her throatily. "Yes, suck me."

Her soft sensuous lips lightly touched the top, her saliva smearing across the glans to make them slide easily over the velvety skin.

Pinching her thumb tightly on his base to prevent him coming, she enveloped the head of his cock with her soft warm mouth and drilled the tip of her tongue into his eyehole.

He cried-out and shuddered, his body racked with the spasms of orgasm that couldn't be fulfilled. The desperate need for release tearing at him but outside his control.

"Let go!" he demanded.

Jenny's pussy was throbbing incessantly, the nagging ache in her clitoris was building to a tremendous pitch, she was close herself just by doing these things to him. She felt her pussy juices flowing readily as she delighted in his demise.

Maintaining the pressure with her thumb and holding his gaze with her smouldering eyes, she slid her soft lips down the side of his shaft. Open and lose, sensual and rubbery, her red lips moved along it, she murmured softly to add to the effect.

"Please! Let me come. Please!"

Again Jenny ignored him, continuing to wet his pulsing shaft with her saliva. Using her tongue occasionally to flick beneath the head to send him into renewed series of spasms. Four or five times she repeated the process before at last licking his lubrication blobs that appeared from the eyehole of his cock.

"Is this just Sir's and Cynthia's little secret?" she asked and then covered the head of his cock again with her mouth. Down and down she lowered her head, feeding his length into the back of her throat.

"Yes," he cried-out, his body twitching in convulsions of ecstasy and pained pleasure. He grunted and sobbed in a desperate plea to be released and be able to come to his climax.

Jenny released her thumb pressure and he came. A forceful great spurt of his sperm hitting the back of her throat to be followed by another and then another. His cock jerking in gripping spasms so powerful and strong.

She gulped his seed greedily and sucked his creamy liquid into her mouth, savouring the salty taste.

Jenny withdrew, pulled the gusset of her panties to one side, straddled him and lowered her pussy to take his cock inside her. She held his head with both hands, kissed him full on the lips and pushed his sperm into his own mouth with her soft tongue. Then she began to ride him.

Fast and desperately she lunged her hips back and forth on his softening cock. Her need urgent and all consuming, she bucked and thrust frantically, her long finger nails digging into his shoulders and scraping his skin in her urgency. The kiss continued, her mouth never breaking contact with him, her internal muscles gripping him to maintain his erection, until finally she came in a shuddering orgasm that ripped violently through her slender frame, Jenny slumped against him sated and drained. She rested against his warm body, twitching with involuntary little ripples of after pleasure as her powerful orgasm subsided and the wonderful sensations lessened in their intensity.

"Slut," he breathed softly in her ear.

She roused herself, with long slim fingers she brushed a bead of sweat from her forehead.

"Good?" she asked.

"Paula?" he enquired as to the source of her knowledge.

She smiled and kissed his wet forehead.

"And who else would know of our little secret professor?" she asked playfully.

"Tonight will bring the severest of punishment, you realise that don't you?"

Jenny looked directly into his eyes, a longing and dutiful look.

"Promises, promises," she giggled and gripped her internal muscles tightly around his soft cock. For a few moments they lay together savouring the after-glow, then at the professor's command Jenny slid off him, untied him and then undressed and adopted a submissive pose by the side of the bench, her head hanging down and hands clasped behind her back. She waited whilst the professor roused himself, selected a long thin cane from beside the bench and moved to her side. She drew a gasp as he rested the cane across the swell of her breasts, the hard bamboo touching across both her soft orbs.

"Punishment I warned you would get and severe punishment it will be you little slut. Are you ready to receive it?"

Jenny simply swallowed hard, the thought of the thin cane stinging at her breasts made her heart beat in fearful anticipation and her throat constrict to make her answer inaudible. But at his command she lay down on her back and allowed herself to be tied, her arms raised to the bar over her head. She whimpered as the cane raised high above his shoulder.

"Answer me bitch!" he snapped impatiently.

Jenny could only nod in response, she tensed, bracing herself for the pain to come but the professor was in no hurry.

The cane fell, a powerful descending slash that landed across both her breasts close to the nipples. The professor's cock jerked in involuntary reaction as the girl screamed her pain. Again he raised the cane and paused.

"Filthy little slut - aren't you?"

A sobbed response was all that was heard before he brought the cane down again on her tender breasts. His cock jerked again as her body bucked, her back arching to cope with the searing pain. He was gaining another erection, the sight of the young girl in such excruciating pain delighted him. Twice more he lashed savagely at her breasts before she broke.

"Please no more!" she sobbed, "please professor."

"You took command - that I won't allow slut."

She sobbed her reply pitifully, willing as always to please and hurting at his displeasure of her.

"I did it for your pleasure - not only mine."

"Then you understand that this is part of my pleasure."

"Yes, professor," Jenny agreed humbly, aware that under the pounding heat at her breasts her sex was moistening at the knowledge that worse pain was to come.

He was silent. The professor took a step back, positioned the very end of the cane on her left nipple to gain his aim and raised the cane high.

"Oh God no please!" Jenny pleaded pitifully.

"Who is in control slut?" the professor demanded.

"You are! Always," she cried aloud in an attempt to appease him and to avoid the threatened agony to come.

The cane cut down sharply, to cut harshly across the firm bud of her nipple. Jenny emitted a pained wailing scream that turned to a low, defeated but fulfilled gurgling from deep in her throat and then she passed out.

CHAPTER ELEVEN

The mini-bus drew to a halt in the lay-by, the professor switched off the engine and turned around to distribute the velvet blindfolds amongst the girls.

"Secret stuff eh, professor," Natalie offered as she took hers from him.

"I am relying on you all to observe my wishes and not to peep."

"You can rely on us," Caroline answered dutifully as the eldest.

The others sniggered at her, she wouldn't change, and perhaps she simply couldn't. Always playing the wise-old owl of the flock.

Dress for the ceremony had been left to each individual girl, trousers or the like, being the only item of clothing outlawed. All had chosen short dresses or skirts with tight clinging tops, clothes that showed their slim bodies and legs off to perfection, the professor had approved even if he hadn't told them so.

The girls giggled and chatted idly as the professor drove around in circles for the next half-an-hour, taking turn after turn so as to disorientate the girls and thereby ensure that the location of the barn remained secret until they were initiated.

At last, the roads became bumpier, the mini-bus slowing at times to almost a crawl, it indicated to the girls that they were now close to the famed and much heard-of Buckinghamshire barn. The girls fell silent as the moment of truth for them approached; each filled with pangs of apprehension and a little fear of the unknown. It was a strange atmosphere inside the back of the mini-bus, a mix of excited anticipation tinged with a kind of dread that none of them felt strong enough to challenge.

The mini-bus finally drew to a halt, the professor got out and opened the back doors for them to file out, helping each of them to find safe footing.

The professor was on edge, they all sensed it in him, and they recognised tonight's importance to him as he shepherded them into the barn. He was excited and a little nervous, he was doing all he could to calm any fear in the girls whilst seemingly unable to do that for himself. It had become a silent understanding between them, a subject no one felt they wanted to raise.

They all stood unseeing and waiting patiently as the movements close to them in the small foyer of the barn seemed louder and more acute than they normally would have.

"You may remove your blindfolds now," the professor said in a level tone.

As their blurred visions cleared and they were able to see again, the rustic charm of the building became apparent, heavy beams above them and a closed-off area that served as the foyer surrounded them. A naked man in a black velvet hood stood before them, a red number stitched to the mask at about his forehead height.

The professor also had stripped naked and taking a similar hood from a long rack partially filled with them, he pulled it over his head. A silver number attached to his mask distinguished his rank of senator from the red of the ordinary members.

"Anonymity is essential here," the professor offered in explanation. "The door-man's privilege is to handle the goods on entry, you will all stand still whilst this is done."

The over-weight naked man moved forward, his semi-flaccid cock swinging lazily between his thighs. His hand gripped Sasha's buttocks through her short tartan kilt and then lifted it to stroke her buttocks through her small panties. His podgy fingers felt between her silky smooth cheeks to probe at her labia before moving on to Caroline to fondle her breasts through her tight fitting blouse. Caressing and feeling he enjoyed his perk, his thick fingers roaming all over her breasts and covered nipples.

Each girl in turn was subjected to his groping before the professor called a halt to his pleasure; he obediently turned back to resume his place by the door.

Geraldine noted that he had a full hard-on by now and smiled at the way they had brought his cock to stand to attention.

The professor had given them a detailed briefing as to the

series of events once they reached the barn. A step-by-step guide through the procedure so that they didn't feel threatened or unsure. He had refused point blank however, to discuss what happened during the ceremony or quite what form it would take.

Caroline had secretly related her experiences at the barn to the other girls, emphasising that the model horse as part of the ceremony was now defunct, and to be replaced by - she didn't know what. Her revelations as to the extreme pleasure that she had experienced astride the huge mount had kept them enthralled for a long time with many questions being fired at her in rapid succession.

As part of his little talk, the professor had stressed that no ceremony had ever involved more than one girl at a time, five was unthinkable and they should be prepared for an exceptionally noisy reaction from the crowd of members.

As part of his build-up to and planning for the ceremony, the professor - out of courtesy - had informed the present principal as to his plan, no other person knew of his intentions. He had however, circulated leaflets to the whole of the membership, promising a very different evening of sexual delight that should ensure full attendance to vote on his behalf tonight. He had left little to chance.

"Okay girls," the professor said suddenly, breaking the silence and moved slowly off down the narrow wooden corridor to the right of the door.

As it followed the outside wall, it was not difficult to work out that they were moving to the back of the huge barn. Small flights of steps first down, then up, led them towards the stage until finally they stood in a line, ushered by the professor to face the heavy velvet curtain.

The nervous girls looked from one to the other as the professor stepped through the gap in the curtain and onto the stage itself. They listened intently as he addressed the waiting audience in a loud, but proud voice.

"Tonight, members and principal. I make my bid for the highest post within the organisation."

A loud chorus of gasped surprise rippled around the hundreds of members present in the well of the barn floor, black hooded heads turning to one another to express their surprise at the announcement. It took several minutes to die down sufficiently so that the professor could continue.

"As you all know, it is a requirement that I offer for your approval, a total of five recruits. It is usual - though not a requirement - that these five are offered individually over a period of time, credits gained and used at the time of the bid being made."

"Get on with it," someone shouted to an accompanying ripple of laughter. A loud thumping from the principal's platform at the other side of the barn brought silence once again so that the professor could finish his presentation.

"I have tonight however, decided and prepared for your delight," the professor built the volume and the excitement in his voice to imitate a ringmaster whipping up the crowd. "Not one young and delectable girl - but all five at once!"

He stood back with a theatrical sweep of his arm as the curtains pulled back to reveal the five girls; the crowd erupted into a thunderous cheering and hooting. A surge in the baying crowd moved the naked and hooded mass forward towards the stage and catwalk. They loved it, it was new and unknown, the professor glowed with pride at his masterstroke, this surely now would ensure the vote would go his way.

The loudspeaker system crackled into life as the principal's irritated voice commanded that order and silence be retained. However many minutes passed before any kind of order was restored to the proceedings and the principal was again able to take his seat and allow the professor to continue.

The girls looked out across the crowd. Naked bodies of all shapes and sizes, some young and some old. Male and even a few female. Sasha thought she recognised one pair of women's boobs on a particularly slim and shapely body.

All of the girls felt a tremendous thrill at the reaction they received from the membership. Without exception their nipples and clitoris' were hard and excited. A throbbing growing feeling of anticipation ran through the five. The heady pounding of being desired by so many men filled them with a tremendous driving charge to spur them onward.

At the professor's prompt, Jenny led off, walking slowly down the long catwalk to the small stage area at the end that was surrounded by the heaving and pushing crowd. She thrilled as she walked, the heels of her long black boots striking the wooden boards in confident and deliberate strides. Her short blue dress hid little of her thighs as she towered above the crowd. Hooded figures with heads at her ankle level looked up her skirt as she passed.

Posing and strutting for the benefit of the crowd, Jenny reached the end of the catwalk and stood in position on her initial chalked on the boards. Beaming broadly, she drank in the fantastic feelings of being the centre of attraction for the audience.

Her body shivered with delight, a heavy pounding in her head, fed by the sight of erect and semi-erect cocks in the naked mass. One man had gripped a woman around the waist and was entering her from behind as they stood watching her. That gave Jenny a terrific jolt in her vulva, so strong that it made her gasp for breath.

Caroline moved down the catwalk, her flared skirt billowing out as she walked, displaying her upper thighs and panties to the whistling and shouting crowd. Her neat breasts bouncing under the thin crew-necked jumper that she wore. She felt so good and desirable, to be the object of their attention and their lust. Parading like a fashion model with so many men wondering what her body was like beneath her clothing, wondering what it would be like to come into contact with her warm soft flesh. She felt her pussy moisten as her excited juices flowed, blood rushed to her breasts to excite her already hard nipples further, pounding in her brain made her slightly dizzy with the heady excitement.

Natalie next, strutting and giving a wave in response to the loud cheers that greeted her walk down the catwalk. She too bathed in the attention and rousing greeting that she received, it made her wet as she slowed her pace to make the very most of it. The tall girl strode casually, swinging her hips and moving her body at the waist to give good emphasis to her breasts.

Geraldine drew as many encouraging cheers during her voyage to the end of the catwalk and stood with the other two as the members inspected them from below. So many men liked redheads, she thought as she posed sexily, they certainly seemed to like her. Playfully she lifted her skirt quickly to give a brief flash of her thighs and panties beneath; the crowd loved that and showed their approval noisily.

The house erupted as one in terrific thunderous applause that turned into an unruly and noisy screaming as the olive-skinned Sasha stepped forward. In her mini-kilt and ruffled white blouse to complete her pseudo-Scottish look, she wiggled her hips in delight as she strolled casually down the long catwalk. Her bright smile that showed her white teeth against the red of her lipstick was well received. Her slim body moved gracefully, her long brown neck against the fluffy white of her blouse added to her sensual look. Her even and olive-coloured thighs against the black and white check of her tartan skirt made her positively adorable. Sasha bathed in the attention, feeling that she above all the others was their favourite.

Later, as the noise lessened, the signal was given and the bench was lifted onto the stage. Placed before the line of girls, it was long and strong, with thick leather straps at the sides. Geraldine looked across at Natalie, who licked her lips in response, bringing a huge smile to Geraldine's face.

"Strip!" the professor commanded loudly above the noise. "The bidding starts now with Jenny."

He moved to Jenny's side as she undressed, indicating to the crowd that she was the first of the girls on offer.

"Two!" someone shouted loudly followed by a round of derisory remarks from other members of the crowd.

"Two-and-a-half," another hopeful offered loudly and added,

"If I can lick her arse."

Much laughter and varied remarks followed before the professor held up his arms in an effort to bring silence. He succeeded after a few moments and again addressed the audience.

"Members!" he said loudly in a disappointed tone. "This is an exceptional night and these are exceptionally young, beautiful and above all, innocent girls - I expect sensible offers or they will be withdrawn."

"Three!" another voice shouted.

All the girls were naked now, standing proudly as the hundreds of hungry eyes roamed their firm flesh, lusting and wanting. Searching the array of firm young breasts and hairy covered mons displayed before them.

"Three? That's not much!" Natalie whispered to Geraldine.

"Hundreds, you twit," came the whispered reply.

A whirring sound took the attention of the crowd and from above a set of heavy beams lowered down into position in front of the girls. Five sets of stocks were fixed by their bases to the beams that now rested on the stage. Made of thick and well-used wood, each of the stocks had three holes in the upright panel, one larger one for their necks and the smaller ones either side of it for their hands. The beefy attendant removed the cables that had lowered the framework and guided each girl to her own set of stocks.

Jenny remained with the professor as each of the other naked girls was bent forward to rest their arms and necks in the cutouts before the tops were lowered. Securing them in a standing position with only their heads and hands through to face the majority of the crowd, their backside's pushed out and presented so temptingly behind. The attendants took full advantage and felt the young bodies often as they worked.

The girls were alive with sexual arousal, pinioned naked, they were helpless and at the mercy of the baying crowd, with only the professor to temper the level of the sexual abuse that would surely follow.

The professor held up a large card to the crowd, the girls

couldn't see what was written on it. A low whistling and grumbling came from the membership as they took in the amount being asked.

"Tonight members, this is the total figure I wish to receive for the pleasures of the five young girls here. I offer in return for your money, sexual delight unlimited and in addition - entertainment."

"Four!" a man called waving his hand to attract attention to his bid.

The professor nodded and the man stepped forward, his way blocked by one of the big attendants, to wait until the full amount was reached before he could pass and claim his prize.

The other attendant, who grabbed at and felt her naked backside on the way, to lie back on the wooden bench, led Jenny. He inserted an angled board behind her so that she could rest back in a semi-sitting and half-lying position; he then secured her wrists into the thick straps at her side and her ankles at the end of the bench.

This action had increased the interest of the crowd. The bidding had increased and the number of paying members grew as they waited at the foot of the steps that led up and onto the catwalk.

Jenny was pinioned, her legs spread either side of the bench in her half-sitting position, her pussy ached and she pounded with excitement as the many hungry eyes searched her most intimate parts. An attendant stepped forward as the bidding continued around them, he took full advantage and began feeling and groping at Jenny's presented pussy. His thick fingers worked all around her labia, taking more time on her hard little clitoris, feeling her as he leered down at her. His thick cock showed signs of arousal as his hand roamed freely between the sweet young girl's parted thighs.

The crowd fell silent as a third hooded attendant pushed his way through them and up the short steps, and then mayhem erupted. Loud shouting and delighted howling filled the big room, the crowd went mad. They surged forward again, making the situation border on getting out of control, only prompt action from the principal's voice over the loudspeaker brought some stability to the situation.

Jenny, straining at her bonds to see what was happening, groaned loudly and then screamed, pulling frantically a the straps holding her. Fear filled her; she wriggled and bucked, cowering as her real sense of dread increased.

The latest attendant wore a gigantic dildo strapped around his waist and buttocks, so huge was it that it that no woman could possibly accept the thing without injury. Cartoon - like in its great proportion it was so long that it needed the attendant's hand to steady it. He stood over her gloating at her fear as the crowd bayed loudly for him to fuck her. He smiled down, parted his lips and pushed out his tongue. The crowd broke into wild laughter as the extraordinarily long tongue hung down his jaw and curled up under his chin.

Jenny was still straining fearfully, the tongue she could ñ would cope with and with much pleasure at that but the enormous dildo?

The professor knelt, his mouth close to her ear.

"His little joke Jenny, never fear, the professor is here."

The dildo was discarded and the attendant knelt between her thighs, his snake-like tongue flicking out long and curling.

Jenny bucked and tensed at the contact was made, the long tongue licking up and over the lips of her labia. She screamed her pleasure above the noise of the crowd as the expert attendant teased her senses. The rough tongue dipped and lapped, scraping harshly over the tip of her hard clitoris to send jarring sensations of raw pleasure tearing through her.

The crowd were chanting now, clapping and cheering, stamping their feet as they urged both the tonguing man and Jenny onward.

Fear gripped Jenny still, the delightful and excruciating rubbing and slobbering that excited her pussy took second place to what might come after.

The professor knelt bringing his face close to Jenny's ear.

"The dildo won't be used my hungry little slut."

His words were sweet relief, the fear dispersed almost instantly. That threat gone, Jenny relaxed into the wonderful feelings that the rough tongue was bringing to her. Gripping sensations filled her as his tongue brushed her warm flesh, hot breath between her thighs and that ever-so long and rough tongue then pushed fully up inside her.

"My god," Caroline gasped in disbelief from her tethered position as she watched the erotic spectacle.

The total amount of money had been reached and the first of the lucky members stepped forward to take their positions behind the bending girls. With a nod from the professor they began.

Eager and excited hands felt and groped the pinioned young girls, pulling and squeezing at their nipples, fingers feeling and entering their offered and defenceless orifices. Stroking and caressing they sampled the firm young flesh as their lead-up to their ultimate pleasure.

Natalie turned her head within her wooden prison to glance across at Sasha who was being well and truly ridden. The man behind her had hold of her slim hips and was ramming hard into her. The brown face with bright red painted lips contorted with a mix of pain and pleasure as she endured his frantic thrusting.

Each girl, now that the initial groping was over and done, had a cock inside them, battering and thrusting, the grunting men rammed their cocks hard into the soft warm interiors of the young girls.

Jenny screamed aloud and tensed, urged on by the chanting crowd. Her head was muzzy with excitement; the raw sexual way that she was being pleased before so many people made her body tingle with satisfaction. The wet tongue rasped incessantly over her hard clitoris and in and around her labia. The long tongue wriggling so far up inside her she almost came as it flicked over certain parts of her soft interior.

"Yes!" she cried out and the crowd responded as one.

"Yes!" they chanted in reply to her pleasure.

"Yes!" Jenny cried out again as she pulled at her straps and thrashed her head around in heady sex-crazed pleasure. Again and again she cried-out and then screamed. Her body locked and her head threw back, her back arched to receive the wonderful pounding waves of orgasm as they crashed over her. She gurgled and then gagged as the powerful sensations gripped her, she gasped hard for breath and sucked in air hungrily as her slim body endured the tearing sensations of pleasure.

The man licked on unconcerned as Jenny shuddered in violent spasms of orgasm, all the time the delighted crowd baying for more. Her climax reached, the man pulled back and walked away, Jenny slumped exhausted onto the surface of the hard bench to savour the tingling ripples of after pleasure that pulled lightly at her sated body.

Each of the girls stood bent and held in the stocks, sperm dribbling from their pussies from the wonderful and sometimes brutal ministrations of the men.

Natalie moaned as she felt another cock pressing against her buttocks, moving and searching for the way into her wet warm pussy. Caroline screamed aloud, much to the delight of the crowd as the cock behind her pressed into her anus. She cried out as it entered her, shouting her protests to the noisy membership. Her face contorted and her fists clenched tight, she could do nothing to prevent the invasion of her tight and previously unexplored anus.

As each man shot his seed inside one of the girls, he was replaced by another. Some indulged themselves in a little spanking of the soft firm bottoms of the girls before pushing their cocks inside. Many men took advantage also of the sweet soft mouths on offer and took their pleasure at the front, leaving the girls the taste of their sperm to savour before the next cock brushed its excited way in.

Jenny had been released and led to be secured into the stocks to take her turn at being the subject of pleasure for the waiting men.

To a loud cheering, Sasha was released and led to the front of the stage. Face down on the hard strong bench, she was strapped securely to the frame with her pert little backside pushed up into the air.

A slim and attractive woman walked slowly up the steps and onto the catwalk. The crowd fell silent as she stood proudly and confidently waiting for her audience to quieten. Long black leather boots hugged her slim legs, thick laces all down the front pulled them tightly into place. Shiny leather straps criss-crossed her body, pulling harshly between her thighs and under her ample breasts. She was naked, her pussy and long rubbery nipples clearly on view as the straps pulled tightly to the sides, she carried a thick riding crop, her face covered with a leather mask. Jenny smiled her recognition of the tall elegant girl with the blonde hair.

In two long strides of her slender legs the leather-clad woman was beside the bench. Without hesitation, she raised the crop above her shoulder and brought it down hard to lash a stinging blow on Sasha's soft firm buttocks.

Sasha screamed her mouth fell open and her eyes bulged as the excruciating pain shot through her. Even after the initial shock the searing pain in her backside remained. Her body movements as she jerked in response to the next lash thrust her along the hard surface of the wooden bench, her mons and breasts rubbing cruelly on the rough grained surface.

The other girls watched her receive her beating, each being had from behind, the pumping cocks inside them adding to the pleasure they were all now experiencing as the queue to have them lessened slightly.

Geraldine had come twice; she was fast approaching her third wonderful orgasm despite the thick finger being forced inside her anus as the man thrust into her. Natalie had another excited cock in her mouth as she was being serviced from the back. The excited man at her front standing on a small box to gain the required height before her. How many cocks she had had in her she didn't know or care, she just enjoyed the present and the wonderful sensations and emotions that she was experiencing.

Sasha screamed again, loud and long, a pitiful wailing noise as her thrashing continued. Many times the cruel crop had stung at her soft flesh and now the pain was at its peak. A warming and glowing pleasure began to spread through her lower regions to arouse her even in such extreme pain. Twice more the lashes bit into her flesh and then stopped.

The leather-clad woman knelt behind Sasha and began gently licking the red weals on the young girl's flesh. Each of her red stripes was tended carefully. The woman's tongue, so warm and soft, tickling yet exciting brought Sasha closer to her peak. Down the tongue travelled, tracing a path between her firm buttocks to lap and taste at the entrance to her open and wet pussy.

Sasha gasped at the exquisite pleasure she received and the tongue entered her soft folds, long delicate fingers rubbed at her hard clitoris from below. Lapping at the mix of her juices and the sperm that remained inside; the tongue searched every soft fold of her warm wet interior.

Gripped by involuntary spasms of intense pleasure, Sasha arrived at her climax. She gasped and shuddered, her mouth fell open and she came. A crashing and gripping orgasm of such intensity that her body was jerked around many times before at last the jarring convulsions of pleasure began to subside.

To loud cheering, Sasha felt the velvety head of a cock nudging at her mouth; she opened her lips to receive it willingly and sucked hungrily on the throbbing member as another man entered her pussy from the rear. She slipped into a warm swirling mist of pure sexual abandon as the cocks abused her before the crowd. She felt detached and distant, only the wonderful feelings served as a reminder of her delightful situation.

Geraldine delighted the crowd with her performance. Pinned to the bench, she received her treatment with an animal-like hunger that whipped the crowd into frenzy as they watched. The bidding increased as a result of her hunger, as did the number of takers as the evening progressed and the entertainment continued.

A double dildo was used on her, a thick shaft inserted in her pussy and an attached pencil-thin probe in her anus at the same time. Her hard clitoris was rubbed throughout with a powerful vibrator that brought her to a thrashing orgasm as she sucked on a series of hard cocks in succession.

Natalie too delighted the crowd by riding an upright dildo fixed to a chair. Then she was hung upside down by her ankles suspended on ropes from the ceiling; her pussy was filled with champagne and the contents drunk by both men and women. She delighted the audience further by coming several times during her turn as the cabaret.

Caroline had came last and had, for a few moments at least, threatened to put a damper on the evening's festivities. As soon as she was free from the stocks, the older woman, naked and her breasts bouncing, stalked angrily down the steps to seek out the man that had invaded her anus. The crowd fell silent as she searched the hoods for the number she sought.

When at last she found him, Caroline landed a powerful and stinging slap across his face, so hard that it jarred his head to the side.

A stunned silence followed, the professor groaned in dismay and then the hooded man burst out laughing loudly. The audience squealed their delight as he lifted Caroline's slight body and lie her across his knee; there he spanked her mercilessly as she screamed vile abuse at him. Others joined in and soon her body was coated in sperm and bruises as she suffered every indignity possible. On the floor she now lay, held down and screaming, cocks entered her and filled her with sperm or withdrew and spurted over her thrashing body. Several more times her anus was stretched wide as she paid the price for rebellion.

Stinging lashes bit at her body in a free-for-all that many of the baying crowd took advantage of to take their pleasure. In many ways, the impromptu event was one of the best events of the evening and was well received by the members before at length the professor stepped in to end her punishment.

Freed and standing naked in the centre of the barn floor with the crowd pushed back in a full circle around them, the girls were subjected to a hosing-down. Freezing cold water in powerful jets that moved over their bruised and sated bodies made them shiver and huddle together.

At last, the principal called the meeting to order and asked for a vote as to whether or not the professor's bid should be allowed as successful. It was a resounding yes from the crowd, if there were any votes against, they certainly didn't show. The bid had been successful, as had the entire evening.

CHAPTER TWELVE

The atmosphere was tense as the out-going principal settled himself in the deeply upholstered settee in the professor's lounge. He accepted the generously filled cut-glass tumbler of whiskey offered by the professor.

"It was a shambles!" the man said angrily to the professor. "Never in my time as principal nor in fact, in my time as a member, did I witness such a breakdown of order within the membership."

The professor crossed his legs casually and sipped at his glass of whiskey, he listened intently as the man rambled on. When he paused for a moment in his onslaught, the professor seized his chance; he spoke casually with a hint of mockery in his tone.

"But then you are no longer principal - and I am."

The man's face reddened, his expression thunderous, extreme anger boiling inside him. He slammed his glass down noisily on the coffee table between them and shifted to the edge of his seat.

"You deliberately set out to humiliate me just as I was coming to the end of my term as principal. You couldn't even allow me to bow-out gracefully could you?"

The professor shook his head.

"I simply offered the five girls together to ensure that my bid was successful, and for no other reason. You cannot deny that the evening was a huge success, the reaction of the members and the final vote should be sufficient to confirm that."

The man shifted uncomfortably, his mind distracted as the tall and elegant Natalie entered precisely on cue, just as the professor had asked her to. She walked casually over to the two men, posed momentarily before settling herself on the arm of the settee close to the man. Her heady perfume filled his nostrils to give a hint of the delights she possessed, it excited him instantly.

Natalie wore a tight black Lycra skirt that pulled itself around her narrow hips and slim thighs. It rode up as she sat, the thin hem stopping just short of her groin to reveal tight white panties hugging her bulging pussy beneath. She looked adorably sexy, a tight red top that showed her bare mid-driff and breasts to good effect and enhancing her broad smile.

"Am I interrupting?" she asked sweetly.

The man's eyes roamed her slender thighs hungrily; peering up between them at the sweet tight mound of her pussy that was delightfully covered by the thin material.

"I have no wish to quarrel with you," the professor addressed the now silent man. "Perhaps Natalie could show you the gymnasium and help to clear your mind a little."

His reaction was instant, a lightening smile came across his face, he stood slowly and followed Natalie from the room, watching her backside wiggle as she walked.

***

Geraldine lathered herself in the shower, turning and posing to direct the hot water to spray down over her hair and body. The bright red of her pubic hair glowing against the whiteness of her skin between her creamy slim thighs.

She became aware of someone opening the door of the shower cubicle and rubbed the water from her eyes to see more clearly.

"You did say any time," Sasha purred.

She was naked, her olive-skinned body, lithe and sensual. Thick black hair touching her shoulders and bright-red lipstick to showed off the white of her teeth as she smiled.

Geraldine groaned with desire, the girl was radiant and so beautiful. Her dark rubbery nipples jutting out so temptingly from her beautifully rounded and symmetrical breasts. It aroused her instantly even to think of touching the soft velvety skin of the girl. Sasha's ability to use her tongue to such good effect gave a rippling charge that throbbed in Geraldine's pussy at the very thought.

"Join me?" Geraldine asked hesitantly, fearing rejection.

Sasha smiled broadly and stepped into the cubicle, fine droplets of water falling onto her breasts and running in rivulets down her cleavage between the swell of her firm breasts. Immediately her hands went to Geraldine's breasts, covering them, her fingers feeling and caressing lovingly as she massaged the foamy soapsuds all over the firm orbs.

Geraldine moaned in pleasure, arching her back to force her chest out towards Sasha in an offering of total compliance and submission. The thrilling sensations that the slim fingers produced were indescribable, mixed with the tingling naughtiness of being with another woman gave a series of pleasurable jolts to Geraldine's hard clitoris.

Two sexually aroused young women, alone and in need of each other to satisfy their hot craving for satisfaction.

The soft red lips descended, enveloping one of Geraldine's firm nipples as the other was pulled and pinched by tender fingers. This was warm, sensual love-making as opposed to being simply sex, the tenderness and the feeling was transmitted through their bodies to further relax and excite them both.

Geraldine rested back against the tiled cubicle wall as the water cascaded down on the two of them. Shifting her feet apart, Geraldine adopted a wide-legged stance that Sasha took full advantage of and moved her hand between the open thighs. Cupping Geraldine's pussy, Sasha's hand pressed in against the lips of her sweet labia. The heel of the hand pressing hard against the panting girl's clitoris, her fingers stroking gently at the pink inner lips as they were offered so readily.

Geraldine's shoulders were against the wall, her head fell back to rest against the tiles as the water and the pleasure washed over her. Fingers inside her now, searching and probing. Long slender fingers with equally long hard nails explored the soft moist interior of her intimate depths. Moaning and sighing, Geraldine moved her hips to meet the hand of the raven-haired beauty whose touch was so delightful. The soft nuzzling lips and tongue that played on her nipple brought wave after wave of pounding excitement rushing through her.

"Do it to me," Geraldine murmured pleadingly as her head rocked from side to side in hot passion.

"Do what?" Sasha's husky voice teased, then bit gently on the erect nipple.

Geraldine cried-out and shuddered.

"You know, do it to me please."

Gripping the nipple between her top teeth and tongue, Sasha rolled the nipple side to side and pushed another finger up inside Geraldine's wet pussy.

Geraldine tensed and her body convulsed as the exquisite sensations rushed through her.

"Please, Sasha - please.

Several more minutes of extreme pleasure followed before Sasha broke away and holding Geraldine's hand guided her to the bed. Both girls, wet and dripping, stood and embraced, mons against mons and breasts against breasts they pressed hard onto one another.

Sasha's full lips came close and then kissed Geraldine full on the lips, her tongue searching all around the inside of Geraldine's soft mouth.

Responding hungrily, her need now driving her onward, Geraldine held Sasha tightly around the waist and hips, feeding her own tongue back into the soft cavern of Sasha's open mouth. Her hand slid down the back to cup and to squeeze the firm flesh of Sasha's buttocks, fingers moving into the tight crease between them to feel and to savour the young firm flesh.

***

The man was tied hand and foot to the wall-bars in the gymnasium. Star-shaped, his arms were pulled out wide and above his head, his feet pulled apart and tied as his wrists were, with strong soft rope. He remained there helpless, naked with only his throbbing erection sticking out from his body. He was in great need; his cock twitched involuntarily as it awaited the touch of the tall elegant girl who had tied him there. Expectant and hopeful, longing for sexual bliss and that wonderful final release.

"Please," he begged earnestly.

Natalie knelt in front of him, her wide eyes looking up as his sweating and pleading face. She gathered the skin of his shaft into a bunch, her delicate fingers cool and sensual on his throbbing shaft. Natalie attached the strong bulldog clip around the gathered flesh along its length, then she released the jaws.

His body bucked and thrashed as he screamed in agony. The skin around his cock pulled so tight it looked as though it might split, his pulsing excitement simply compounded the pain for him. Several drops of lubricant squeezed from the eyehole of his cock as the pain and pleasure combined in wonderful excited sensations that both hurt and pleased. For pain at the hands of such a young and beautiful girl could after all, only contain much pleasure in a sexual context.

"Fucking little bitch!" he cursed through gritted teeth. "I should be in command!"

"Oh but you are, you pathetic little wimp - but not today."

Natalie stood and watched him wriggle and squirm in helpless pain. It was good to see this little shit suffer; she didn't like him, not one bit. She owed her allegiance to the professor, not to this man.

Calmly, she attached two further strong clips, one to each of his nipples and watched smiling as he struggled against his bonds. The jaws of the powerful clips squashing his nipples almost flat as they pressed hard together, sending searing pain through him to tear at his senses to accompany the already severe pain produced by the clip on his cock.

As his thrashing around began to subside and she had his full attention once again, Natalie undid the crossover top and pulled it apart to reveal her neat breasts. Held within the constraints of her small black lacy bra, her soft breasts were pulled together to form a deep and swelling cleavage.

His eyes lingered on her soft flesh as she discarded the top altogether.

"Hard are we?" Natalie toyed sexily. "Like a feel of them would you?"

"Fucking bitch, I'll get you for this," he spat angrily in response.

Natalie unfastened the back strap and shrugged her shoulders forward to allow the bra to drop from her body. Firm soft breasts with long hard nipples sticking out from the centre took his attention. She moved close, pressing the warm and scented inside cups of her bra onto his face.

"Can you feel my warmth?" she asked, her voice thick with arousal. "Sniff them you little shit!"

It excited her immensely to tease him like this. Her body trembled with sexual pleasure and thrilling excitement. Her pussy throbbed and her juices flooded readily as she made him want her. He was desperate for her, wanting to feel her and to get inside her, she would make him suffer much more before she was ready herself.

With a casual ease, Natalie threw the bra aside and moved closer, her hard nipples brushing against his chest to further excite the bound and helpless man. She moved her hips back slightly so as to keep clear of his pulsing erection, his agony was about to begin.

Gripping the hem of her tight little skirt at the front, she pulled it up to her waist and shifted her feet apart. Gradually she moved towards to him, rubbing the tightly covered mound of her pussy against the head of his throbbing cock. Lightly, she began a back and forth rocking motion with her hips. The thin material pulled tightly into the shape of her labia beneath, the head of his cock sliding within the crease of her labia to produce a delightfully different set of sensations.

He groaned in pleasure and frustration. His mouth fell open at her touch as the feelings raced through him. He was breathing hard and rapidly as his pleasure increased.

"Good?" Natalie teased her smiling face close to his.

He nodded and half-closed his eyes as he drank in the heady sensations that were pounding through him. His cock twitched and jerked in little spasms of extreme pleasure through the pain of the clips that gripped it so tightly. Then Natalie stopped and stepped back. He groaned loudly in disappointment, the wonderful feelings of her warm moist body against him now ended.

Slowly and sexily, Natalie stood before him removing the tight little skirt. Her long legs seemed endless as her slender thighs and hips came exposed, just her small tight panties pulling high on her hips to cover her nakedness. He gasped as she slipped the panties off and faced him. A neat triangle of dark soft pubic hair nestled between her slim thighs, she looked stunning and so desirable. His cock twitched against the restriction of the clip holding it.

Natalie rubbed the gusset of her panties hard into his face, forcing him to smell her most intimate juices and taste her as the thin material was pushed into his mouth. She giggled at his expression when at last she removed them.

He was flushed, his look excited and so very urgent now, it pleased her immensely to watch him.

Dropping her little panties to hang over his throbbing erection, Natalie gripped his stiff cock through the material and received a terrific jolt in her vulva at his loud groan of sheer pleasure. Gripping hard, she moved her hand slowly on his pulsing member using the material of her panties as the means of lubrication.

He went wild. Moaning and sighing his pleasure which heightened as his arousal increased. Natalie took him forward towards his peak; she watched and carefully studied his movements and expressions as she rubbed him. At the first indication of his body tensing in the initial stages of orgasm, she stopped and withdrew.

"You will suffer severely when I am free," he threatened, his face and stare full of menace.

Unconcerned, she moved close and repeated the rubbing of her pussy on the head of his cock, this time her soft downy pussy was naked. She began the sensual hip movements, staring into his face all the time and revelling in his discomfort. Her juices aiding the sliding motion of the big head over her swollen lips, Natalie increased the pace.

"Good?" she teased softly. "Like to get inside me?"

He nodded, cleared his throat and answered again.

"Yes, so good. So very good, let me in you now."

"Beg."

He hesitated as she rubbed against him.

"Please, Natalie. Let me fuck you."

She increased the movement of her hips and the pressure on the tip of his aching cock.

"Pretty please," she prompted.

With a look of distaste and then a groan of pleasure, he relented.

"Pretty please, lovely Natalie, let me fuck you. Let me inside your sweet little pussy, Please!"

"Ahh," she moaned sweetly as if giving in to his pleadings and giving hope to the suffering man.

"As you asked so sweetly."

She moved back to stand before him. Her voice low and calm.

"The answer is no."

His shouting echoed around the hollow sounding room. Natalie laughed loudly in equal volume to his cursing and name calling, enjoying the many insults he threw at her.

Holding up the tiny silver clip and squeezing the jaws for his benefit, she knelt and gripped his cock with her left hand. Long and thin, about the size and thickness of a matchstick, the metal clip had sprung jaws that closed when the pressure was released and opened when pressure was added.

He screamed, almost crying as she pushed the clip into the eyehole in the end of his cock. Natalie smiled, grinning sweetly as she pressed on the clip. The tiny jaws opened inside his small tube, forcing it apart inside him. The frantic thrashing of his body rattled against the wooden bars that held firm at his back. He gagged as he struggled to cope with the searing pain. His shouted insults had now changed to a pitiful and whining pleading for her to stop.

Again and again Natalie repeated the process, delighting in his pain as she came to an involuntary but welcome orgasm.

Thumping surges of intense power racked her body; simultaneous charges hit her clitoris and deep in her pussy, tugging at her insides to bring sweet and warming feelings of such intense pleasure. She cried-out softly, her body shuddered before slumping back on the cold wooden floor to quiver in light shudders of after-pleasure. Moaning and mewing, she drank in the light convulsions of exquisite bliss that filled her. In her distant and dreamy state, Natalie was aware of his angry voice shouting loudly from his pinioned position, the words she couldn't make out - she really didn't care what he was saying.

***

Sasha tied the last of the knots that bound Geraldine hand and foot. Seated on the small stool of the bedroom, Geraldine's feet were stretched either side of the stool, thighs wide apart and her feet secured to the legs. Behind her back, both wrists were tightly tied together and her elbows, linked by a third rope, were pulled harshly inward to bind her helpless and immovably.

Gently, Geraldine was pushed back to rest her elbows on the dressing table behind, her mons pushed up and forward as her hips shifted to accept her new position. She sat open and presented with nothing to hinder access to her offered pussy.

"Don't make me wait any longer Sasha," Geraldine whined. "I need you to do it. To lick to me!"

The tops of Sasha's inner thighs were still damp from the shower; her body glistened in the light from the large window to show it to full and beautiful splendour. She moved gracefully to the dressing table and picked up the hairbrush.

"Patience, patience," Sasha soothed the desperate girl. "First a little lesson for you that will increase the power of any climax you will have from now on."

Sasha stood before the bound Geraldine; she adopted a wide-legged stance, bent her knees slightly and inserted the handle of the brush up inside her pussy.

"Look! No hands," Sasha beamed as she released the brush.

Staring in amazement, Geraldine watched as the bristle part of the brush that protruded from the girl's pussy began to vibrate slightly.

"My internal muscles, Geraldine. Much practice is needed for this part, but you can easily learn to grip it just I have."

The brush moved as if under its own power, moving in small jerky movements as though Sasha was fucking herself.

"Let me try!"

Sasha smiled at her interest and removed the brush from her pussy. The brown plastic handle wet with her juices. She knelt and stroked Geraldine's slim thigh with one hand as she manoeuvred the brush handle with the other hand, towards the girl's open pussy.

Wet and rigid, the initial contact of the handle made Geraldine tense.

"Relax," Sasha soothed. "It doesn't hurt."

The thick brown handle pushed in between the open labia of Geraldine's pussy, then the inner lips and into her secret interior. Up and up it travelled, soothing and coaxing words from Sasha combined with a sensual stroking of her thigh, relaxed Geraldine to allow easy passage for the rigid handle.

"There!" Sasha stated. "It's right up you now, grip it with your muscles."

"I can't, I don't know how!"

"Try."

"I can't I tell you!"

Sasha's long fingernail probed at the entrance to Geraldine's anus.

The red headed girl tensed and gasped her body muscles contracting to grip the handle inside her.

"No, that's not it, not the way you did it. It just doesn't seem right somehow."

Sasha smiled as she spoke. "You're gripping it now."

A look of bewildered disbelief came over Geraldine's face as she realised that she was now holding the brush handle inside her with her own muscles.

"Relax now and then grip again. Good! Very good! Imagine that you have a stiff cock inside you."

"I am!" Geraldine grunted half-laughing.

"Then imagine the ecstasy that you would give him by doing this to him."

Geraldine's face was flushed with excitement; her voice trembled as she spoke.

"I am! I am!"

Sasha smiled and moved back to sit on the floor and watch.

"Don't leave me, lick me please," Geraldine implored.

Idly rubbing her clitoris with the tip of her long middle finger, Sasha sat open-legged on the floor in front of the girl.

"I only like to lick a pussy that has had at least one orgasm," she teased. "I like to taste everything and miss nothing."

Faster and faster Geraldine's muscles worked to first grip and then release the thick handle inside her. Her excitement grew as her pace increased; she was building, bringing herself to orgasm by gripping the brush handle inside her. Her body shook as she tensed and relaxed, her hips giving little light thrusts as she worked, her breasts jiggled and her facial expression was one of pained pleasure as she strove to bring herself off.

"Can you feel him inside you?" Sasha coaxed huskily. "His rigid cock that you are milking. He's ecstatic, his eyes are rolling, his body heaving and he is panting heavily as you draw his sperm from him. Can you feel it?"

"Yes," came the low reply. "Yes, yes."

"I'm rubbing myself, Natalie. Mmm, it feels so good. I can't wait to taste your pussy juices and lick at your hard little clitty."

Geraldine groaned deeply from within the base of her throat. She drew breath and sighed. Her body tensed and twitched, her hips raised and then she screamed. A loud and satisfying wail that echoed around the room. Geraldine's body was racked by a series of shuddering tremors; she gasped at their intensity. Her head and shoulders strained forwards as she received the final powerful surges of her orgasm. On and on the convulsions went, draining her body of every last drop sensation, pulling every last wonderful feeling from the experience, her internal muscles still pumping vigorously on the handle inside her.

***

Natalie had, stage-by-stage untied and re-tied the man in a kneeling position on the gymnasium floor. First his hands, untied and re-tied behind his back, then his feet, giving no opportunity for him to grab or to strike out at her. It had been over two hours since he had first undressed in delighted hope of sex with the tall girl, his torture had lasted all of that time; his orgasm seemed a million miles away, perhaps never to arrive at all.

A collar around his neck with a dog-leash attached to the front D-ring; the man knelt on the hard wooden floor. His wrists bound tightly behind him, arms pulled cruelly high up his back, he could do nothing to end this humiliating experience that he was being subjected to. His feet, bound yet free to take half steps by the restricting ropes which linked them made his demise a little easier now. His head was bowed low, his eyes averted as she had instructed him, he feared the thin cane that she now carried.

Natalie towered over him, her long leather boots shone in the bright natural light of the gymnasium, her thin high heels clicking harshly on the wooden floor as she moved slowly and deliberately around him; she otherwise, was totally naked.

"Ready to come yet, you shit?"

She tapped at his stiff erection with the end of the thin cane and he winced as the attached clip brought a fresh series of stabbing pain to his aching cock.

He nodded his agreement in a defeated and servile manner.

"Good," Natalie stated firmly. "But first you dance for me."

He raised his head to look at her questioningly.

She struck instantly, landing a stinging blow with the thin cane that bit cruelly into the soft tender flesh of his buttocks.

"I told you not to look up," she reminded gently and slashed at him again.

His trembling body jerked as the cane cut into him, the searing pain shooting to his brain to register his discomfort and to add to his suffering.

"Stand up!" Natalie barked harshly in command.

He struggled to gain his feet; the restricting ropes making the movement difficult in the extreme.

Unconcerned, Natalie landed blow after blow on his body to urge him on, paying no heed to target areas of his body; where she lashed was where the pain was felt, a cruel and sadistic thrashing that excited her immensely.

Once on his feet, she guided him by the leash to move around her in a circle as a horse or circus animal would be trained in an arena. Her hand pulling at the leash to guide him by the collar to her required direction.

"Faster!" Natalie barked, swiping at his bare buttocks with the long cane.

He broke into a run, moving his legs in small fast steps as the restricting rope would allow. He looked ridiculous, his overweight naked body bumbling along in a frantic effort to avoid further punishment; his stiff cock with attached clip bouncing painfully as he ran.

"Faster! Run!" Natalie shouted angrily to show her displeasure, she lashed harshly at his bouncing buttocks with the cane, bright red marks appearing on his flesh to bear testament to the severity of her caning.

On and on he ran, circling her many times before at last dropping to his knees in exhausted defeat.

Natalie raised her leg, pressing the thin sharp heel of her boot into his shoulder, she kicked him to roll onto his side. Wide-legged, she towered over him as he cowered fearfully on the floor.

"Who am I you shit! Answer me!"

"Mistress!" He blurted fearfully. "My mistress!"

"Good," the satisfaction sounded in her voice. "Now, my slave will be allowed to come."

Her body throbbing with sheer excitement of the command that she had exercised, Natalie knelt beside him. Her delicate hands removed the strong clip from his cock and her mouth descended to envelope the head in her soft sweet moistness. He came instantly, his sperm jetting out forcefully into her mouth. He groaned and moaned as little jets of his seed spurted out of his sore eyehole to end his agony so sweetly.

The professor entered and released the man, throwing his clothes down onto the quivering wreck on the floor.

"You abused the hospitality of my house, that I can never forgive. I will allow you to remain within the organisation - but as an ordinary member, never to attain a higher rank than that. You will immediately resign from your rank of senator and vote in Paula or Louise in your place. Do you agree?"

The man nodded, clutching his clothes against his body as some little protection against the anger that radiated from the professor.

"Very well," the professor said calmly. "Then never have the occasion to come to this house again - you will not be welcome. The video of this session today remains -shall we say - on file."

They watched as the man scurried out, then the professor turned to Natalie and held out his hand. She bent to pick up the cane from where she had dropped it and handed it to him.

"You were a real bitch Natalie," he said quietly.

"I was wasn't I?" she purred, licking her lips to savour the last of the man's sperm. "And I can't expect to get away with it can I?"

The professor smiled. "Over against the wall bars I think Natalie."

Calm and submissive, she walked over to them and held her arms up and out to have her wrists tied with the same straps she herself had used. When the professor had finished he kicked her legs apart and bound her ankles so that she was now spread, star shaped, just as her victim had been. But she was facing the bars and tied so tightly that her breasts were crushed up against one of the bars and her hardened nipples, now compressed sent shards of pleasure darting through her. She tried wiggling her shoulders and found she could rub them a little, that would make the punishment which was coming her way all the sweeter!

The professor swished the cane through the air a couple of times. Anticipation! Let her hear it and wait for it before she got it. He surveyed the graceful contours of her back and buttocks.

"How many lashes did you give him?" he asked.

She glanced back over one shoulder, a mischievous light in her eyes. "Ooh, at least twenty, maybe more."

"Thirty then. Plus ten to teach you your place, and you will count them."

Natalie felt a surge of excitement throb in her vulva. This was going to be a long and wonderful punishment, driving her slowly through the mists of pain to the peaks of delight that only the professor could take her to. She heard the cane swish and then a blaze of pain exploded across her shoulders while a loud Crack! echoed round the gym. She bit down on the scream that threatened to erupt from her throat and managed to croak, "One!" in a shocked whisper.

The cane whistled through the air again........and again.........and again. Natalie tried desperately to keep count while she drowned in the surges of pain which engulfed her and set her body throbbing with strange pleasure. And she knew that best of all, when the caning was done, he would fuck her without mercy.

***

Sasha knelt before the small stool in the bedroom, one hand on each of Geraldine's open thighs. Her soft wet tongue licking, in long cat-like strokes from the very bottom of Geraldine's labia, up its entire length and over her erect clitoris.

"Oh god! Harder, please harder," Geraldine pleaded as she approached her second orgasm.

Ignoring the pleading, Sasha continued the slow and light strokes of her tongue, occasionally dipping the tip of her tongue into the wet inner lips of Geraldine's soft pussy. Her delicate, slim fingers caressing at the soft flesh of the young girl's inner thighs, mewing softly her pleasure as she tasted the musky juices.

Geraldine tensed, her body filled with surges of rippling pleasure as she built. The sensations stronger now, the wonderful feelings coming to her faster and faster. She was close, her heart pounded in her chest, her breathing rapid, she urged her climax towards her with a growing enthusiasm.

Sasha parted her teeth and gripped the hard bud of a clitoris between them, pulling gently, she teased the throbbing bud to unknown heights and Geraldine came to a noisy and thrashing orgasm.

Many minutes passed. Sasha remained kneeling before the girl, he head resting on the open thighs whilst Geraldine savoured her orgasm.

"Two down," Sasha said brightly raising her head. "And more to come."

Geraldine moaned softly as Sasha again dipped her head and she felt the soft wet probe circling her swollen labia on its way to the centre of her pleasure. Geraldine rested back, her warm and sated body beginning to respond already to the light and delightful touch of the gentle tongue on her skin. She liked Sasha very much, it made it all the better, her strong feelings for the lovely girl were in addition to the wonderfully powerful orgasms that she could bring her. Geraldine felt that there was more, much more that the oriental girl could teach her, she looked forward to that very much indeed.

CHAPTER THIRTEEN

It was a pleasing sight to the professor as he drove down the country lanes towards Sussex Downs. He could just make out the large house on the rise within the thickly wooded estate nestling at the foot of the downs. He steered the large Mercedes around the final bend in the lane and turned onto the gravelled area in front of the gates to the estate.

High stone walls topped by rows of newly fitted barbed wire surrounded the whole of the grounds to preserve a private existence for the organisation's future meetings. Tall, wrought-iron gates faced him, standing as an impenetrable barrier to all who had no business at the house. He pressed the entrance phone buzzer set into the strong brick pillar and waited, kicking idly at the deep gravel with the toe of his polished shoe.

"Yes?" The female voice crackled over the intercom.

"Paula, it's me. Are all the girls here yet?"

"Already in and waiting for your arrival, sir."

The professor sighed in irritation; Paula could never resist exercising a little sarcasm.

"I specifically asked you to keep them out of the house Paula. I wanted to show them around the place myself. You know how important this is to me."

A mischievous giggle preceded the cryptic reply.

"Who said they were in the house?"

Before he could answer, the buzzer clicked and an electric motor burst into life, the great black gates began to swing open as if unaided.

Cursing under his breath, the professor got back into the car and drove into the estate, the wheels of the Mercedes crunching on the gravel of the driveway as it purred majestically along.

Thick woods covered the major part of the large estate, the house; built on a slight rise was surrounded by a large lawn area in the centre of the trees and accessed only by the driveway.

Private and remote, seemingly cut-off from the outside world and modern living, the professor congratulated himself at having found such a fitting location.

The light flickered quickly on the windscreen from the sun breaking through the thick over-hanging branches of the trees that formed a dark foliage tunnel along the length of the wide driveway. At last the front of the house came into view; the professor steered the car to the front porch and parked the car along side it.

His suspicions were roused immediately when no one came out to greet him. Slowly, he got out of the car and surveyed the front of the house, his eyes searching every window of the large house for signs of life Ê∑ there were none. Again his gaze flicked rapidly to each of the windows in turn, double-checking that he hadn't perhaps missed even the slightest movement.

His mood darkening, he stomped up the wide stone steps and into the front lobby. A loud groan emitted from him when he saw the note pinned the enormous wooden front door, part irritation and part relief.

'Look in the rooms above the garages' was the neatly handwritten message on the paper.

He whirled around and strode purposefully back down the wide steps and along the front of the house, in long strides he turned the corner around the side and walked quickly to the old stable block at the back of the house that now served as garages. His mood had darkened considerably more, silly hide-and-seek games he simply didn't have time for. It was with the thought of severely reprimanding Paula on his mind that he moved swiftly up the stone stairs at the side of the garage block that led to the rooms above.

As he opened the door and ducked under the low beam that formed the ceiling of the entrance, he froze; stunned into silence by the sight that greeted him.

All of the girls, Paula and Louise included, bringing the number of them present to seven, stood-up from behind their low school desks and sang-out together in high-pitched voices.

"Good morning sir, congratulations sir."

All were dressed in identical school uniform. Short pleated skirts in light-grey, white long-sleeve blouses with striped ties loosened at different angles and little white socks around their ankles. Ponytails and pigtails in their hair gave all of them a look of youthful innocence that radiated from their smiling faces. Pert breasts thrust hard against the white material of their blouses to stretch the thin material so tantalisingly and tanned legs that looked so smooth and velvety against the grey of their short little skirts. They stood behind their desks obediently awaiting his reaction.

Confused at first, a conflict of emotions filled him. Anger that his secret fantasy had been revealed, yet pounding and thrilling excitement that his girls had gone to the trouble of setting up this fantastic scenario for him. One that he loved, the thought of some of his many students over the years that had teased him almost to the point of agony as they had shifted their slim thighs beneath their desks at the colleges and high-schools at which he had taught.

The horny little sluts that were aware of their bodies and the effect they could have on him, flaunting themselves, blatantly at times, to arouse him as he took their classes. Never allowing himself to weaken, it had been a monumental effort at times not to succumb to their youthful bodies. The universities had been similar if lacking the uniforms, the young girls deliberately leaving buttons undone to give tantalising flashes of their firm cleavages. Crossing and re-crossing their legs, short skirts riding high up their thighs to offer themselves secretly to him beneath their desks. He remembered too the sweet and knowing smiles they gave him as he ogled the offered young bodies. Now, it was all here for him, a step back in time, the opportunity to re-live his earlier teaching days and to do the things he always dreamt of with those young and fresh bodies before him.

Gathering this thoughts and composing himself after the initial shock, the professor dropped willingly into the role and strode slowly down the row between the desks. His body erect and shoulders back, he paced slowly, his eyes roaming the beautiful young girls under his supervision, delighting in their youth and innocent looks. The tight and short clothing, the firm swell of their breasts, those ever-so long legs and thighs to tease him and the sweet firm flesh that lay beneath their skimpy clothing. It was just like it was many years before - only better now, for now, he could touch. He could control and dictate, coax and order them to do what he wanted. His cock stiffened to full hardness and that pounding throb of extreme excitement began.

"Who is responsible for this charade?" he snapped angrily.

None of the girls answered. A soft tittering was the only sound to be heard in the otherwise silent room.

"Paula?"

She shook her head, the pigtails at the sides of her head swinging sexily with the movements of her head. Her mischievous smile and the way she used her eyes to smoulder sexual telepathy gave him a charge that made his cock jerk suddenly within the confines of his trousers.

"Jenny, then."

"Not me sir," Jenny giggled.

Frowning deeply, his face bearing a set and serious expression, he turned and walked back to the front of the group, his hands clasped tightly behind his back.

"Come here Jenny," he said flatly, pointing to the required spot. "Come and stand at the front."

She complied, looking solemn; her head hung down so that her chin rested on her chest, Jenny walked between the desks towards the front of the class. The short grey skirt clung to her upper thighs, moulding itself to the slender shape beneath and falling so invitingly in-between her legs. She stood sheepishly before the glowering professor at the front of the class, guilt-ridden and ashamed.

He made much of picking up the thick cane from the small table set at the side of the door and bent the cane, bending it with both hands to test the whip and flexibility of the stout rod.

"Bend over," he said as though it were the most natural thing to follow her passage through the desks.

Jenny obeyed dutifully, bending over to lean forward so that she rested her hands on her knees. Long slender legs ran up from the white socks, her little skirt pulled high up at the back to show half of her buttocks tightly covered by thick navy-blue knickers that pulled tightly across her neat firm backside. The bulge of her covered labia visible between the tops of her slim thighs.

The room was silent, filled with anticipation and charged with a sexual headiness that pounded through every person in the room. An electrifying silent suspension in time as the eager eyes of the girls flicked from Jenny's excited face to the professor's groin and the thick hard bulge of his erection that pressed hard against the front of his trousers. Without exception, all of their clitorises were erect and aching, those delightful feelings pumping through them to further excite the young girls.

"Naughty girl," he breathed excitedly and raised the cane with his right hand.

He paused to lift her little skirt with his left hand and to pull it up to rest on the small of her back, the pert little bottom and the full amount of her knickers now on show to all with nothing hidden. Then he lashed her, the thick cane slicing through the air to sting savagely at her soft firm buttocks.

Jenny cried out as the stinging pain bit at her flesh through the thick knickers. The pulsing in her vulva changing instantly to a jolting surge of pained pleasure, the thought of the other girls watching made it all the better. Her nipples were hard and pressing into the soft lining of her tight bra, the coarse material of her thick knickers pulled tightly across and into her swollen labia. She was wet, wet and aching for satisfaction. Jenny knew well the effect her uniform could have on the professor, that simply added to her high state of arousal.

Again he struck and she whimpered as the dull pain now crept through her, spreading out to throb deeply across her presented buttocks. Tearing at her insides to jar her innermost feelings and to add further tingling excitement to her expectant clitoris.

He paused to grip the sides of her blue knickers and to pull them down just as far as was needed to clear her buttock cheeks leaving them bunched-up high on her thighs; the thick gusset pressing still against her thick labia. Reddened areas on her soft cheeks showed the severity of his caning even after so few strokes. His big hand stroked and felt the creamy young flesh before lovingly before he stepped back and swung the cane down harshly upon the waiting girl.

Jenny screamed and gagged, the searing pain tearing at her body to sent electric spears of jarring pleasure through her to mix with the agony and to raise her level of sexual arousal and anticipation still higher. Her head spun with the heady mix of sensations, the pounding pleasure and desperate need filling her mind to bring numbing warmth that urged total submission.

"Oh god!" she blurted in reaction.

"Silence Girl!" he snapped angrily and struck again.

The thick cane making a high-pitched cracking sound as it contacted with her flesh. Five more times he lashed in frenzied excitement at her before again pausing to stroke her now fully red buttocks, allowing himself the pleasure of slipping his fingers down between the tops of her thighs to feel at her swollen labia. She was wet; the dirty little slut was so wet!

"Was it you?" he asked softly, coaxing the girl to admit her part in the organising of his welcome. His index finger pushed inside her to feel the moist warmth of her pussy, he had never known her so aroused. Her juices were slick and plentiful, his finger slid easily over the lubricant quality of her moisture.

"Me! It was me!" Louise said loudly from the back of the room.

The professor removed his hand from between Jenny's thighs and stormed to the back of the room.

"Bend over!" he shouted, shoving her roughly in the centre of her back to propel her forwards over the low desk. Without hesitation he began a rapidly caning on her backside, without waiting to lift her skirt or to remove her knickers.

He was panting, his face flushed with high excitement, much effort being channelled into the beating of the tall young girl with the long slim legs. Each stroke of the cane bit through the pleats of her little skirt and the material of her knickers.

Several minutes passed before he stopped and stood back panting. His face fully red with pounding excitement, his brow coated with sweat from his exertions. His hand slid beneath the short skirt, thick trembling fingers searching along the thick elasticated edge to find their way beneath and to savour the firm silky flesh beneath. His fingers probed and stroked at the flesh he had known, but hadn't tasted for some little while now, she was sensual and felt wonderful.

Louise was every man's fantasy, tall and slim, blonde and pretty with big blue eyes and large breasts; thoughts of her exceptionally long nipples came back to him as he felt and touched the passive girl.

Many minutes passed as he stroked and felt, exploring Louise's wet pussy and tickling at her hard clitoris. He allowed himself several strokes of her tight puckered anus with his wet fingers before withdrawing his hand and pressing himself against her. Groaning and moaning his pleasure, the professor thrust hard inward against her; his stiff cock resting in the crease of her soft buttocks whilst his hands stroked up and down the outsides of her slender young thighs.

Slowly, he took great pleasure in lifting her little skirt and sliding her knickers down over her firm backside, standing back from her to take in the wonderful sight of her slim young body. The rosy-pink of her little anus, the soft downy pubic hair that coated her swollen labia as labia pushed through from between her soft slender thighs. Again he stroked her, bare flesh that felt so good and fresh, so much better when he could also see her shape and tantalising posture.

Louise yelped loudly as the cane struck her across the soft cheeks of her presented backside. Her body jolting forwards momentarily as the pain registered, her mouth dropped open, red-painted lips opening so sensually as she bore the agony and the extreme pleasure. Again he struck, the thick cane leaving a wide red welt across her white skin, the soft flesh wobbling as it received the impact. His strokes were slower now, more deliberate and calculated, his arousal so high that his heart beat fast and his throat rasped dry. The professor lashed at her once more and stopped.

"Sit!" he blustered unsteadily trying to compose himself. "All of you sit."

As he walked back between the desks he noted that their blouses had been undone several buttons. He paused beside the desk at which Caroline was seated. Her firm neat little breasts bulged together in a tight cleavage clearly visible at the open neck of the white blouse; a rush of memories flooded back to him and his head spun with the pounding excitement. He was sweating and shaking, the pulsing excitement making his body tense and relax in a jolting series of spasms.

She turned her head and looked up at him with wide searching eyes, just as many of his students had done in the past. Questioning looks that transmitted more to him than just the subject of discussion within the class, sexual looks of pleading innocence that offered themselves to the more experienced man without words being spoken.

He groaned loudly and shuddered visibly, he rested his hand on the desk to support and steady himself as the wet stain spread out through the thin material of his light-grey trousers, to create a spreading dark stain that grew bigger by the moment. He moaned softly to himself as his orgasm continued and his sperm jetted against the inside of his trousers.

"Told you he wouldn't last," Jenny whispered across to Geraldine in the front row as she maintained her bowed position at the front of the class.

"God! Neither can I," came the hushed reply. "By Christ do I need some attention!"

***

Showered and dried but totally naked, the professor allowed himself to be led by two of the girls back into the adjoining room above the garages. He complied unresistingly as he was made to sit on the upright dining chair to be bound hand and foot to the chair, ropes pulled tightly also around his chest and upper thighs. The professor was helpless and unable to move his body or limbs even a fraction; he had taught his students well.

The desks had been cleared to the sides of the room leaving the centre and most of the space free, all the girls lined-up next to one another with Paula at the front facing them. She took control and began.

"Knees bend," she said in a voice that could have come from a straight-laced P.E teacher.

All the girls obeyed, moving as one they bent their knees low, squatting down with thighs apart to show tightly covered pussies between open thighs beneath their little grey skirts. Thick navy-blue material pulling tight and showing dark against the whiteness of the upper thighs and little white socks.

The professor groaned aloud as he watched them, his eyes flicking quickly from one girl's open thighs to another in sequence as they first stood up and then squatted again, setting a steady rhythm at Paula's barked commands.

"Turn and touch toes!" Paula sang-out cheerily.

All of the girls turned, some giggling, and bent at the waist. Six wonderful pairs of long legs and backs of their thighs were presented to him, leading up to firm little bottoms covered by the navy-blue knickers that stretched tightly around the cheeks of their buttocks.

The professor groaned loudly, his cock twitched and shifted as it began to harden to erection. The head taking on a purplish colour as the blood pumped into the thick member to swell its shaft and length. It continued twitching involuntarily as he watched the lithe young bodies before him exercising in a display of pure sexual tantalising.

"Up," Paula commanded.

They all stood upright, shifted their feet apart and at the command dipped again at the waist to touch their hands on the floor in front of them. They began a steady routine of standing and bending. As they moved, the gussets of the knickers worked themselves deeper in between moist and swollen pussy lips; one - Caroline's, pulled aside to squeeze one side of her labia out of the restraining elastic; an event that didn't go unnoticed by the professor's searching gaze. Her dark pubic hair displayed for him as the elastic cut deep between her labia and pulled tightly across her hardened clitoris.

His cock was rigid now, standing up from his lap as he watch the horny spectacle of the young girls' physical exertions. Alternating and tantalising glimpses of thigh and knickers then teasingly short skirts that hid them from his view. It was wonderful, truly wonderful; he wanted to touch but couldn't move. It was a blissful agony that he endured so very willingly as the little sluts moved their bodies in the full knowledge that he was wanting to get his cock up inside each and every one of them.

Groan after groan came from him as he stared intently at the wonderful scene. The foreskin stretching hard back and around the excited shaft of his cock to squeeze a blob of transparent lubrication from the very tip.

At Paula's command they all stood and faced him. Moving as one, they pulled open their blouses to reveal slim naked waists and tight black lacy bras that restricted their breasts to swell teasingly within. One at a time they stepped forward, slowly peeling off their little knickers from beneath the short skirts and working to a pre-planned sequence.

Geraldine first, removed her knickers, squatted before him and lowered her soft mouth down over the entire length of his hard cock.

He moaned in satisfaction as the head of his cock pushed deep into the top of her throat, his entire length buried in her soft wet cavern of a mouth. His head fell back and his mouth opened, he savoured the wonderful warm feel of her on his throbbing cock.

Geraldine didn't suck or move, she just remained still, covering his cock with her soft mouth for a moment and then pulled back and off. She straddled him, lifting her short skirt with both hands and lowering herself to let his cock bury itself deep inside her warm and wet pussy, pushing slowly down to take the whole of him inside her. Again without moving, she allowed him to savour her moist warmth before kissing him full on the lips. A long and passionate kiss full of meaning and emotion, then she broke off and freed herself to stand clear.

He groaned as her pussy slipped off his erect cock, the wonderful wetness of the hot youthful body leaving his cock wanting more. It was a tingling and throbbing mix of sensation and need, tinged with disappointment as the sweet feelings ended.

Natalie stepped forward, repeating the same series of actions as Geraldine. Removing her knickers, taking his cock in her mouth for a moment, then straddling him to accept his cock in her as she too, kissed him passionately and then got off him.

Caroline next, then Jenny, then Sasha and Louise following. Paula was last, his favourite of all of the little bitches. She sat astride him, his cock buried deep inside her warm pussy, and she kissed him, her soft tongue entering his mouth as she mewed softly her pleasure and excitement. Her hands cupping his head tenderly, delicate fingertips stroking at the lobes of his ears. She began to move her hips, pushing them forwards slightly in a slow and sensual rhythm to bring him to his peak.

His cock jerked inside her, exploding in powerful jerks to ejaculate deep inside her moist interior as she shifted her hips in sharp jerks to aid him. The kiss continued to the applause of the other watching girls. He grunted and moaned, spurting his seed into her until he was finished and Paula ended the kiss. She remained sitting astride him, his softening cock still held in her wet and sperm-filled pussy.

"Just a little ceremony to show our gratitude and appreciation of the best teacher a young girl could ever have," Paula purred.

Before he could reply, she placed a silencing finger to his

lips.

"Your little secret remains just that. It stays within these four walls, never to be known to anyone else. We are all your little Cynthias, in awe of our teacher. And in case you wondered - I'm responsible for telling the others."

He frowned at her.

"But remember, we are your girls, committed to serve and to obey as we always will be."

Paula kissed him again. "Congratulations on gaining the post of principal - you deserved it."

He smiled broadly looking first at Paula and then at Louise.

"Thank you, senators," he looked then to the other girls in turn. "And other, now fully-fledged members."

***

The house had once been the country mansion and estate of a Lord of the Realm, used for hunting and country jaunts for the privileged classes; changing hands several times through a number of millionaire owners but always remaining in private ownership. Its idyllic and private situation close to the popular coastal town of Brighton and the rolling Sussex Downs made it a much sought-after estate whenever it was offered for sale. The professor, even by pulling all the strings and calling all the favours he could with his many high-placed connections, was fortunate indeed in securing the estate on behalf of the organisation.

The twenty-six roomed house and two large stable blocks, one now converted and the newer one still used as such, were the main buildings on the estate. Other smaller and little-used buildings dotted the grounds in various locations; the gatehouse, two tied cottages for estate workers and an old abandoned woodcutter's hut in the centre of the woods being the main ones. Others were just barns and outbuildings for the small farm on the estate that provided a fair income to help support the sprawling grounds and the huge cost of running such an operation.

The professor proudly gave the girls a room-by-room guided

tour of the big house, pointing out all alterations that he had both planned and supervised throughout the works being carried out. Reception rooms, lounges, a study and two offices plus a kitchen and a large dining room made up the main of the ground floor in the older part of the house, the newer extension housed the swimming pool and gymnasium.

"What's in the basement?" Caroline enquired naively.

A round of giggling from the group made her blush deeply in her foolishness.

"You, Caroline," the professor said, smiling at her question. "Will be the first to sample the delights of the secrets that the basement holds."

Another round of laughter echoed in the high-ceiling corridor as they moved-off chattering excitedly towards the staircase. The upstairs of the house consisted of many bedrooms, all tastefully decorated and furnished to suit the character of the house, and each having its own en-suite bathroom; several rooms being locked and deemed out of bounds to all except the principal.

A grand and long lunch followed the tour, the professor having gone to considerable trouble to lay on a splendid meal that all of the party thoroughly enjoyed. The wine flowed freely and was consumed equally as freely. A loud series of drink- enhanced groans came from the girls as the professor announced his intention to 'give a little speech.' He waited patiently and smiling until the noise had died down, then he began.

"I should like to begin with a hearty thank you to all of you girls - my very special girls."

A cheer filled the room accompanied by clapping and shouted comments. Again he waited and then continued.

"It is essential that you all know the plans I have for the organisation, some of the changes may not be well received by some of the membership and I will need your support in carrying out my proposed changes."

"You've got it!" Natalie shouted in support, the others adding their agreement in a loud and noisy chorus.

"As you may have gathered, the barn in Buckinghamshire

will now be sold off and the monthly meetings transferred down here, hence the vast amount of bedroom space for over-nighting members who may travel far."

"Is that all they are to be used for?" Geraldine shouted in a disappointed tone. The others loved her quip and loud drunken laughter echoed around the room.

The professor waited and then continued his speech.

"All of you newer members have a choice. You may have a permanent room here - plus the run of the house of course, you may live with me in Hampstead..."

Shouted remarks and much nudging and winking followed his remarks.

"Or - as I said originally - you may have your own separate property in which to make your homes. Please give it careful thought and let me know your decisions within a week so that I may make the necessary arrangements."

"Here he goes - getting all serious again," Louise murmured.

"Thank you, Louise," the professor said frostily in response that brought yet more chattering as the other girls sided with one or the other of the verbal fencers.

"Can we hear the rest now?" Caroline added, sighing loudly to show her impatience with the remarks from the girls that prevented the professor from speaking.

The professor cleared his throat and began speaking once again as the room fell silent.

"Obviously the woods give many opportunities for the membership to engage in other...outdoor activities."

"Only during the summer I hope," Natalie offered to a loud burst of laughter from the others that degenerated into a noisy round of giggling and sniggered talking amongst themselves.

In a rare show of humour the professor joined in the merriment and gave up trying to talk sensibly to the gathered girls, he re-charged his glass and sat down again to join them. Jenny moved swiftly to sit in his lap and wrap her arms comfortingly around his neck.

"I think you know my answer already," she breathed in his

ear. "After all, who would turn back your sheets at night?"

One hand slid around to his front and gripped his cock through the material of his trousers, squeezing steadily in a teasingly erotic rhythm.

"Little bitch," he murmured so that the others couldn't hear him.

Her soft wet tongue probed at the entrance to his ear, her warm breath floating over the side of his neck to bring him to erection.

"Aren't I just?" she giggled.

CHAPTER FOURTEEN

Caroline stood at the top of the stairs leading down to the basement. She was tethered by the thick leather collar around her neck to the long leash that the professor held. A black, skin-tight latex suit covered her entire body, moulding itself to her shape to reveal every contour of her neat and petite frame. Only her hands and face were left uncovered by the thin second skin. Red painted fingernails and bright red lipstick stood-out against the white of her skin and contrasted with the shiny black suit. High-heeled boots with slender stiletto heels added to her height and overall sensual look.

It was a strange feeling being inside the suit, Caroline felt. Her naked body beneath having been liberally coated with talcum powder before the suit had been fitted onto her. Slippery baby oil had then been poured down the neck to spread all over the body. Her skin seemed to move slightly within the suit despite the restricting covering; agitating her nipples to erection and squashing so erotically around her pussy lips and anus where the tight material pulled into her crevices. Moist and lubricated, her body tingled with a warm erotic glow that spread over her whole slim body.

She felt good, so horny and powerful, the suit made her body look so good and well proportioned, presenting a shapely and seductive look that any man - or woman - would find difficult to resist, she was pleased with the result. Her throbbing need had grown steadily since she had faced the professor for the first time dressed as she was, his instant erection simply confirmed her thoughts and feelings. A conservative dresser most of the time, Caroline felt this was wild, so unlike her but so wonderful. She was ecstatic too that the professor had chosen her above the other younger girls to the very first down in this part of the house. Inwardly she hoped that the professor found her maturity desirable, matching the deep feelings she held for him.

He led the way down into the basement, the heels of Caroline's boots clicking noisily on the well-worn stone steps as they both descended into the gloom below. Her pussy and clitoris further aroused as she moved in the tight suit, the baby-oil around her aching pussy squelching so sensually.

A slightly musty odour filled Caroline's nostrils as they reached the lower steps; she stood obediently in the darkness as the professor groped to find the light switch on the side of the wall. Standing in the silent darkness tuned her senses, she could both imagine what movements the professor was making by the sounds he made; she also felt that he was taking a lot longer than was necessary so as the bring her senses to a good level of awareness.

Brightness dazzled Caroline momentarily as the lights finally came on, a long stone-floored corridor stretched out before them with many doors both to the left and to the right of the narrow passageway. Old yet freshly decorated the smell of paint mixed with the mustiness of age to produce a strange odour that further teased her senses.

"Kneel bitch," the professor said firmly. "I hold to my promise that you shall be the first to see and to taste the delights of the lower floor."

He set off down the corridor, pulling at the least to half-drag Caroline along with him. She grabbed at the leash with one hand, close to her collar and struggled against his pulling, resisting him whilst moving quickly on both knees and her free hand in an effort to keep-up with him.

"Ouch! My knees - it's hurting me!" she wailed as he tugged at the leash.

Using the thin cane in his other hand, the professor landed a stinging slash across her shiny tight buttocks, the thin latex suit doing little to absorb or to cushion the stinging pain. She silenced herself, still resisting, she increased the pace of her shuffling in an effort to avoid further caning, her knees scraping harshly on the rough stone floor.

At last he stopped and opened the door to one of the many rooms along the corridor. It contained simply a dog-bowl filled with milk on the floor in the centre of the small room.

"Drink!" he commanded curtly.

Caroline stared back at him in horror.

"I most certainly will not!" she stated indignantly.

He launched into a series of wild swings with the short cane, lashing at her thinly covered body.

She screamed pitifully as she received the punishment, the searing and biting pain burning into her body though the coating of latex. Caroline rolled onto her side on the floor in a vain effort to evade the stinging blows. Her thighs, back and buttocks all bearing the brunt of his attack on her. At length he stopped, panting heavily, his cock pressing hard against the inside of his trousers.

"Learn well, bitch. That in the basement the rules change."

His voice took on a more serious and menacing tone. "Total and unequivocal obedience is required here, the punishments are severe indeed for non-compliance. Today you will taste just the very tip of the delights that the basement holds, you will accept it or resist it at your peril."

Glad at least that the thrashing had stopped, Caroline cautiously crawled towards the bowl, looking around her hesitantly, she bent and lapped at the milk, as a cat would drink from the bowl. She felt it demeaning and humiliating to be knelt and bowed, acting like a tame animal for the pleasure of her master.

"All of it!" the professor warned harshly.

His hand slid down over her raised buttocks, feeling and

caressing her through the shiny material, his fingers stroking the bulge of her latex covered pussy lips.

Caroline groaned her pleasure at his touch. Her throbbing ache deep inside her pussy made all the better by knowing that his fingers couldn't enter her although she desperately wanted him to do just that. She lapped noisily at the milk as the rhythmic stroking over her pussy took greater effect, gasping loudly whenever pressure touched her hard little clitoris through the rubber covering. Pain and anger, then soft caresses to delight her, the mix was so powerful, so very, very sexy.

"Faster bitch!" he snapped and increased the pressure of his stroking.

Caroline obeyed and gulped hungrily at the milk, complying eagerly to urge on the sensual rubbing of her pussy. Rubber against oil and oil against her skin, wet and slippery, warm and lubricating as it mixed with her pussy juices to spread down her thighs and around to her anus.

Aware that the stroking had now stopped, Caroline felt disappointment at the lack of touch on her aching pussy, he would be undressing, she guessed. Those wonderful pounding sensations from the feel of his caressing had stopped; she wanted more, much more.

The milk finished, she shuffled around on her knees to face him. Dribbles of the creamy liquid tricking down her chin to drip onto the black shiny material that stretched so tightly across her prominent breasts.

He was indeed naked but with a thin leather strap apparatus around the base of his erect cock. It surrounded his scrotum and another thin strap circled the base of his shaft, small silver buckles pulled it tight to restrict any flow of fluids from him.

"What are you?" he asked pulling the tension on the leash and raising the cane threateningly above his shoulder.

Caroline cowered, raising her arms in front of her face defensively.

"A bitch."

"More!"

He lashed at her.

"A slut, I'm a slut."

"More!" he demanded raising his voice angrily.

Again he struck, the thwack of the blow resounding in the small low-ceiling room.

"A slut, a cock-sucking little slut that likes being fucked hard."

He lowered the cane slowly and grunted his approval.

"And do you enjoy it, slut?"

"Cock-sucking you mean?"

He slashed savagely at her, the stinging blow slicing agonisingly across the upper part of her thigh. She screamed, falling back on the floor, both her hands clutching at the affected area. Caroline sobbed as the numbing pain continued to burn its way through her slim thigh.

"Being fucked," she screamed loudly to prevent a second lash of the brutal cane. "Yes, yes! I love it. A hard cock is what I need."

He stood over her menacingly.

"Good," his voice took on that velvety tone once again. "For that is exactly what you will get my little slut."

Pulling her roughly, he walked from the room, Caroline shuffling quickly on all fours to keep pace with him, the burning pain in her thigh forgotten momentarily in her eagerness to comply. Into the corridor they went before turning into another room on the opposite side of the narrow passageway.

"Remove the suit," he ordered her.

The professor released the leash from the collar and stood back a pace with his arms folded across his chest like a jailer watching his prisoner; the short cane still held menacingly in his hand.

With great difficulty Caroline struggled with the suit, it clung to her body, resisting every attempt to prise it from the suction the oil had created with her skin. Panting and sighing she managed to peel one shoulder free and pull it partially off the other before he lost patience and struck at her with the cane.

She yelped as the pain shot, hot and searing through her

tightly covered buttocks, Caroline increased her efforts to free herself. Bending and shifting she wriggled the clinging suit down over her hips and thighs, her oiled body shimmering in the bright light cast down from the ceiling above her.

"Put the boots back on," he stated simply and seemingly uninterested as she struggled to pull her feet free of the rubber covering. His eyes roamed her body, probing at her open pussy when she sat on the floor to pull them back on. An inelegant posture that left nothing to the imagination.

At last she stood before him in her boots, her naked body glistening with a mix of sweat and baby oil to give her skin a velvety and smooth appearance.

"Feet apart," he said in a flat tone and knelt before her.

Caroline groaned aloud and shuddered as he untangled the thin cord that joined the small triangular lead weight to the jaws of the small silver spring-clip. He pressed open the jaws of the clip with his right hand and used his left hand to separate the lips of her labia to expose her hard little bud. He then attached the clip to her hard clitoris as it jutted out from between her swollen lips and released his grip on the sprung jaws.

Caroline whimpered as the searing pain charged through her, it increased many-fold when he released the weight to hang down full-weight on the securing cord. She stood erect, her legs apart and the weighted cord hanging down from her clitoris. The pain it produced was intense, a tugging on her soft skin that seemed to threaten to tear her flesh from her, it throbbed through her in heavy waves of agony that tore at every nerve-end. She gritted her teeth and tensed her body to try to cope with the stabbing pain she was being subjected to.

The professor selected a wide wooden paddle from the rack on the wall and slapped it hard across her tensed buttocks.

Caroline gasped at the different sense of pain, trying not to move her hips or body and thereby minimise any further painful surges from the clip clamped to her clitoris. A jarring and powerful slap that jolted her whole body and forced the breath from her for a split second.

"Talk."

"But about what?" she asked nervously.

He struck again; the flat wooden paddle slapping harshly across both of her pert oiled buttocks. A harsh and brutal blow designed as a reprimand for her question.

Caroline whimpered and drew breath as a new sort of agony rushed through her; she tensed her hips to keep the weight from swinging and in turn tugging harder on her sore clitoris.

"I like your big cock," she purred in the sexiest tone she could muster. "I like the taste of it. The taste of your thick sperm drives me wild as it slips down my throat. I love to touch it and feel it, the hard throbbing of your big cock."

He hit her again, then again and again; all the time she talked. Her pussy responding to the pain that was forcing through her. That warm and wonderful feeling when the glow in the tops of the thighs and groin turns to an exquisite blend of heightened sexual arousal. She talked continually as he spanked her soft reddened buttocks, bearing the agony of the swinging weight between her legs. Caroline found herself gently moving her hips to receive the slaps of the wooden paddle, the movements of the weight tearing at her clitoris to send searing shards of exquisite pain surging through her.

Faster she talked as he lashed at her, her head swimming in a misty haze of extreme excitement. Blood rushed to her brain making her legs feel weak and unsteady. She panted heavily and had stopped talking. She could hear his shouting as he swung the paddle cruelly at her firm buttocks; she stood erect accepting the wonderful sensations it produced for her. Expectantly and eagerly awaiting the next slap of the paddle to bring those dreamy sensations rushing through her.

"Slut! Whore! Cock-sucker," his words rang in her ears to urge her ever forward to her peak.

To be abused this way was so exciting for her. No one had ever treated her in any other way than courteously - this treatment simply spurred her onward to greater heights of sexual excitement. She found herself calling to him, to strike harder and faster. Panting her urgent pleading to him as her orgasm approached.

He complied, striking her full force to jar her hips and body forward against the swing of the weight. She moaned her pleasure at his response.

The pounding excitement surged through her body. To be standing and accepting such wonderful punishment and sexual feelings from the abuse she was suffering filled Caroline with a throbbing warm feeling of extreme naughtiness and abandonment. She felt so alive, so secret, to be with this man alone and accepting his use of her body brought her to her peak.

Caroline cried out and then screamed as the orgasm came to her. Her head threw back and her back arched as her slim hips thrust forward. She grunted and then screamed again, her head slumped forwards to rest her chin on her chest. She supported her hands on her thighs as her body quivered in shuddering spasms of delight, wavering unsteadily on her feet. Caroline gasped aloud as her knees first bent and then buckled, she slumped to the floor on all fours and then fell onto her side exhausted to shiver gently as the wonderful sensations continued to ripple through her.

She was aware of movement around her as she lay on the floor just as she had fallen, slumbering in the warm comforting feelings of after-orgasm. She roused herself dreamily, rubbing herself and pulling herself up into a sitting position.

The contraption looked horrific to her as the professor manoeuvred it into position in the centre of the room. A thick board served as the base with strong hand straps at one end and knee straps further down the wide board. It lay flat on the floor ready for her to mount and be secured into it, what worried her was the framework behind that the professor was busy attaching to the base.

He was still naked, the thin strap around his cock maintaining his huge erection to stick out angrily from his body as he knelt to fiddle with the securing bolts. He hadn't come himself, his level of arousal remained high, and Caroline was envious in a way of his self-control.

Without waiting to be asked, Caroline moved over to the board and knelt on the wide baseboard. On all fours she positioned her hands within the thick straps and spread her knees to locate them into the lower pair of light-tan coloured straps. So wide were her thighs spread that her hips moved low in an animal-like position that arched her back naturally to push her buttocks high in the air; she knelt there, her pussy open and offered.

The professor tightened the straps around her wrists and secured them with the heavy metal buckles attached around them. He then moved down her body to buckle the straps around the backs of her knees to hold her tightly in position. The last item fitted was a short steel frame that fixed into place beneath her; the two uprights slotted into holes in the baseboard, one to each side, the crossbar pressing against the tops of her thighs at the front to prevent any forward movement.

A terrific surge of excitement and apprehension shot through Caroline as the professor coated her labia and the inside of her pussy with lubricant, his fingers touching sore spots and at the same time bringing arousal again to the pinioned girl.

The rear frame was pushed forward, she gasped as the head of the big latex dildo pressed against the entrance to her pussy and then pushed up. On and on the long dildo was fed into her until its whole length was inside her, stretching her pussy tightly around its great girth.

Caroline panted and breathed hard, her mouth open as if practising contractions in a maternity ward; she tried to allow her body to adjust to the big cock-like phallus inside her. She knelt there, strapped and immovable as she accepted the invasion of her innermost depths.

The professor moved around to her front and knelt before her.

"Well bitch?" he asked with a sneer at her obvious difficulty in adjusting to the huge size of the dildo.

He held up the switch for her to see and then pressed his

thumb on the green button. The electric motor attached to the frame behind her began whirring, Caroline whimpered as he moved the adjustment of the switch and the dildo began to move. Slowly at first, it began a back and forth motion, sliding easily on the lubricant smeared over it.

"Oh god!" Caroline uttered nervously as she felt the huge cock inside her begin its motion. The thick shaft touching every part of her soft insides as it moved first almost out of her, leaving just the bulbous head within her soft lips, and then back up to fill her completely.

"It gets better," he offered and moved the switch again.

Caroline's body jolted as the hard thrust crashed against her from behind. The base of the thick dildo smashing against her clitoris. She cried out several times as the heavy thrusting jerked her slim body hard against the frame across her thighs.

Her eyes widened and her mouth dropped open, her head shook in tandem with her body as the thrusting gained momentum.

"Good?" he asked her with a beaming smile across his face.

She couldn't answer; the heavy jolting thrusts seemed to knock the breath from her as her body was brutally pounded. Faster and faster the thrusting cock moved against and inside her, pulling and pushing within her soft moist interior.

It was erotic, of that there could be no doubt, a pulsing excitement so electric and tingling raced through her. Discomfort forgotten as the feelings turned to sensational pleasure. Within a few minutes, Caroline was panting heavily in extreme pleasure and heady sexual arousal, like an animal she moved with the frantic thrusting of the cock-like dildo urging the pleasure to increase.

The professor shuffled forward on his knees, brushing the head of his stiff cock around her open mouth. She searched hungrily with her lips to locate the head and sucked it in greedily once her soft lips were around the head. Her urgency and sheer lust amazed the professor; this woman was lost in a dizzy world of pure sexual bliss. She sucked on his stiff cock as if it might never be on offer again as she enjoyed the pounding thrusting from behind.

Caroline was mewing and moaning softly, her head moving to allow her tongue to work also on his erect cock, she gobbled at the thick shaft in a hungry frenzy as her slight body shook with the rhythmic pounding it was receiving.

The professor moved his hips in short sharp jerks, forcing his stiff cock further into her mouth, her throat accepting the head as far back as she could without gagging.

She seemed possessed, like a hungry wild animal she grunted with each hard thrust into her, her mouth taking his cock willingly inside the soft wet cavern. Her head bobbed and her back arched, her soft firm buttocks shaking with the battering of the mechanical dildo behind her.

He sensed she was close, the dirty little bitch was coming off on the machine that was fucking her. He too felt the first powerful surges in his own body; he had waited a long time, now he wanted release. The professor groaned and shuddered, his eyelids half-closing in pleasure as the feelings he was experiencing built to a crescendo. His trembling fingers released the small buckle on the strap around the base of his cock and he came instantly. Warm powerful jets of his sperm spurted out from the eyehole of his jerking cock to fill Caroline's soft mouth. Spurt after spurt jetted from him as he moaned in satisfaction and sheer pleasure, the soft skin of her face soaked by thick globules of his seed when she moved her head back in reaction.

She whimpered and moaned as the warm seed shot in spurt after spurt onto her nose and lips to trickle down her face onto her chin. Her long pink tongue circling around the outside of her mouth to taste and to gather his salty seed.

Caroline shuddered, lightly at first, her body then gripped in a sharp series of racking convulsions that squeezed her orgasm from her and a scream from her lips. On and on the pleasure went, her body heaving and bucking as she struggled against her bonds. She trembled and shuddered a final time, her eyes closed and she sighed loudly before falling silent to savour the sensations that were rippling through her.

***

The whole of the membership was gathered, cramming onto the large patio area at the rear of the house and spilling out onto the lawn area beyond. All wore the black hoods required at monthly meetings and all were otherwise naked. The early afternoon sun warming their skin as they awaited the announcement that would begin the proceedings, it would also signal that the very reason for their meetings was about to begin, sex, raw and plentiful. Drinks were offered round and readily accepted before the professor stepped up onto a small wooden rostrum and called them to order.

"Welcome members, to this our first meeting at this new, wonderful and above all, private location. It is also of course, my first as your new principal."

Loud shouting and clapping made it impossible for him to continue for a moment or two; he waited patiently and proudly for the level of noise to drop. The first hurdle was passed, they obviously liked the house and grounds, he felt great relief at that part, and the rest would be easy.

"Today, members and for your delight, we have a meeting with a difference."

Loud cheering greeted his announcement and subsided as the many gathered members waited anxiously to hear precisely the form their sexual practices would take.

"A fox-hunt," the professor announced flatly, deliberately toning his voice down to hint at an uninteresting event. He needed that effect, to later whip them into a frenzy of sexual anticipation that would ensure that his first meeting would be a huge success. Failure at this first meeting could kill off any future chances of his future plans being accepted.

Low groans of disappointment and disapproval were the response, with many less than complimentary remarks shouted from the angry members. The professor stood erect, accepting the abuse being hurled at him, his face serious and expressionless. As the shouting subsided into a low moaning as each member expressed his disgust to the next, the professor made his move.

"But," he raised his voice enthusiastically and beaming his delight. "A fox-hunt with a difference!"

He was the showman now, selling his product to his clients, drawing them in, deflating them and then pleasing them, the sure-fire way of closing a sale.

The audience was unimpressed, the low moaning and mumbled dissatisfaction continued. The professor raised his hands and his voice together, shouting loudly to add emphasis to his next order. His manner now changed to excited enthusiasm that he could hardly contain.

"Bring on the foxes!" he ordered proudly, stepping to one side to add emphasis.

From behind a curtain drawn across the French-windows stepped his five newest students, all naked, their hands bound tightly together in front of them with soft cord.

The crowd went wild, an unruly screaming and shouting erupted from them as they voiced their delight. The noise was deafening and continued as the girls were paraded along a roped-off passage along the patio to a small circle also roped-off to separate them from the baying crowd.

When at last he could be heard above the din, the professor again called for order and slowly the volume of the cheering lessened sufficiently for him to continue.

"The rules, members," he began and was shouted down excitedly as the cheering crowd showed their impatience to start the hunt.

"No member of the hunt, foxes or hounds, may leave the grounds of the estate. The house is out of bounds to the hounds but is sanctuary to the foxes - should they reach it unmolested."

At his final remark the cheering and clapping interrupted his flow once again and he waited for order to be restored.

"The foxes will have thirty minutes head start before the

hounds are let loose."

The cheering was brief but equally as loud as it had previously been, all were anxious to hear what else the professor had to say.

"Once caught, the foxes may suffer any punishments that the hounds may see fit to inflict upon them. Once started, the hunt lasts until five o'clock, it ends then promptly with loss of membership for anyone continuing after that time."

The membership were delighted with the afternoon's planned activities, they displayed it in a long round of applause and shouted comments. Noisy chatter rippled through the crowd as plans began to form and small groups pledged to work together to gain the maximum result for their efforts to come.

"All members please set their watches to the same time in one minute. It is now, one-thirty precisely."

The naked girls huddled in the small rope enclosure; they wore trainers on their feet as the only concession that the professor would allow them. They too quickly tried to form some sort of plan to evade the baying crowd as groping hands reached across to squeeze at breasts and buttocks in the warm sunshine.

The professor had spent time with them explaining the rules, wanting to be certain that they fully understood their role in the forth-coming activities. All of the girls were acutely aware that upward of a hundred men would be searching for them and could possibly capture them - the results of which brought a shudder to them at the very thought. A man alone, when in a high state of sexual arousal could at times be threatening, put more than one together in the same circumstances and their effects could be multiplied many times. That thought alone drew agreement between the girls to do their utmost to evade capture.

An excited murmuring ran through the gathered members as the professor approached the rope enclosure, he raised his hand and checked his watch. A brief nod in readiness to Paula and Louise, as they stood poised, holding the ropes to the enclosure.

"Now!" he said loudly and dropped his arm to his side.

Paula and Louise released the ropes they were holding and the girls set-off running at a fast pace across the lawns towards the thick woods beyond. Naked bodies, breasts and buttocks wobbling as the bare thighs pumped hard to drive their legs fast in escape.

A loud roar erupted from the baying crowd, glasses were raised and many remarks shouted as warnings to the girls as to their intended fate when caught. As the girls disappeared out of sight into the thick undergrowth, the members refilled their glasses to while away the next half-an-hour before they too could set off in pursuit.

CHAPTER FIFTEEN

As soon as the five girls had entered the thick undergrowth they had separated. Sasha and Jenny running as a pair in the rough direction of the farm, Natalie and Caroline heading towards the apparent sanctuary of the abandoned woodcutte'rs hut. Geraldine, more accustomed to life on large estates, had opted to go-it-alone and bide her time before doubling back to the house.

Ducking and weaving, leaping and springing to avoid the overhanging branches and fallen logs, Sasha and Jenny set a fast pace through the thick undergrowth of the woods. Jenny led, Sasha watching the naked buttocks and body in front of her weave her way through the trees and bushes. Small red marks and scratches showed on Jenny's arms and thighs as she ran, the twigs tearing cruelly at her soft skin as she brushed aside the foliage before her.

"Which way now?" Jenny demanded urgently as she stopped in a small clearing to catch her breath.

Sasha lifted her bound hands and pointed briefly through the trees. Her soft breasts and body also were criss-crossed with tiny scratches where the branches had lashed and torn at her body.

"That way," she panted, struggling to regain her breath. "I remember the farm from when we came into the estate, you could just see it in the distance."

Jenny shuddered, sweat covered her body from her exertions but the air now held a chill as the sun had disappeared behind dark and sinister looking clouds.

Taking a few deep breaths whilst they rested a moment, the two girls then again set off at a run, trying to reach the safety of the farm before the pursuers could catch up with them.

"Bollocks!" Natalie cursed sharply as she slid in the mud on the small track through the woods. The rain that had started as a few spots was now lashing down on them to soak and to chill their shivering bodies; every leafy branch seemed to hold fresh chill and dampness for the panting girls as they brushed through the foliage.

Mud streaked Natalie's outer thigh, hip and hands, she regained her feet and again set a fast pace towards the centre of the wood, Caroline trailing a little way back. At last the small clearing came into view and the decrepit old woodsman's hut; set to the side of the grassy clearing, half-covered in foliage was a welcome sight to the rain-soaked pair. Without caution, they prised open the old wooden door and moved inside to take advantage of the shelter it offered.

Geraldine had slowed to a walk as soon as she was out of sight of the house and of the other girls, taking a narrow but well-worn track that circled around to the wooded area close to the driveway at front of the house. She selected with care the tree that she climbed, her naked body scraping against the rough and slimy bark as she hauled herself up with her tethered hands. There she sat, her legs astride a thick branch, waiting her time to return to the house.

The professor checked his watch, raised his arm, paused and then gave the signal; his arm dropped smartly to his side and the hunt began.

The hounds were released to a noisy cheer and hooting as they set-off after the girls, stiff cocks bouncing in erection as the men ran across the grassed area, the younger men reaching the edge of the woods first. Some men broke to the right and the left in small groups that again divided as they neared the woods, each small group hoping to out-think the running girls. Excited yells of what they would do to the girls when they caught them filled the air, the hunt was on and the hounds were hungry.

Sasha and Jenny were just over half way across the open meadow and heading towards the barn when a young man who broke from the woods spotted them. The excited shouting spurred the two girls into a faster pace, running full pelt, their heads down against the driving rain, they ran on. Panting and cursing breathlessly they climbed gingerly through a barbed wire fence, watching constantly as more of the men appeared from the woods and began running toward them.

"Shit, Jenny," Sasha cursed. "We'd better get a move on!"

Jenny needed little prompting, they both began running again as fast as their legs could carry them.

"The barn," Jenny prompted breathing hard. "Head for the barn."

Sasha put on a burst of speed, her breasts bouncing as she ran past Jenny in her haste to evade capture, sobbing as she pumped her naked thighs as fast as she possibly could.

Caroline and Natalie huddled together for warmth in the darkness of the small hut, it reeked of decay and dampness but they didn't care; it offered not only shelter from the rain but a hiding place that they hoped would be their salvation. Time passed slowly as they sat together, Caroline whimpering softly as she buried her face down into the security of Natalie's breasts. Both girls hiding fearfully from the fate that they really didn't want to even think about.

They screamed as one when a heavy kick to the rotting door smashed it from its hinges. Through the haze of years-old dust that was swirling around in the small hut, they could see three hooded men, standing just back from the doorway, their cocks sticking out hard and expectant, their laughter portraying their delight at having found two of the girls so easily.

Geraldine waited patiently for the shouting voices to fade into the distance before climbing down from the tree. Her inner thighs were scratched and scraped as she wriggled and lowered herself between branches to the ground. She was wet, her hair soaked and sticking to her head, small twigs and leaves had glued themselves to her wet body; she felt thoroughly miserable but determined not to be caught. The tight ropes around her wet wrists had rubbed the skin to an irritating soreness.

Remaining within the cover that the thick undergrowth offered, she followed the driveway towards the front of the house. All looked quiet; many cars filled the driveway and gravelled circle beyond the lawns. She just had to cross that and she would be home and safe, a huge grin creased her face as she congratulated herself on having decided to work alone.

She squatted in the thick grass at the edge of the woods as she watched the front of the house for signs of hooded men; none were to be seen. The long wet grass pressing into the backs of her thighs and buttocks, the longer blades rubbing against her swollen pussy lips.

In one swift move, she was on her feet and running quickly, she crossed the lawn and ducked low, using the cars for cover. Weaving and crouching between the expensive cars, the naked girl worked her way towards the front door, her heart beating fast and her spirits raising as she came ever closer to the big front door. Visions of a hot bath and a drink filled her mind, of resting and waiting in comfort for the others at the end of the hunt.

In one great rush, she made her break for the door, heart pounding fast, her feet crunching on the gravel as she neared the stone steps. In two long bounds she ran up the wide stone steps and through the big open door to stand panting heavily with relief and exhaustion in the hallway of the house. A small cry of delight left her lips as she rested her hands on her knees and hung her head forward.

For many minutes she bent forward, allowing her breathing and metabolism to level.

The professor's loud voice took her by surprise; she hadn't seen him there. He was in the hallway near the base of the stairs, silent and menacing.

"You have done well slut!" he said coldly. "Now you will come with me to the basement."

Geraldine panted heavily, dismayed and trying to get her breath.

"But you're not in the hunt, and the house is a safe area," she protested.

"You are of course correct on both counts," he said calmly, unbuttoning his trousers to free his throbbing erection. "This is purely for pleasure. Treat it as a reward for your ingenuity."

He gripped his cock and smiled broadly at her, waiting for her to comply.

Jenny could hear his panting breath, so close was he behind her. She ran in panic, twisting and weaving in her path across the wet grass of the meadow to try to avoid him. Her heart pounded in her chest, her throat dry, she whimpered as she felt he was gaining on her. She saw Sasha slightly ahead of her, brought heavily to the ground by a flying rugby-tackle from one of the pursuers, then they were upon her. Naked and excited men pinning her to the ground and grabbing at her flailing arms and legs as she vainly tried to fend them off.

Jenny felt a grab at her shoulder, the momentum of his grip spun her around and she fell back on the sodden grass before she too was surrounded by several naked and smiling men all sporting stiff erections. She sobbed as they moved nearer to her, then the groping hands reached her, squeezing and pulling, feeling and groping; none of her body escaped their attention. Fingers were pushed into her pussy and anus, other pulled cruelly on her erect nipples as she was lifted shoulder high and carried towards the barn.

In the small basement room, the professor was naked and

strapped tightly to the angled bench. His upper body resting back down the bench below the level of his hips, his legs also in the other direction were below his hips. Forced up high and harshly, his hips positioned his erect cock to stand upright, the bench had been well designed, Geraldine thought as she approached him.

He was so hard, more excited than she could remember. His face flushed and breathing fast, his cock so firm and rigid, it gave her a terrific buzz to see him this way. The sac of his balls was firm and tight; they looked swollen and full, as if they could explode if the pressure wasn't released. The chase had certainly had an effect on him, way above anything that he normally experienced. His request to her that she should strap him down was unusual in itself; it simply confirmed his high level of excitement to her.

She gently curled her delicate long fingers around the thick shaft of his cock, a light and sensual touch that brought a series of deep moans of appreciation from him. The long painted fingernails digging in to the side of his throbbing flesh added an element of pain to his pleasure.

Geraldine rubbed her thumb across the very tip of his cock as she stood over him, she felt so good and in command. It added to her own excitement as he began trying to raise his hips in an effort to increase the pressure and feelings on his cock. Again and again she brushed the tip, scraping across the delicate eyehole with her hard thumbnail.

He winced and groaned at the slight pain. He tensed forcefully and locked his body as she squeezed his cock hard and dug her fingernails brutally into the firm flesh of his cock.

The jolt it gave her made her inner muscles contract in heady spasms. Her pussy throbbed its need as the joy and extreme pleasure of hurting him surged through her. Again and again she squeezed, pushing her nails harder and deeper into him with each firm grip. Her other hand cupped his ball-sac, she squeezed gently and then not so gently to draw a terrifying scream of agony from him.

Her head swam with the excitement it produced; again she repeated the squeezing, both hands working in tandem to inflict the pain upon him. She was wet, her clitoris aching for release, the pleasure she felt from her commanding role made her prolong his suffering and her own pleasure.

Moaning softly and gasping slightly, Geraldine lowered her head to his cock, her soft red lips parted slightly to smear her saliva across the tip of his aching cock. From side to side she moved her head, stroking the very tip of his glans with her soft wetness.

He cried out to her, pleading with her take all of his cock into her warm mouth. An urgent and desperate pleading that she resisted in favour of teasing him for her own pleasure.

She smiled; thrilled that she was teasing him so wickedly, making him wait and him never knowing if she would comply. It sent pulsing shards of electric pleasure surging through her, she felt the first waves of her orgasm building. Little light ripples of pleasure to tease and to tantalise her every nerve-end, it felt so good to Geraldine; being in command certainly was a powerful feeling. To get a man hard and wanting, to touch him, even lightly, could produce such fantastic reactions from him. The sense of power and command that she felt made her not only feel good, but so devilishly sexy.

Her tongue flicked lightly across the head of his thick cock, dipping and circling all around the big bulbous head and teasing beneath his rolled foreskin. A feather-light touch that had his body tensing and gripping as his grunting tried to urge her to the end he sought.

"Do it bitch!" he shouted angrily from his disadvantaged position.

Geraldine simply smiled down at his flushed face, her eyes wide and teasing, she watched his face as her touch on his cock became even lighter. She moaned sexily, sighing and cooing her pleasure to excite him further.

"I feel so sexy," she murmured between the movements of her lips. "My pussy is so wet and in need."

"You rotten little bitch!" he blustered, again trying to force his hips towards her face.

"Does the professor want to get his cock in me?" she breathed sexily, her horny gaze meeting his hungry eyes.

"I'll get you for this, bitch. I'll make you suffer," he warned venomously.

"Nothing to lose then have I?" she said slowly and gave a final grip with her lips on the tip of his cock.

She stopped and stood back smiling; the pounding excitement coursing through her made all the better by his desperation. The waves of heady pounding pleasure washed over and through her, she wanted this to go on and on, her need for sexual satisfaction made it difficult for her to resist, but she did.

Geraldine began massaging her breasts with both hands, teasing at the long firm nipples with her slim fingers. She sighed sexily and gasped her pleasure to add to his torment as his hungry eyes watched her. The flat palms of her hands pushed, stroked and rolled her soft firm orbs for his benefit, the soft silky skin moving so sensually to form a deep and inviting cleavage whenever she pushed them together.

At length, she leaned forwards to grip his stiff cock in her cleavage, pushing her soft breasts together and around to envelope his erection between her warm firm orbs. He groaned his appreciation, his eyes rolling in his sockets as he drank-in the pleasure of her body against him.

"Ready to come are we professor?" she asked huskily, moving her hands to massage her breasts around his throbbing cock. Back and forth she rubbed them, trapping his throbbing erection and massaging it with her warmth. Geraldine panted huskily and sighed, gasping in short little breaths to add to her teasing of him.

"Bitch -just wait..."

Geraldine screamed and jumped back as the door burst open to crash noisily against the wall. The professor raised his head to try to see what had happened.

Jenny strode purposefully into the room, followed by Sasha.

Both were streaked with mud, their hair a tangled and matted mess. Both bodies' soft skin covered in red marks and scratches, no part of them had escaped the abuse to their youthful and formerly perfect skin. The expressions on their faces were of pure hatred and anger.

"You told them!" Jenny screamed angrily at him. She was close to tears as the pent-up emotions began to spill out from her. "You deceived us you rotten bastard!"

She grabbed quickly at the short thin cane, snatching it from the small table by the door and swung it powerfully. A low horizontal swing, that swished as the cane sliced through the air to strike his stiff cock just below the head. A harsh and stinging blow that made his cock jerk when the cane lashed at it.

He screamed and bucked his body, thrashing and pulling against his bonds as the raw agony cut through his body. He gagged and cried-out as the delayed pain rushed through him.

"Bastard!" Jenny screamed at him again, the tears rolling down her cheeks. She struck again, catching him across the top of his thighs and part of his cock. Unaimed and wildly she lashed at him, venting all her anger in her caning of him. Wanting desperately to inflict upon him some of the humiliation and suffering that she had experienced. The most painful part was his deception, that she couldn't take.

Silently, in the corner, Geraldine watched the action before her. One hand massaged her left nipple, the other rubbing furiously on her hard and throbbing clitoris with the heel of her hand; her index finger buried deep up inside her wet pussy. It was wonderful, she felt. The bastard was being ill-treated and she loved it. Terrific surges of wonderful sensation burst through her body to excite her further, the lovely naked women, so angry and powerful made her juices flow and her hand increase its pace in the rubbing. Her body was gripped by a series of light and powerful contractions that gripped her pussy muscles around her finger inside her, Geraldine rested back against the wall, her feet wide apart, ready to accept her approaching orgasm.

Sasha was beating at his chest with both her fists, drumming her anger as she too sobbed her emotions over him. Shouting from time to time between her noisily panted exertions, every swear word and insult she knew came out easily in her anger.

At last Jenny stopped, the cane fell from her hand to rattle noisily on the stone floor. Sasha's knees buckled, she knelt by his side, her head resting on his naked chest as her body shook with racking sobs of relief.

Jenny spoke calmly when at last she had collected herself.

"You did tell them didn't you?"

He smiled back at her knowingly.

Jenny fought hard not to allow her own smile to show. The bastard was enjoying this; it was almost as though he had expected it.

"You are a bastard," she said slowly, a hint of a smile breaking over her face.

"But you love me," was his reply in that thick velvety voice that seemed to melt her very insides every time he used it.

"You know I do you rotten sod!" she answered.

She was laughing now, her humour returning and some of the recent events forgotten as his charm began to work once again on her.

A low sighing and moaning came from the corner; Geraldine leant against the wall and slid slowly down to crumple in a heap on the floor. Her orgasm had been powerful and draining, she murmured softly to herself, otherwise ignored by the others.

"Did they catch you?" he quipped defiantly, an impish expression on his face as he asked the question.

Jenny swiped at his flaccid cock with her hand in a reprimanding but playful slap. Her voice sounded matter-of-fact as she launched into a description of the events.

"Hog-tied and humiliated, dragged through the mud and rain to be tied hanging from the beams in the barn whilst all those horny men used us for their delight! Fucked in every way possible, caned and spanked until we can't sit down! Yes they caught us, you know dammed well that they caught us."

Sasha had got to her feet and stood close to his head, her bushy hair-covered pussy so close to his face that he couldn't resist occasional glances at the wonderful sight. His cock stirred and began to harden once again.

Jenny continued.

"Every object you can think of has been inserted into us! My nipples will need weeks to recover, not to mention my pussy, that will be out of use for months."

"But you came - didn't you?"

Jenny didn't answer.

"Didn't you, bitch?"

She gripped his hardening cock with one hand and smiled.

"Quite a few times actually. I guess we all did, but even so it was a bit much!"

Silence fell in the room as Natalie and Caroline entered, they stood for a moment taking in the scene before them and sensing the atmosphere.

"What do we do with him girls?" Jenny prompted when she saw the anger in the eyes of the two latest arrivals.

If she took the initiative it might prevent later trouble, much as she sympathised with the two girls.

Geraldine stirred sleepily and drew into a sitting position on the floor, her back resting into the corner of the room. Satisfied from her orgasm, she hugged her knees for comfort, her voice thick and still portraying arousal.

"Put a leash on him and take him for a walk - in the woods," she suggested.

"Spank his arse!" Sasha said bitterly. "Bloody hard!"

Caroline offered her suggestion. "Tie him to a tree and whip him with thin branches as we were - and in the pouring rain I might add."

"Yeah!" Natalie agreed. "Haul him through cold wet mud and then shove handfuls of leaves and dirt into his orifices and see how he likes it! They might never have found us if they hadn't been told where to look."

Jenny walked slowly and silently over to the small table,

picking up and playing idly with the large serrated teeth of the crocodile clip in her slim fingers.

"Does anyone mind if I choose his punishment?" she asked politely.

The others gave full agreement as they saw the devilment in Jenny's eyes and in her expression. Her smile and her manner were enough to tell them that she had the solution, they trusted Jenny.

"Good," Jenny announced loudly, walking back to stand over him. "Then we give him what he gave us. A hunt. We set him running and hunt him down."

The girls all clapped and cheered loudly, voicing their delight at the suggestion.

"No rules," Jenny continued holding the strong clip up for them to see and springing the powerful jaws for emphasis. "And the most severe punishment when we catch him."

A loud cheering filled the room, the delighted girls building in their excitement at the very thought of it.

The professor's cock rose to full hardness, sticking up once again to stand hard and upright.

Jenny silenced the cheering, she leaned close over the professor.

"Do you know," she said severely. "That I had three cocks trying to push into my pussy at the same time, two in my mouth and not to mention my ears and arm-pits? My backside was used more times than a bottle opener at a party and my eyelids are still sticky with sperm. I have sperm in my ears, up my nose and enough in my mouth to last a short lifetime."

Sasha stepped forwards, her voice pained and straining to control her emotions.

"Look at me! Rolled in mud, used and abused beyond the normal bounds of acceptance. It will take weeks to get the remnants leaves and twigs out of my backside and pussy. They fucked me in turn, holding me down and using me like a piece of meat. My backside is raw and my nipples stretched by the strings they used on me." Her voice raised as the fury spilled out of her. "A dog would have been better treated, they mocked as I was made to crawl through the woods, whipped and kicked, pushed and beaten. I was hung and stretched ñ you bastard! Made to bark and to howl for their amusement!"

Natalie pushed forward to add her tale of woe, she gripped his balls and squeezed tightly.

"I was made to dance and sing, entertainment they called it whilst they laughed at my fear. I was groped and pulled, sticks and small logs were pushed up into my pussy and backside whilst they hooted their delight. I was made to kiss their feet in turn and squat down and pee ñ it wasn't a nice experience I can tell you. Humiliation in every way, my whole body is sore and raw, it aches in every place possible. How would you like to be made to walk over rough ground bare foot with a small log inserted in your backside and then whipped if you complained?"

Geraldine moved closer, her face close to his, her curled lips spitting pure venom.

"Me? I was hog-tied after being fucked. Like the others my backside was used by all. My body flayed until the skin had broken. My insides are still on fire and have more of the forest floor up inside than there is out there. They even made me lie still whilst they all wanked and shot over my face. I like to suck cock but not when they have been in some of the places they had put theirs. The mud filling in my pussy they found really funny and nearly pissed themselves laughing when I was forced to clamp my muscles and spurt it out of my body. I'm cold, sore, beaten and very, very angry."

The professor smiled, a mocking and disbelieving tone in his voice as he responded.

"I simply cannot believe that even our members would subject you to such indignities."

Sasha tightened her grip on his balls to increase his pain.

"The bastard doesn't believe us!" she shouted in amazement.

"Come on then!" Geraldine enthused. "Set him running and see how he likes it!"

They released the professor, all the girls holding tightly to his arms to prevent him escaping.

"I agree," he announced arrogantly. "To the chase."

All the girls were stunned as his ready agreement.

"But why me? We have two other little foxes here that you girls could demonstrate these alleged indignities on. It would after all be far more authentic and I could gain a true appreciation of the situation. And it would also allow me to estimate the number of times you yourselves came under this abuse."

He broke into a broad smile at their hesitant looks.

"Who? What other foxes?" Geraldine asked.

The girls were perplexed, they looked at one another in bewilderment.

"Who served the drinks today?" the professor hinted smiling.

"Louise and Paula!" Sasha snapped impatiently and then began to smile as the realisation hit home to her.

"Exactly!" the professor stated firmly. "My two, gorgeous previous students would, I am sure, appreciate some of the practices you described."

"But not all," Jenny said with relish.

"Mmmm, all the better then," Natalie added.

The restraining hands of the girls eased to release the professor, all the girls now beaming their delight at the thought of the two beauties running in fear from them.

"I bags shoving some things up Louise's pussy when we catch her!" Geraldine said excitedly.

Sasha added her claim rapidly.

"I want Paula to suffer and I claim my right to give her pain. Those two always reckon they're special!"

"Are we agreed?" the professor said quickly seizing his opportunity.

A chorus of agreement was heard from the girls as they giggled their delight.

"Then kneel my sluts before the hunt and swear alliegance to me."

Silently and obediently the girls formed a line and knelt.

"Ever yours professor," Jenny prompted.

The girls all stated their agreement and bowed their heads before him.

"I know," his velvety voice purred in triumph. "For command I always have - and always will. You are my sluts and will serve - is that not correct?"

His cock jerked to erection as the girls all answered as one.

"Absolutely professor. Yes master."

"Then let the second hunt begin!" the professor said quietly, and began laughing in delight as the naked girls ran to find their quarry.

And now for the opening of next months title "THE CONNOISSEUR" By *Francine Whittaker*

PROLOGUE

Greece

The mother of all storms had those girls who were not secured to their beds, or to some devilish piece of apparatus, huddling together in a subterranean room. Theo, known far and wide simply as The Connoisseur, had a well-stocked gallery of girls, each one special in her own way, and all a delight of sexual servitude. He was thankful there was no rain to mar the show, even though the lightning lit up the midnight sky dramatically for miles around. The flashes, mere seconds apart now, reached eerily into every crevice of what appeared to be an ancient Greek palace or temple.

On the balcony of his room in the living quarters, Theo sat like a prince in a royal box and used the naked, bound and gagged girl as a footstool. Every now and then he applied the heel of his shoe to ram the dildo that stuck from her arse further into her tight, secret channel. And when the tears streamed down her face as she whimpered into the gag, he reminded her with a crack of the dog whip across her buttocks of the purpose of her life.

"Your pain is my pleasure." Then, to further drive the point home, he gave a sharp tug on the chain that was fastened at one end to the arm of his chair, and the other to a crocodile clip that was attached to the girl's labia.

Below them in the centre of the marble expanse that in former days would have been used for ritualistic worship and was tonight unnecessarily floodlit, two naked girls were strung up, face to face, breast to breast. The wrists of each girl were secured together by means of leather cuffs around her wrists, and then fiendishly attached by a metal ring to the wrists of the other girl. Chains had been fastened to their cuffs, and by a series of pulleys which stretched the girls' arms tautly above their heads, the chains were themselves attached to the overhead bar of the wooden structure, erected hastily earlier in the day for the sole purpose of tonight's significantly private entertainment. But worse still were the painful nipple clamps that tugged the girls' cruelly extended nipples upward by other chains, also fastened to the overhead bar. Together, these restraints kept the girls balancing precariously on tip-toe, as too did the seething mass of snakes which slithered and coiled at their feet. While they were not venomous and could inflict no harm, both girls were piteously unaware of this fact. The overall effect was devastating and showed off the sensuous curves of their lithe, young bodies most pleasingly.

There was no doubt in Theo's mind that their pain, both physical and mental, was agonising, as indeed it had been designed to be. His thin lips twisted into a half-smile.

The black-hooded guards, wearing the leather harnesses that served as a uniform on this beautiful, decadent island, stood one behind each girl. With ferocious accuracy, they wielded their whips to strike in sadistic synchronization with each lightning flash, adding to the magnificent theatre of the occasion. Strike upon terrible strike had the girls writhing, and jerking on their chains like puppets on strings while the snakes coiled and uncoiled around their ankles; their shrill cries rang out and were lost across the Aegean.

Theo watched the scene with mounting excitement. Pumping his cock in his fist while holding the telephone receiver in his free hand, he gloried in the scene below him. Each ear-splitting scream and fall of the lash filled him with a lust that his caller in England could only begin to imagine.

"I had you installed there, Flynn, to do a job, not to procure pussy. What makes you think this... this temptress you've discovered will amuse me? I require at least a degree of subservience from new blood." He jerked on the chain and the girl beneath his feet screamed into her gag as the clip bit into her tender flesh. "If she's as sure of herself as you say, why should I give a fuck?"

Yet even as he said it, Theo's lust was sharpened. Surrounded by adoring slaves, he began to relish the idea of such a challenge, to turn a sexually confident woman into a subjugated slut. It was one thing to dominate a born submissive, but to break and enslave a cock-teasing seducer of men was another thing entirely. It might even have its compensations.

"Ok, the idea intrigues me. Have your own sport with her by all means, but don't damage the goods. I'll take control when I come to London in a couple of weeks-"Theo swallowed hard as the lash cut across the girls' breasts. When he spoke again, his voice came out in ragged gasps. "I'll want daily reports from someone I can trust... I'll have someone on a plane in the morning."

Theo kept his eyes rivetted to the two naked girls as they twisted and turned to evade the lash, and the thought of a new girl undergoing the same treatment made him pump his considerable shaft faster. He took a deep, steadying breath before giving his final instructions to the Englishman.

"Find out if this... what's her name?... Vivienne's got family- we don't want any extra baggage. Sever all her relationships. Don't do anything to alert her suspicions. You'll be rewarded if she lives up to expectations."

He slammed down the phone. In one frenzied moment of lust, the final blows crashed down on the two beautiful girls, he kicked at the half-obscured dildo and drove it deeper, the girl collapsed in a heap and Theo spurted his hot come over her trembling body.

Exhausted, having taken as much punishment as they could stand in one night, only the two girls' bonds prevented them from falling as they passed into the comforting blackness of unconsciousness.

Theo smiled and reached for his metaxas.

CHAPTER ONE

As her heart rate returned to normal, Vivienne splashed cold water onto her face. Her dusky-gold skin was positively glowing. Deftly applying fresh make-up, she told herself smilingly that no one save herself and Adrian, the eighteen-year-old "new boy" from Marketing, would ever know about their lunch time quickie in the new Divisional Manager's empty office.

Tiny arrows of elation caused her breath to catch in her throat as she remembered Adrian's virgin cock entering her hot, wet quim from behind. Her feline body had leaned over the photocopier, her full breasts flattened against the unyielding metal. Now she smiled as she looked back at his clumsy attempt to withdraw once he had come. She gave a little laugh and wondered if the cleaners would guess the cause of the stain on the new beige carpet.

In a characteristic gesture, she slipped her hand beneath her hair at her nape. First tilting, then throwing back her head, she flicked her thick, raven hair over her shoulder. Long and silky, she wore her hair brushed back from her face, and let it hang down her back like a shining curtain to her waist.

Her glowing, golden skin was unblemished. Blessed with high cheek bones, and almond shaped eyes that were an unusual shade of green, her appearance had often been described as "exotic."

After checking one final time in the mirror, she left the Ladies to return to her desk in Customer Services.

Smiling teasingly at the Credit Control supervisor as she passed his desk, she accepted his invitation for after work "drinks" with an almost imperceptible nod of her head. She had always felt an attraction for him, and now that he was free she would be quite happy to step into his wife's shoes, for a short while at least. In her way she felt quite sorry for him- it was common knowledge that his wife of twenty-five years had left him... for another woman! Vivienne bit into her bottom lip, unable to imagine what possessed one woman to fancy another. You certainly wouldn't catch me making love to a woman, she avowed silently.

What Vivienne wanted was a man, a real man. For fond as she was of Nathan, her live-in boyfriend, there was something missing in their relationship. She wasn't sure when it had happened, but somewhere along the line, passionate fuck had turned into textbook copulation. That first night in his hotel room at the conference had been wonderful, and she had been more than willing when he had suggested moving in with her. He had been living with Vivienne for approximately six months now, but things had gone rapidly downhill after the first couple of weeks; she was already beginning to feel trapped.

For Vivienne, it had never been the same since he had declared his love for her, maybe that was what had killed it. She couldn't help but feel it was that nice, safe, dependable love, or the cloying love of an ill-suited marriage; there was no magic, no sparkle. It wasn't love that she was looking for - it was something far more potent than that.

Smoothing her short, black skirt that showed off her bare legs to an advantage, Vivienne settled herself behind her work station. She hit the mouse button and immediately the screen saver was replaced by a table of half-yearly sales figures. She checked her watch. There was just about time to study the figures and make a start on her report before Denise-something-or-other turned up for her interview.

***

Something made Vivienne swivel round in her chair to look out of the window. Flynn Pallister stepped from his BMW in the car park, seven storeys below. Now there was a real man!

Tall, suntanned and blond, Flynn was in his mid thirties. Vivienne found him sexy, in a well-groomed, well-spoken sort of way. Even the thought of him made her large nipples stiffen. Dark brown, they were clearly visible as they pushed against the flimsy fabric of her pale blue silk blouse.

Flynn had recently been flown in from the New York office by the powers-that-be. Now he was Divisional Manager of the Southeastern region at Head Office, twenty-five miles from London. It was all change since the company take over.

No one was sure where Flynn came from originally, though it was rumoured he came from a well-to-do family somewhere in the North of England. He could have come from the moon for all Vivienne cared; it was his potential performance in bed that intrigued her.

A short while later Vivienne glanced up as Adrian flitted past her desk in Customer Services and scurried through the large, open plan office in the general direction of Flynn's. It was with a certain pride that she mulled over how he would always remember Vivienne Trevayne as the woman who had led him from youth to manhood in a single lunch time. While she had been delighted by his firm, young body, in truth it had been something of a kindness on her part. Adrian was pathetically shy of women, and had often been heard to complain that he had "never got anywhere with girls". And as he had been following her around like a lost puppy for the past couple of weeks, she had felt almost obliged to reward him.

Glancing up again, Vivienne was surprised to see two security guards on their way through the office. They were probably doing one of their periodical checks to make sure that everyone was wearing their ID.

When she received a phone call from Flynn requesting her presence in his office immediately, Vivienne left her table of figures and set off for his office. He had earned the reputation within the company as a hard task-master. He expected, and usually achieved, nothing less than complete efficiency and total commitment from his staff. While she had no intention of being at any man's beck and call, even Flynn's, it seemed unwise to upset him so early in their acquaintance.

Flynn's work station comprised two desks placed at right angles, one housing his computer and other equipment, while the second desk, running parallel with the wall, was covered in paperwork. Sitting behind his desk that faced the door, he sprawled sideways in his chair, one arm across the back. He gave her a broad, sexy smile.

She flicked her eyes to the photocopier, then the stain on the carpet, and smiled a secret smile.

"Hi, Flynn. If it's about the report, I was just about to start-" Vivienne began in her ususal, somewhat husky tones that men found incredibly sexy, while Vivienne thought it made her sound as if she were constantly suffering from laryngitis.

"Come in. Close the door." There was a note of authority in his urbane voice. "Draw the blinds." Sectioned off from the main office by floor to ceiling panels that could be easily taken down and re-erected elsewhere, there was one window that enabled Flynn to monitor most of the activities of the department. With the blinds drawn, as when Vivienne had been here earlier, it gave the illusion that Flynn's office was more private than it really was.

"I know you're conducting an interview in a few minutes, so I'll keep this brief-" his eyes travelled upward from her ankles to her thighs "as is your skirt."

Vivienne smiled. She knew she had good legs, and if a man wanted to eyeball them, it was fine by her. It gave her a thrill when a man looked at her the way Flynn was looking at her now, and she couldn't resist the temptation to flirt. Using the tip of her tongue to wet her lips, she looked at him coquettishly from beneath her long eyelashes. Transferring her weight from one leg to the other, she took up a provocative pose with her hand on her hip.

Flynn beckoned her towards him. Taking a metal rule from his desk drawer, he used it as a school teacher might to point to the floor beside his chair, indicating the spot where he wanted her to stand. What made Flynn different? When he said "jump" Why did she want to take up pole vaulting? It never occurred to her to refuse. Instead, she savoured the feeling of contentment that washed over her as she took up the required position beside him.

Facing him, she could see an assortment of objects scattered among the paperwork on his desk, including a collection of bulldog clips of various sizes, a wide leather belt and the leather tip of something sticking out from underneath a file. Following the line of her gaze, he slowly pushed back the file, to reveal a riding crop.

"I might go riding," he said by way of explanation.

"Oh. Have you got your own horse?"

"Who said anything about horses?" He picked it up, flexed it, then brought it swishing down across his open palm. Replacing it on the desk top, Flynn selected one of the large bulldog clips and held it up to her eyes. He opened it and held it poised within inches of her eyes, then snapped it closed. There was a menacing undertone to his voice as he said "I find these quite useful, too."

He lowered his hand and brushed it against her skirt, pushing the fabric against her mons. She smiled down at him, happy to feel his light touch at last. Hoisting up her skirt, she guided his hand toward the elastic of her flimsy, pink panties, intending to steer his fingers towards her hairy mound. Her heart sank as he pulled her hand away.

"We'll do this my way or not at all." He brought the bulldog clip down between her legs and held it against her nylon covered crotch. He opened it, then snapped it closed.

Instinct made her jump backwards.

Flynn merely laughed, let her skirt fall back into place and dropped the clip on the floor. He held out his hand and gently pulled her back into position.

Feeling stupid, she smiled down into his suntanned face. She could see the hunger there in his eyes- she could also see the huge bulge in his trousers.

"You're beautiful, Vivienne," he reached out and cupped her full breast in his hand, kneading it gently through her blouse "but you already know that. And you want every man in the place to know it, too, don't you? It gives you a thrill to know that men lust after you and can scarcely control their desire to master your body."

Vivienne had always rejoiced silently in the knowledge that hers was a body that could drive a man insane. After all, if you had been blessed with good looks, you could hardly fail to notice, could you? And hers were exceptionally good looks.

Of medium height, she had narrow shoulders and a long, elegant neck; her full breasts gave emphasis to her narrow waist and sensual, rounded buttocks, and her hips and thighs narrowed to long, shapely legs. The whole, stunning effect gave the illusion that she was taller than her five feet four inches.

Releasing her breast, Flynn ran his fingers up the insides of her thigh, making her quiver deliciously. Already she could feel her sex moistening as the familiar stirrings of arousal coiled and uncoiled in her belly. Then he repeated the process, except this time he scraped his fingernails into the soft, yielding flesh.

"Ouch!"

He dug his nails deeper, making her gasp.

"Turn around, Vivienne."

Well, if he wanted to play games that was fine by her. Besides, she thought it might turn out to be fun. She turned so that her back was towards him. A delicious warmth spread from her breasts to her pussy as she imagined how much he wanted her.

Using the tip of the metal rule, he hoisted up her skirt at the back to reveal the pink thong of her panties that separated her rounded buttocks. She felt the cold, hard edge of the rule as he used it to force her thighs apart. He rubbed it back and forth, back and forth against her pussy lips, which to her shame were already leaking juice and making her panties damp.

He withdrew the rule and she waited with a smile on her lips as she wondered what he would do next. But nothing had prepared her for the sudden shock and she screamed out at the blaze of pain as he slapped the rule sharply across her thigh. Then with lightning speed, he caught hold of her right wrist and wrenched her arm backward. Startled, she tugged to free herself, but he held it securely with one hand, level with her narrow waist.

"What are you doing, Flynn? That hurts!"

"Really? What about this?" He struck her again with the rule and again she screamed.

She gave a sharp cry as he yanked her arm upwards so that her hand was between her shoulder blades. He made no move to release her. Nor did she make a move to pull away.

Flynn's fingers dug into her wrist as he held her tightly, while the fingers of his free hand found her labia lips as they pressed against her fine, damp panties. With finger and thumb, he gave them a sharp pinch. Then she heard a sharp snapping sound and was lacerated by sudden pain as the bulldog clip closed over her panties.

"Argh!"

"Be quiet-" once again the rule cracked against her thigh "or I'll put it on without your panties."

"God no! Take it off! Please, it hurts. Let go of me, Flynn, or I'll scream."

"Go ahead- no one will hear you. I've arranged for a special showing of the safety at work video to be shown in one of the conference rooms on the second floor. People should be leaving about now."

Even as he squeezed tightly on her other wrist and yanked her arm upward, her lips curved of their own accord into a kitten smile. She didn't know why he was being so spiteful, nor did she care. She guessed it was nothing but some sort of power game he was playing.

But more was to come. She felt something touch her wrists, then to her horror he began to bind them together. The belt! She tried to pull her hands free, but he had bound them tightly.

"You may lower your arms now, Vivienne."

Only slightly relieved, she stood trembling with her secured hands resting on her bottom and the bulldog clip dangling from her labia, only slightly protected by the nylon. The metal cut into the tender flesh, bringing tears to her eyes. Never had she known such pain, nor so spiteful a man.

"Okay Flynn," she began bravely, "you've had your fun. Now let me go."

She made to turn round, but his hand shot out at once to stop her.

"It's come to my attention, Vivienne that you have something of a reputation", he admonished her. "In fact, you're something of a slut."

The allegation stung her. "That's a bit strong! How dare you bring me in here to discuss my sex life. I really can't see that it's any of your business. I don't need your approval as to how I should conduct my private life. I would have thought a man like you would know better than to listen to idle gossip."

Vivienne knew that her sex life had been a subject of tittle-tattle among work colleagues. She had heard herself referred to as "the fuck-patrol" and "cock chaser" by some of the men in the office, notably those who hadn't made it to her bed. But as Flynn's fingers began to swirl in tiny circles over her soft flesh, she was unable to tell from his tone whether he was taking disciplinary measures into his own hands, about to issue a formal warning or merely trying it on. To make matters worse, she knew her golden-toned features were beginning to turn rosy, not a usual occurrence since she was seldom embarrassed.

"For that reason, I've had Security remove your little friend, Adrian, from the premises. Thanks to you, he's now out of a job."

"Bastard!" Her heart set up an erratic thumping in her chest as her anger took hold. "You can't do that!"

"Oh, but I can. And I'll go on doing it. So unless you want anyone else to face life on the dole, I suggest you keep your favours to yourself."

Thunderstruck, no words came to her. But even as her blood rebelled through her veins, she slowly became accustomed to the virulent pain of the metal that imprisoned her burning labia. His madness and uncertain temper left her little choice- she must get out of here. Yet somehow, she couldn't find the will in her legs to make a run for it. Instead, she stood stock still, and vowed to report him to the authorities. Until then, she would play him at his own game.

His fingers left a feathery trail across her buttocks. His breathing became heavier as he reached between her legs and cruelly twisted the clip, forcing another cry from her lips. He laughed, twisted again, and on the third twist he yanked it off. Before she could react his hands were at her waist. Gripping hold of her panties, he pulled them down around her knees. His forefinger traced a line along the deep crease of her buttocks, then pressed against the tightly puckered hole of her anus. She swallowed hard. No one had ever entered that private place, and every nerve in her body stiffened at the very thought of it. She would die if he-

"Tell me, Miss Trevayne ... is your pussy as tight as your nerves?"

The formal use of her surname, along with his curious line of questioning caused an uncharacteristic bout of nerves that set her trembling. Yet afraid as she was, she heard herself respond as if instead of hurting her, he were merely setting out to seduce her.

"There's only one way to find out," she whispered foxily, looking at him over her shoulder.

Flynn raised an eyebrow questioningly. "We understand each other?"

Even as she silently cursed him, she revelled in the knowledge that he wanted her. All she had to do, she reasoned, to get back at him was to lead him on a bit- it wouldn't hurt him to wait a bit longer, would it?

"I hate to rush things, Flynn- perhaps another time, another place- I have an interview, remember. And I still have that report."

Flynn's attitude seemed to change. He withdrew his fingers and with a quick movement, released her hands. He flicked the belt in the air- it made a terrible cracking sound- and every part of her body tensed as she waited for it to come cracking down on her flesh. But Flynn seemed to have lost interest and pushed her away roughly. With her panties around her knees, she lost her balance and stumbled. To her shame, there was juice trickling down her thighs.

To be continued............

The cover photograph for this book and many others are available as limited edition prints.
Write to:-

Viewfinders Photography
PO Box 200,
Reepham
Norfolk
NR10 4SY

for details, or see,

www.viewfinders.org.uk

TITLES IN PRINT

Silver Mink

ISBN 1-897809-22-0	The Captive	*Amber Jameson*
ISBN 1-897809-24-7	Dear Master	*Terry Smith*
ISBN 1-897809-26-3	Sisters in Servitude	*Nicole Dere*
ISBN 1-897809-28-X	Cradle of Pain	*Krys Antarakis*
ISBN 1-897809-32-8	The Contract	*Sarah Fisher*
ISBN 1-897809-33-6	Virgin for Sale	*Nicole Dere*
ISBN 1-897809-39-5	Training Jenny	*Rosetta Stone*
ISBN 1-897898-45-X	Dominating Obsession	*Terry Smith*
ISBN 1-897809-49-2	The Penitent	*Charles Arnold**
ISBN 1-897809-56-5	Please Save Me!	*Dr. Gerald Rochelle**
ISBN 1-897809-58-1	Private Tuition	*Jay Merson**
ISBN 1-897809-61-1	Little One	*Rachel Hurst**
ISBN 1-897809-63-8	Naked Truth II	*Nicole Dere**
ISBN 1-897809-67-0	Tales from the Lodge	*Bridges/O'Kane**
ISBN 1-897809-68-9	Your Obedient Servant Charlotte	*Anna Grant**
ISBN 1-897809-70-0	Bush Slave II	*Lia Anderssen**

UK £4.99 except *£5.99 --USA $8.95 except *$9.95

All titles, both in print and out of print, are available as electronic downloads at:

http://www.silvermoon.co.uk

**e-mail submissions to:
Editor@Silvermoon.co.uk**

TITLES IN PRINT

Silver Moon

ISBN 1-897809-16-6	Rorigs Dawn	*Ray Arneson*
ISBN 1-897809-17-4	Bikers Girl on the Run	*Lia Anderssen*
ISBN 1-897809-23-9	Slave to the System	*Rosetta Stone*
ISBN 1-897809-25-5	Barbary Revenge	*Allan Aldiss*
ISBN 1-897809-27-1	White Slavers	*Jack Norman*
ISBN 1-897809-31-X	Slave to the State	*Rosetta Stone*
ISBN 1-897809-36-0	Island of Slavegirls	*Mark Slade*
ISBN 1-897809-37-9	Bush Slave	*Lia Anderssen*
ISBN 1-897809-38-7	Desert Discipline	*Mark Stewart*
ISBN 1-897809-40-9	Voyage of Shame	*Nicole Dere*
ISBN 1-897809-41-7	Plantation Punishment	*Rick Adams*
ISBN 1-897809-42-5	Naked Plunder	*J.T. Pearce*
ISBN 1-897809-43-3	Selling Stephanie	*Rosetta Stone*
ISBN 1-897809-44-1	SM Double value (Olivia/Lucy)	*Graham/Slade**
ISBN 1-897809-46-8	Eliska	*von Metchingen*
ISBN 1-897809-47-6	Hacienda,	*Allan Aldiss*
ISBN 1-897809-48-4	Angel of Lust,	*Lia Anderssen**
ISBN 1-897809-50-6	Naked Truth,	*Nicole Dere**
ISBN 1-897809-51-4	I Confess!,	*Dr Gerald Rochelle**
ISBN 1-897809-52-2	Barbary Slavedriver,	*Allan Aldiss**
ISBN 1-897809-53-0	A Toy for Jay,	*J.T. Pearce**
ISBN 1-897809-54-9	The Confessions of Amy Mansfield,	*R. Hurst**
ISBN 1-897809-55-7	Gentleman's Club,	*John Angus**
ISBN 1-897809-57-3	Sinfinder General	*Johnathan Tate**
ISBN 1-897809-59-X	Slaves for the Sheik	*Allan Aldiss**
ISBN 1-897809-60-3	Church of Chains	*Sean O'Kane**
ISBN 1-897809-62-X	Slavegirl from Suburbia	*Mark Slade**
ISBN 1-897809-64-6	Submission of a Clan Girl	*Mark Stewart**
ISBN 1-897809-65-4	Taming the Brat	*Sean O'Kane**
ISBN 1-897809-66-2	Slave for Sale	*J.T. Pearce**
ISBN 1-897809-69-7	Caged!	*Dr. Gerald Rochelle**
ISBN 1-897809-71-9	Rachel in servitude	*J.L. Jones**
ISBN 1-897809-72-2	Beaucastel	*Caroline Swift**
ISBN 1-897809-73-5	Slaveworld	*Steven Douglas**

UK £4.99 except *£5.99 --USA $8.95 except *$9.95